To Die For
TRUTH
SCARLETT FINN

Also by Scarlett Finn

TO DIE FOR...
TO DIE FOR TRUTH
TO DIE FOR HONOR
TO DIE FOR VIRTUE
TO DIE FOR DUTY
TO DIE FOR LOVE

GO NOVELS
GO WITH IT
GO IT ALONE
GO ALL OUT
GO ALL IN
GO FULL CIRCLE

KINDRED SERIES
RAVEN
SWALLOW
CUCKOO
SWIFT
FALCON
FINCH

LOVE AGAINST THE ODDS STANDALONE COLLECTION
SWEET SEAS
HEIR'S AFFAIR
RESCUED
MAESTRO'S MUSE
GETTING TRICKY
THIRTEEN
REMEMBER WHEN...
RELUCTANT SUSPICION
XY FACTOR

EXILE
HIDE & SEEK
KISS CHASE

THE EXPLICIT SERIES
EXPLICIT INSTRUCTION
EXPLICIT DETAIL
EXPLICIT MEMORY

WRECK & RUIN
RUIN ME
RUIN HIM

MISTAKE DUET
MISTAKE ME NOT
SLEIGHT MISTAKE

NOTHING TO...
NOTHING TO HIDE
NOTHING TO LOSE
NOTHING TO DECLARE
NOTHING TO US
NOTHING TO SAY
NOTHING TO GAIN
NOTHING TO YOU
NOTHING TO THIS
NOTHING TO DO

THE BRANDED SERIES
BRANDED
SCARRED
MARKED

RISQUÉ & HARROW INTERTWINED
TAKE A RISK
FIGHTING FATE
RISK IT ALL
FIGHTING BACK
GAME OF RISK

FORBIDDEN PREQUEL DUET
ALL. ONLY.
ONLY YOURS

THE FORBIDDEN NOVELS
FORBIDDEN DESIRE
FORBIDDEN WANT
FORBIDDEN WISH
FORBIDDEN NEED
FORBIDDEN BOND

LOST & FOUND
LOST
FOUND

ONE

TESS ANDERSON WAS AWARE of her mom rushing in and out, packing their possessions into the suitcases scattered around the living room. Headphones spared her the matriarch's accompanying monologue. She cared. She did. There just wasn't time to humor anyone. Clients' alterations had to be delivered before her nightclub shift.

The headphones were yanked off her head and tossed to the desk. "Are you listening to me?"

"I am not listening to you, Mom. I'm listening to Prince." Tess switched her focus back to the sewing machine. "He makes more sense."

"Please do not mutter at me, I despise the muttering."

Concentrating on her work, she pressed the foot pedal and ran the last seam into the needle. "You know I'm no good at subtle. If you want to tell me something, tell me."

Frustration seasoned Anne's next exhale. "Twenty-seven years I've been keeping you alive. One of these days, you'll be responsible for yourself."

Like she'd never heard that before.

Tess smiled. "Momma didn't raise no fool."

Her mother sinking to a crouch was a signal to pay closer attention.

"Light-Sprite…" Anne took her daughter's hand from the table. "I would never want to worry you."

And that was the beacon, the message came through loud and clear. "It's time to go?"

"The things we do for love," her mom said on a sigh, referencing one of her favorite songs.

Taking a deep breath, Tess adjusted to the development. "When? How much time?"

The moment of hesitation on Anne's lips contradicted the meager smile that followed. "We don't have to leave immediately."

"But soon?"

"Soon."

Soon could mean later that night or the next day. Maybe they'd leave in a week. Whenever it was, Anne had just issued the final warning. It was time to say goodbye to yet another city.

***

AFTER RUNNING ERRANDS and slinging drinks for a few hours, Tess came home in the dead of night. As usual, her mom had fallen asleep reading in bed. She put the book on the nightstand and tucked her mother in, kissing her cheek before flicking off the lamp.

Inhale and out. Her mom's breathing was so even. So peaceful.

Their perpetual cycle had to be a burden. Something had to come next, had to change, eventually. At some point, Anne would get bored with the constant moving, the never staying still. Wouldn't she? Her whole life, the same question.

Tess went to bed and slept late the next day. Her mom was already out, so she went about completing alterations for various stores. Several sold the apparel she made on consignment too. The lamp next to her worktable countered the shadow of her body as hours passed. Until a loud knock drew her attention, she didn't realize just how many. Night blackened the windows, despite the streetlights' efforts to keep the neighborhood safe.

Anne never forgot her keys. It wasn't like her to be out late either. As Tess reached the hall, the knock came again. The only keys on the hook by the front door were hers. Something must've happened.

Figuring she'd hear quite a tale, Tess opened the door wearing a smile that quickly faded. Two police officers stood on the threshold, rain pouring down behind them.

"Ms. Anderson?" She had no memory of reacting to the question. "I'm sorry to tell you we have bad news."

TWO

CLUTCHING THE URN TO her chest, Tess dropped her weight against the front door to close it. The wall clock in the kitchen ticked. Even in the hall, she could hear it. The solitary sound. Ticking. The seconds of her life dwindling away.

The stairs straight ahead led to rooms she shared with her mother.

Had shared.

They didn't share anything anymore. Never would again.

It took every ounce of energy to draw her next breath.

The only world Tess knew was the one her mom created.

What was her world without its creator?

They didn't need anyone else.

Except now she was alone.

Alone.

News of the car accident had stopped her world on its axis. From two to just one, Tess had been halved. Her life was half gone.

What to do next? Her well of inner strength was parched; her knees ached to buckle. It was a test. Collapsing into her grief would be the easy option. Easy didn't mean right.

Giving up in that pivotal moment meant never getting back up again.

It was a choice. Every step she took was a choice, every decision. Tess wouldn't fall down, she'd stand tall. Even when it was hard, they had to keep going, like Anne taught her.

Pushing away from the door, Tess strode to the stairs, beset by a new determination. Her mom had said "*soon*." For her, soon was that minute.

There were rules about leaving an abode for the last time. Clear rules. They couldn't leave anything behind. Nothing that could identify them.

First thing was laundry. The beds had to be stripped, towels collected, and everything was put through the highest temperature cycle in the washer.

In her mom's room, she threw the comforter off the end of the bed and flipped over a pillow. Something fluttered to the floor. What was…? Folded paper. She tossed the pillow onto the bed and bent down to pick it up.

The words on the crinkled paper took her breath. "It's a love letter."

Sinking onto the floor, she read on. With each new word, her intrigue grew. It didn't have a name at the beginning and was signed with only an H.

Tess read the words before the final letter, "Forever yours."

Running her thumb over the sentiment, the blurred watermark beneath could only be the circle of a fallen teardrop. Who was H? Who was he writing to? It stood to reason that her mother was the recipient, except her name didn't appear.

> "*Even after all these years. You're the
> only one, C.*"

C? Anne didn't begin with a C. Who was the letter for?

Other odd references perplexed her.

"I wanted you to have a fresh start, to have a chance at a real normal life. Crazy, right? I stole any chance you had for that after ML's."

"I fantasize about Miami, about how it was when our eyes met, when you took my hand."

While the letter wasn't quite written in code, it wasn't explicit either… Well, no, it was explicit in a different way, intimately explicit.

"Just your touch got me hard, I don't know how you did that, h   ow you still do. You've mesmerized me. I am yours, Angel."

The paper wasn't new. Without an envelope, it was impossible to tell which of their many addresses it had been sent to. Damn. A postmark would've narrowed down the date of receipt too.

"Even after all these years…" the sender had written.

How many years? And why pick up contact again?

Pouncing onto her knees, Tess set the letter on the nightstand and opened the top drawer. Without knowing exactly what she was looking for, her hands ran through makeup and medications. Nothing unusual jumped out, so she checked the other drawers.

An envelope, or semi-finished response, would give her a better chance at figuring out the mysterious H. It didn't make sense. Anne wasn't a letter writer. They weren't allowed to have computers or phones, other than the occasional burner for work purposes. Limiting their use of technology was one of her mother's strictest rules.

On occasion, they would go to an internet café, but it wasn't like she had anyone to email. Even if people gave contact information, Tess wasn't allowed to use it. In fact,

Anne would burn anything that might identify anyone they'd interacted with.

The letter was so against the "rules" that it ignited a need to know more. After rifling through the closet and clothes, Tess came up empty. They traveled light. They weren't supposed to have sentimental attachments to objects. In previous cities, her mother had packed and readied them to flee before Tess got home from work. Sometimes it happened that fast.

Concentrate. Concentrate.

The urn was by the letter on the nightstand.

Her mom was gone.

Despite going through the procedures of identifying her mom's body and arranging the cremation, it was still difficult to grasp that Anne wasn't around anymore.

"Who is H, Momma? What were you hiding?"

Anne could be tight-lipped to the point of infuriating. It wasn't a revelation that there were secrets between them. Protecting Tess when she was a child, sure, understandable, but Anne could've been more open in her later years.

Her later years. It was insane. Dead at fifty-one. They weren't supposed to be the later years of Anne's life. The woman was supposed to be in her prime. Happy. Free.

They would never be free. No, not "they." *She* would never be free.

Determination crackled and gathered mass, heating her insides. Tess didn't understand. Wouldn't understand until she knew the truth. Why had they been running her whole life?

Angry resolve wrapped around her heart, fracturing and exploding, forcing her onto her feet. Fear and doubt faded. Losing her mom was a high price to pay, but it meant there was nothing left to lose. A woman without ties was without vulnerability.

If the letter was intended for her mother, it was a consolation to learn Anne had experienced love. Not that romance was a life goal. Control was the ultimate purpose. She wouldn't spiral, wouldn't keep running until the day a random event stole her life. The futility was as glaring as a neon billboard on a dark street. Anne chose to run. Tess wouldn't.

Ah! An epiphany. There was one thing her mom took everywhere. On the occasions they'd fled with only what they could grab, Anne always snatched the small hard-shell cosmetics case that fit in her hand. The backpack under the bed. It was kept in the backpack.

Dropping to her knees, she dragged out the bag. In the past, she'd never been allowed to touch the cosmetics case, which explained why guilt swamped her when she fished it out. Like a child sneaking a hand into the cookie jar, she glanced around as she pressed the button to release the clasp.

When it popped, the edges fell open, sending a flutter of paper to the floor. Something solid hit the hardwood, but all she could see was faded white. Regaining her senses, she picked up the closest sheet. The writing inside matched that of the first letter. All of them bore identical handwriting.

Prying into the personal papers at any other time would be wrong. Tess didn't see that she had any other choice. Putting the case on the floor, she gathered up the scattered pages and began to read. One after the other, after the other. Letter upon letter. None were dated, and none contained any names.

> *"As long as I'm a slave to the Darkness, nothing will be right and the Light will never be free."*

> *"I've seen what the Darkness has done to PK."*

> *"Remember the glitter? When you're ready, you know our code."*

The pages weren't in order. Even if they were organized, she doubted they'd be easier to follow. Still, the words drew her in.

> *"...rambling about our past and the mistakes I made. You're the only one who*

suffers. I got all the positives and none of the burden. You shoulder it all and I'm not there to carry it with you."

Questions mounted up about H and his affair with C.

"Your gorgeous smile, your satin smooth skin, the sweet taste of your kiss. You torment me, even from a thousand miles away. One day I will have your kiss again, that's all that keeps me going."

"Everything I am is because of you, every cell in my body aches for yours. I would've left this earth long ago if I hadn't..."

"Saying goodbye to you is more than I ever thought I'd live to endure. You were right, they won."

Love shone from H's words.

"...I dream of you, of us being together like we were before."

"I have no right to ask you to wait. I can't tell you when or how I'll be with you again. I have taken too much from you already. You deserve happiness. You deserve the world and I wish I could give it to you. I wish I could've been a man worthy of you."

The couple's intimacy haunted him.

"That's what I see when I close my eyes at night, when I think of you, of being with you, all I can feel is love."

"Memories of your body, of being inside you, it is my curse and my salvation."

"You don't deserve this and I can make it right. I can free the Light. Give me purpose, Angel. I can get us back together again. It's time. I miss you too much to wait any longer. I've already missed my chance to be with you. One day I'll turn around and you'll be gone for good."

Emotion wasn't the only thing revealed. Hints of knowledge teased her.

"You are my meaning and my reason. Tearing me away from you ignited a fire they'll never be able to control."

"Angel, I pledge my love to you, but can only promise you vengeance."

"If they suspect anything, I'm worried they will take preemptive steps. You need to get out. Leave where you are as soon as you get this message."

"You can't snatch a man's hope from him and expect to get away easy."

The vague statements frustrated her desire for answers.

"You hid yourself well, but you can't stay put, it's still too dangerous."

"They have no fucking idea what you saved them from."

"...life wouldn't hurt you that I ever

would've let you go? That sacrifice wasn't for nothing. I won't let you erase two decades of sacrifice."

Wearing a persistent frown was giving her a headache. Rubbing her forehead, Tess went back and forth on whether the letters belonged to her mom. A big piece of the puzzle was missing. Figuring it out would take more than reading a few letters. Her focus snagged on the urn.

"Who is he?"

If she'd found the letters while her mother was alive, maybe a reply would've been forthcoming. Reading H's absorbing words again, Tess tried to get a deeper sense of him.

"My word is steel that was no lie."

"You told me I didn't have to choose, that you would never ask me to."

He carried a burden of his own.

"My nightmares are filled with images of your devastation, of witnessing your heart breaking. Watching you walk away broke mine."

"I don't doubt that we'll go down one day, maybe soon, who knows? When we do, we'll go together. I have to be there, C. I have to."

Anne had always been aware of something behind them, something chasing them, watching them, tracking them. The letters confirmed the danger was real. Whatever the threat, it was no fantasy. Maybe it was this H. Maybe he was their pursuer; the shadow stalking them.

"Run far away, as far as you can get, as fast as you can. Lose yourself so I will

never be able to find you."

"Don't tell me to admit any truth! I love you and if I have to smother the Darkness with my own bare hands to keep you safe that's what I'll do. This isn't over, C. No fucking way. If you think that I'm going to give up and forget…"

Tess wouldn't forget either. The journey ahead would have to be thought out one step at a time. Her mom didn't carry a purse, but the cops had given Tess what they found in their Corvette. At least what was found by people who weren't really looking.

Gathering up the letters, she put them back in the cosmetics clutch and shoved it to the back of a nightstand drawer. After a quick stop in her room to grab the necessary ID, Tess was down the stairs and out the door on a mission.

Her purpose was to identify the threat. It may be one Anne never wished her to have, but she would live with disappointing her mother's memory if it meant uncovering the truth.

THREE

IT DIDN'T OCCUR TO Tess to look for a payphone; her mother's conditioning was still in full force. There probably weren't any nearby anyway. She'd been at the police precinct asking questions when the sight of one on the wall put the idea in her head.

The desk clerk initially tried to redirect her to their website and requested she send an email. No one understood another person not having an email address or a smartphone. Faced with her dogged persistence, the guy relented and gave her the answer that she wanted.

Pausing at the open chain-link gates, Tess read the sign. "Buckhorn Parts and Towing," she said. "Salvage and scrap."

High wooden and chain-link fences enclosed the perimeter. The twine of razor-wire on top suggested the site was in tune with its security needs… or paranoid. The office was a single level unit, quite small considering the substantial size of the junkyard. The curve of a silver Airstream trailer protruded from behind the structure. Maybe someone lived on the land, or stuck around to protect it after hours. That was a relief. With the time already passed five, Tess had worried the business might be closed.

The door handle of the concrete building was stiff, but she pushed it down and yanked open the heavy door. Inside it became clear that the person responsible for running Buckhorn Parts and Towing didn't care much about cleanliness. The thin industrial carpet was caked with trodden in muck. So much so that she couldn't hazard a guess as to its original color.

All around, on every wall, were posters of cars, price lists and specs. Interspersed were a few posters advertising different car related products. Behind the cluttered counter was a calendar open to an unashamed centerfold, wearing only the tiniest thong. Like Barbie, but bustier and with glistening come-to-bed eyes. The model had so much weight on top that Tess doubted she'd be able to stand up.

A small section of the L-shaped counter was cleared, just enough to keep a button on show. The crusty laminated note above said, *"Ring for attention."* So that was exactly what she did.

With the distraction of the blonde and the posters, it was difficult to make out the narrow door on the opposite wall. Few people would notice it. Staying alert in a new environment was second nature for Tess.

The door opened, releasing a cloud of white smoke. Waving her hand in front of her face, she tried to waft the obvious smell away while a tall, dark-haired guy moseyed in. Coupling the scent to his heavy eyes, it didn't take long to put the pieces together.

Shock powered her voice. "Are you high?"

He didn't focus. His grubby coveralls were open to his hips showing that his tee-shirt was in pretty much the same state as the carpet.

Smacking his lips, he yawned and laid a hand on the center of his torso. "Hmm?"

Her grief hung as a weighted anger in her gut. Dragging it around took effort, but the heat of it fueled her resolve.

Setting both hands on the counter, Tess wasn't in the mood to play. "Are you the person in charge?"

"Right now, I think, yeah," he said, flexing his

shoulders to stretch his back. "Work's a bitch, right? There's gotta be a better way than slogging all day." From where she was standing, he didn't let work prevent him from taking it easy. "Lay it on me."

"Excuse me?"

He propped himself against the closed door. "Can't give you what you want until you ask for it," he said, one corner of his mouth quirking in a brief lazy smile.

When he folded his thick arms over his broad chest, Tess noticed the patch on his left pec bearing a name. "Danny? Is that your name?"

He tipped his shoulder her way, as if to present the name on his coveralls. "'Less I put on someone else's duds yesterday."

"Yesterday?" she said, wrinkling her nose in disgust.

On a shrug, he licked his lips again. "Just messin'. Wanna get something to eat?"

"What? No!"

"I'm hungry," he muttered, looking left and right like he might find something delicious lying around.

Tess rubbed her temple. "What is wrong with you?"

"Geez, lady, loosen up," he said like she was killing his buzz. "Who fucking died?"

Well, if that wasn't just the absolute wrong thing to say.

Slamming a hand on the counter, Tess lunged toward him. "Funny you should ask, my mom did. I am trying to find the vehicle she died in. Cops said it was here."

He took the news in his stride, with no sign of contrition or humility. "Makes you Little Red," he said, boosting his shoulder off the wall.

"What?"

"Corvette."

"Oh," she said, realizing he was paying attention. "Yeah. It's a Corvette."

Slapping a heavy hand onto the book that lay by the register, he dragged it along the counter toward himself. "Obviously not a music fan."

"I know Little Red Corvette, thank you very much."

Opening the book, he licked his dirty fingers to leaf through the smudged pages. Mechanics dealt with a lot of grime, grease, and oil. Filth, she supposed, was part of the job.

"Offend you?" he asked, glancing up.

"If you're calling me easy, yes."

Though, in truth, all of her sexual encounters were of the brief and easy variety. Necessity kept them that way. Tess and her mom adopted a "don't-ask, don't-tell" policy on that score.

"Free spirited," he said, trying to show her a smile. The lines on his brow suggested his smoking was starting to catch up with him. "If you were easy, we'd be in my trailer already."

"That's you who lives back there?"

He flicked over another page. "Surprised?"

"Yeah," she said without shame. "I figured whoever stayed back there had to be responsible for security… You don't seem like the type."

"To handle myself?"

"Uh, no," Tess said because she couldn't deny the strength of his physique. "The type to care."

He snickered. "Yeah, maybe, Little Red…" Slapping a hand onto the page, he ran a fingertip along a line of text. "We've got it in the yard, not much left."

Her gusto shrank. "I knew that."

The guy at the morgue had resisted providing a list of injuries. At that point, all they had were the cursory results, but those were enough to make the truth obvious. Her mom hadn't stood a chance.

"Come on, I'll show you."

Lost in her own thoughts, Tess hadn't noticed him coming around the counter. His eyes were still heavy and his hair a mess, but his solid form was more commanding than she'd given him credit for on first sight. The guy was ridiculously tall. In that moment, there was something comforting about his height and obvious capability. So comforting that for a split second, she envied him. Maybe not giving a crap wouldn't be such a bad way to live.

Since learning about the accident, she'd had no one

to talk to, no one to comfort her. She hadn't even cried. Not really. Every time sadness crept in, she pushed it aside to focus on the practical. Things needed to be done. Places visited. Arrangements made.

When she caught a glimmer of discernment in Danny, she cleared her throat and took a step back. The last thing she needed to do was gain the curiosity of the junkyard lackey, even if there was zero chance of ever seeing him again.

"Lead the way," she said.

He might not care that her mother was dead, but he'd done her a favor by skipping over the expected ID requirement. The car was registered to her. To one of her identities. The ID she'd brought was fake, they all were. Tess didn't even know her real last name.

Danny took her outside and led her past a few rows of crushed cars. "Want to grab a drink later?"

Women probably weren't common around a junkyard, so Tess didn't read too much into the invitation. Being an attractive guy, he wouldn't have to work hard for attention from the opposite sex.

"Do you ask out every woman who comes by here?" she asked to avoid answering the question.

He puffed out his cheeks. "Sometimes they ask me."

Watching the ground, she hid her smile. "I'll bet."

"Cut loose, Little Red. Let's go crazy."

At least the guy was a Prince fan; there was hope for him yet.

"Thanks," she said, trying not to focus on his heat permeating her way. "But I'm seeing someone tonight."

The yard opened out beyond the trailer. A bunch of heavy machines and equipment were intermingled with piles of twisted, gnarled metal.

Danny stopped and pointed. At first, Tess didn't have a clue what he was pointing at. When she saw the streak of red paint and realized that was her car, her mouth opened in shock.

"Need us to tow it somewhere for you?"

"No, I..." Tess was in a daze. "You can keep it. I just... I have to check something."

"Need help?"

"No," she said, forcing herself to smile at him. "You've been very helpful, Danny. Thank you."

Bobbing his head in acceptance, he walked backwards. "I'm always around if you change your mind." She widened her tight smile and nodded. "Food, drink, whatever…" Opening his arms at his sides, the corner of his mouth rose, revealing an endearing dimple. "Stop by the trailer sometime, Little Red. I'll rev your engine. No charge."

At a different time, the blatant invitation may have made her laugh. It just wasn't in her, so Tess raised a hand to wave instead.

Surveying the damaged vehicle, only one word came to mind: horrifying. Once it was the ultimate birthday gift. How her mom saved money and kept the purchase a secret still impressed her. A little red Corvette. Just like she'd always wanted… Its glory days were gone. Long gone.

Without question, there had been impact in more than one place. Did the car spin out and pinball off every obstacle in its careening path? She couldn't imagine the terror. Fear like that, so complete and consuming… warmth gathered at her lashes.

At times, the turbulence of their life caused friction between them. Even though "normal" didn't feature in her upbringing, Tess shouldn't have taken their relationship for granted. Anne's last thought would've been reserved for her daughter. Tess didn't doubt it. She should've been there, should've been with her…

Guilt roused her anger again. Squeezing her eyes closed, Tess got it together. Giving in to emotion wouldn't help either of them. Anne, if she was looking down, needed to witness her daughter's strength. Anything less than complete fortitude would be an insult to her memory. Forging on, no matter what, was imperative.

Putting aside the devastating mental images of her mother's last moments, she refused to be a victim to grief.

Grabbing the warped car door to yank it out of her way, she crouched down and examined every crevice. After going through all the usual places in the door, center console and ashtray, she went to the other side and did the same again. Nothing in the glovebox, nothing under the seats.

The frame was so twisted that the trunk release didn't work. She found a crowbar by one of the machines and wedged it into the space between lid and chassis. The damn thing wouldn't budge. Her muscles worked overtime until her feet lifted from the ground, but she wouldn't be defeated. Even if it took all night, Tess would get the trunk open.

"Don't fucking test me," she growled, ignoring the burn in her arms.

It yielded to her command and burst open. Dropping the crowbar, she grabbed the edge of the car so she wouldn't follow it down.

The triumph was short-lived. No clues lay around in the trunk, above or below the liner. It was empty.

But Tess wasn't done yet.

Returning to the body of the car, she hauled out the mats. That was when she saw it. In the passenger foot-well, a small, white rectangle.

Sinking onto the hard ground by the car, Tess picked it up and whispered the printed word. "Pandora."

Touching the letters, she wondered what they meant. On the other side was another name in smaller, bolder print. "*Russell Figgs, PI.*"

No answers. Nothing made sense. Her mother would never go to a PI, not in a zillion years. Unless… Maybe she didn't know what the letters meant either. But using an outsider meant making a connection. Telling a story. Anne wouldn't tell her own daughter; it was unlikely she'd tell a stranger. Would she?

As Tess stared at the black letters, she caught sight of the time on her watch. "Shit," she said, leaping to her feet, brushing the dirt from her jeans.

Friday meant drinks with Patrick. They had a standing date. It was Tess's habit to keep everyone at arm's length, but a sounding board may help her make sense of what she'd found that day.

FOUR

GOING HOME TO CHANGE for her date was a blur. Preoccupied, Tess could only think about the letters and vague business card. That was probably why she'd blurted out their discovery to Patrick.

Seated opposite each other at a table in the window of the bar, she'd held court most of the night. "It just feels like..."

"Your mom was keeping secrets," Patrick said and shrugged. "Most people do, Tess."

"I know, but we were close. Why wouldn't she tell me if there was something I needed to know?"

"Maybe you didn't need to know. Your mom got a few love letters, you don't even know what year they were from. They could've been written decades ago... or maybe she just found them somewhere and liked the sentiment. You said her name wasn't in them. Maybe it felt wrong leaving them behind. You moved a lot, right?"

Her shoulders sagged as she sank back in her chair. "I know."

That possibility had occurred to her too. They couldn't have new relationships, not lasting ones. Why wouldn't her mom hold onto the old ones or embrace the fantasy of someone else's?

"If they were hers, it should feel good that she had someone who cared for her like that."

In frustration, Tess balled her fists on the table and sat up straight again. "I know. Don't you think I know that? I just… When did it change? Does that mean she had this whole other life before me? That she…"

Patrick didn't know her past. No one would understand it. Her mother always dissuaded her from telling any one person too much. During her retelling of the day, of the week, the sensitive details were omitted on purpose. It wasn't Patrick's fault that she was tired and frustrated. On hearing of her mother's death, he'd said all the right things, but he didn't get it. No one could.

"Maybe they are from before you or maybe she had a relationship while you were a kid or something," he said, obviously trying to appease her. "You weren't together twenty-four seven and no one remembers much from when they were super young."

Maybe. Maybe. Everything was maybe. That wasn't good enough.

Her anchor was gone. Aimless drifting wasn't her style. Without her mom, she needed stability, something to lean on. She didn't know how to be alone. What it was to be completely alone.

Her future alone. Just like her mom's past… alone. Anne never spoke of parents or siblings, or any other family. She'd assumed that there wasn't any. What had her mom's life looked like before becoming "mom"?

When had it changed?

They'd always been on the run. Had her mom's life always been the same?

Losing her mother was a sucker punch, but that was no excuse for believing they'd always have time. Complacency was to blame. Questions were met with "*there isn't time for that now*" while her mom packed or panicked. In her naivety, it was easy to think her mother would get around to telling her everything sometime.

In spite of the mantras, the awareness, the vigilance,

Tess hadn't understood the urgency. She hadn't grasped how precious life was or how quickly it could be snuffed out. Apparently, neither had her mom.

"You need to relax," Patrick said, reaching over the table to take her hand. "You're grieving. I remember when Toby passed, it was such a shock. Took me weeks to come to terms with it."

Unimpressed, her attention ascended. "Toby was your mom's dog."

"Yeah," he said and shrugged. "But we'd had him since I was a kid. Place just wasn't the same without him." Patrick smiled. "You need to relax. Just go crazy. Do something fun and insane… We can go to that club across town, the one with the podiums. We'll dance the night away."

Her idea of a nightmare. Picking up her drink, Tess downed the rest of her cocktail. "Thanks, but I… I'm just not in the mood."

"Trust me," he said, gathering their empty glasses. "We'll get another one here and then head over there. Letting loose really makes a difference. It helps you forget for a while and that's exactly what you need."

He got up to walk over to the bar, leaving her alone. Tess couldn't think of anything worse than being in a crush of people, screaming over music trying to be heard. Though forgetting for a while sounded incredible, oblivion wouldn't be easy to reach. She'd have to do something really nuts or get really drunk. Alcohol didn't usually make her forget anything. Going overboard with booze wasn't smart. Her mother had drummed in the importance of keeping her wits.

"Someone always wants to hurt you," Tess whispered, her focus drifting to the street. "Everyone is a threat. Paranoia keeps us alive."

Her mother's mantras seemed ironic now. In the end, Anne had been the one to hurt herself. Not on purpose, sure, but still. Paranoia hadn't kept her alive. Paranoia probably contributed to her death. If her mom's concentration had been on the road, maybe she wouldn't have skidded off.

What Tess really needed was to feel something other than the grinding pressure of unknowns piling up. Sex was the only thing ever capable of taking her out of the moment and erasing her worries… temporarily anyway.

Patrick was still at the bar. They'd met a few weeks ago during one of her nightclub shifts. No doubt the guy was cute, but people insinuating themselves into her life was her mother's biggest red flag. He was the closest thing to a friend she'd had for a long time. They'd enjoyed a few make out sessions with some heavy petting, but she'd never been tempted to bring him to her bed.

Cute wouldn't untie her knot of frustration and grief. Friendship wasn't the remedy either. Patrick was not the definition of going crazy. He was synonymous for vanilla. Okay, so she didn't want anything kinky, but she did want something… wild. Something completely insane. Being safe wasn't all it was cracked up to be.

Anne's warnings were like tribal drums beating in the back of her brain.

"Be in control," Tess repeated another of her mother's mantras. "Never be led. Be the leader."

Anyone could be a threat, which was why no man had warmed her sheets more than once. Patrick was on the precipice and didn't know it. Sleeping with him would be a terrible idea. After so many dates, he'd think they were beginning something. In truth, if she talked to a guy, she'd never sleep with him. Sex had to be quick and dirty. Had to be once and never followed up. In short, if they did it, they'd be done. She couldn't bring herself to cut loose the only other living person who knew her name.

Grabbing her shawl from the back of her chair, she kept her attention on Patrick. With his back to her, he had the attention of the bartender. Good, so she could just… Tess swept her clutch from the tabletop and dashed out. The guy didn't deserve to be ditched, but that didn't make him what she needed.

Wrapping her shawl around her shoulders to fend off the night, she folded her arms. It wasn't too cold; the air smelled good. Any free air smelled good. Wait. Free? No. There was no such thing.

Nothing made sense.

After a few blocks, she stopped on a corner and cursed herself. This wasn't living. It wasn't life. Worrying about her mother's past and the secret message in the car was driving her nuts. Go crazy. Twice she'd been told that. Maybe everyone was right. Maybe her mom wasn't the one with the mental health problem.

If Tess hadn't had one before, one would be creeping up on her soon.

She needed to clear her mind. To let loose. Talking was overrated. Going into any of the bars would involve playing the flirting game. She'd have to catch someone's eye, smile, look away, look back, bat her eyelashes. Be funny. Be charming, alluring, seductive.

"Fuck that," she said to herself and marched across the street, away from the bustle.

Small talk and flirtations were unnecessary. All she wanted was to be pushed down and taken hard. To clear her senses, sharpen her view of the big picture. Feeling anything other than numb despair or infuriating frustration would be an improvement.

Keyed up, she raised a hand to hail a cab. Adrenaline was rising. Faster. Faster. The cab took less than ten minutes to get to her destination. The gates were open, and a light shone from inside the office. Though a huge tow truck blocked the majority of the building. If her plan didn't come to fruition, she'd be even more frustrated. The potent, pressurized need for release was reaching fever pitch.

Without breaking her step, Tess pulled the clip from her hair and threw it away. Flipping her head forward, she tossed it back and popped open her clutch to retrieve what she needed from inside.

Rounding the office building, she almost squealed at the sight of the light in the trailer. So far, so good. Two steps led to the door, she leaned over them to knock loud and sure.

A second passed, something clattered inside then a shadow crossed the lit window. Her heart hammered. Excitement? Anxiety? Who cares?

She moistened her lips and set her determination.

The door was pushed open. Leaning forward, with a

flat hand on the door, Danny wore nothing but a pair of jeans. His wet hair was slicked back, curling a little around his ears. Bingo. This was what she needed. In the office, she'd known he was fit, but seeing him half naked upgraded that assessment to ripped.

His brow arched in question. Her answer? The condom between her first two fingers. Without much of a reaction, he stepped back, holding the door open.

Licking her lips again, she went up the stairs to slip inside. Face to chest, just a few inches between them, she closed her eyes in a sultry blink and tossed her purse onto the seat next to them.

"Rev my engine, Danny Boy," she murmured, stepping out of her shoes and shedding the shawl.

As his eyes grew drowsy, a dimple slowly formed in his cheek. Yes. That was what she needed. Mischief. Abandon. Insanity. Her drawing down the zip of her dress gave Danny the cue to slide her spaghetti straps from her shoulders at an excruciating pace. After forever, her dress drifted to the floor. Gentle wasn't right, it didn't need to be drawn out. It needed to be now.

Somehow he sensed the slow tease didn't fit her mood and flipped the pace. In a rush, he crouched to pick her up, squeezing her ass hard.

Her whole body clenched in response.

Yes. That was it. Hard. Rough. Wild. Desire. Success.

Their mouths met as her legs wound around his torso. No longer lazy, their frantic need ignited an instant inferno. Tess coiled her arms around his head, losing her fingers in his hair, clutching him close and tipping her head to the side to push her mouth harder to his.

The kiss was enough to consume her. Nothing plagued her. There was nothing but this. His tongue, the sweet taste of him, the urgency of his commanding lips. Danny wanted her, though not as much as she wanted him.

They fell to the bed; he pushed her higher to take his mouth to her throat. He slipped the condom from her fingers and from that point, there was only one driver.

With her eyes closed, her head rose and moved to

grant him any access he wanted. She needed this. Exactly this. This man, his mouth, and that incredible body. Nothing else existed. The whole world was in that trailer, in the sensations firing through their nerves. He didn't even expect her to do anything.

Scooping an arm around her, he held her off the bed to peel her bra from her body. Her panties were next to go. When he dropped back down to kiss each of her inner thighs; she gasped and grabbed his hair in both fists. Whatever he wanted to do down there would wait. She needed him, his mouth, his cock, every part of her screamed with need.

"Danny," she panted, just managing to find his narrow eyes with hers. "Your cock. Give me your cock."

His primal groan warmed her as he dipped down to lick the seam of her body. Driving her fingers deep into his hair, she dragged him up, his mouth ascending all of her before rediscovering her kiss. Sucking his tongue hard, the clamp of her legs tightened around him.

Some odd, ancient instinct fired through her. She'd never wanted to possess anything or anyone in her life. But there she was, heart pounding against his hard chest, thinking that she never wanted to be anywhere else ever again.

All of her strength wasn't enough to subdue him. While still kissing her, Danny took her knees and forced them away. She couldn't prevent him from opening her up to him. Not that she wanted to. Her muscles were still tight, yet he was arranging her like she was his doll.

"Breathe in, Little Red," he groaned in a deep voice that vibrated her every atom.

There was a tease in that command. Seeking meaning, her eyes opened at the same moment he surged forward and impaled himself inside her. On an involuntary shocked inhale, her world narrowed to exist in that one place between her thighs. No man had ever occupied her so completely. He was everything. Her everything. Just like that, in their fixed stare on each other, she lost some part of herself. Something came loose. Something she should keep secure.

That wasn't good, but she couldn't concentrate enough to care. Danny slid back and forward in a slow rocking motion, stroking her inside and out. The movement of his hips sped up and slowed down. It wasn't a quick, frenzied fuck, but he wasn't making love to her either.

Watching him watching her, she read his need to get inside her. He was evaluating her. Judging her. Lost in the chasm of arousal, her only goal was to be whatever he needed her to be. Seemed only fair when he was doing such an incredible job of giving her what she needed.

"Danny," she whispered in a half whine, raising a heavy hand to his cheek.

He put his hand over hers to direct it away from his stubble, down his chest until he guided her fingers to her clit, right above where he dominated her. Using her fingers to caress the spot he'd already pampered with the movement of his pelvis, he kept going for a few seconds until she was gasping and yelping, close to climax.

"Right there," he said under his breath and pulled back only to slam into her again.

She came so hard and suddenly that she couldn't breathe for half a minute. Lost in the depths of an ocean, her whole body tightened in a spasm that blocked air from her lungs. He kept on going, moving fast and hard, pleasing himself in her submission.

"Danny!" she called out again when another orgasm devoured her.

If he didn't come soon, she'd have to beg for mercy.

No. She couldn't handle it, couldn't breathe, couldn't think. Nothing made sense. Nothing about the world was real. All she wanted was—on the crest of another orgasm, Danny surged forward with such force that she was shunted up the bed, smacking her head against something hard. The growling expression on his face relaxed, though she couldn't focus her eyes to take in any more than that.

His form vanished. She was left lying there, sweating, out of breath, and completely off-balance. What the hell just happened?

FIVE

"WANT A BEER?"

Who asked that? What was going on?

Raising her head, she looked between her crooked knees to see Danny further down the trailer, fridge open, holding a beer toward her.

Her legs collapsed to the side. She couldn't even muster the energy to straighten her limbs. "Uh… sure."

Already she'd said something stupid. Sex was over; she was supposed to leave. A hiss signaled the caps popping off the beers, but she still wasn't breathing right when he came over to wave one above her.

"Need some help?"

"No," she said, registering the smile in his voice.

Though she didn't appreciate his amusement, there was no quick retort. In fact, despite the top of the bed being right there to support her, it took a few attempts to even sit up. The blinds were shut, thank God. She appreciated not being on view to the wider world, but couldn't gather herself enough to cover up.

Just taking the beer was difficult.

The cool liquid felt good sliding down her throat. The hydration was definitely welcome.

Danny either hadn't taken his jeans off at all, or he'd

put them back on and fastened the top button. As he sank down to sit on the foot of the bed, Tess extended her legs and pulled her ass toward her feet, scooching to the end to put her feet on the floor. It felt good to remind herself there was something solid beneath her. Drinking some more beer, she stood up and wandered down the trailer, taking in the environment she hadn't absorbed before.

Strolling past the distorted glass that disguised the shower, she enjoyed the masculine scent that betrayed it hadn't been long since he'd used it.

"What happened to the boyfriend?"

Running a fingertip across the width of a closet, Tess let it fall to the stove by the counter and glanced back, without getting as far as actually looking at him.

"Hmm?"

"The dude you're dating. He didn't get to take you home… or he did and couldn't finish the job?"

The swaggering snicker in those last words earned him no points.

"You got laid, what do you care?" she asked, touching the towel he'd tossed on an otherwise clear kitchen counter.

"Don't. Just makin' conversation."

"Stick to what you're good at."

"Whoa, sex and abuse," he said on a gruff laugh. "You offer a full service, baby. Crack that whip."

Insulting him wasn't fair. Turning her back to the sink, Tess wasn't upset to see his smile. He lay on his side on the bed she'd vacated, his head propped on a sure fist, his beer loose in his other hand, hanging over the edge of the mattress.

"I'm sorry, that was rude."

"Go ahead, be rude," he said, sinking back to tip beer into his mouth. "Don't matter to me."

On a smile, she appreciated him for his uncomplicated self. Danny was a guy without a care. Taking the world as it came. The simplicity of his existence was enviable. A fantasy for another day.

All good things had to end. She took another mouthful of beer and then set it on the counter to go retrieve her dress.

"Yo, you don't need that."

She bent down to step into it. Before Tess could straighten up, she was being scooped off the floor and carried back to the bed.

"Danny," she said, laughing. "I have to go."

"Little Red, Little Red," he said, climbing onto the bed on his knees to dump her in the middle. "That was just the warm-up."

"No, I'm through," she said without moving. "I've had enough."

"Cool, then the next time will be for me," he said, lying against her side, his fingertips playing at her inner thigh.

Taking his hand away from its playground, she wrapped both of hers around it to stop him tormenting her. "You're supposed to be easy."

He exhaled a laugh. "Your seduction was showing me a condom. How much easier you want?"

Clasping his hand in her cleavage, she smiled. "Simple I mean."

"A dumb grease monkey?"

Sucking in a breath, she winced. "Oh," she said, bringing her knees up. "I'm not doing too good here."

"You just keep the insults coming," he said, freeing up his hand to reach for the beer he'd put on the windowsill behind them. "If it's angry sex you want, you should be more explicit… I'm not that easily offended, but I can fake it."

Resting a hand on his stomach while he drained the beer bottle, she appreciated how down-to-earth the guy was. So laid back he was literally horizontal, Tess couldn't imagine him getting upset or reading too much into anything. That last thought led her to a question.

"Do you think paranoia can kill?" she murmured, tracing a fingertip around the ridges of his muscles.

"Sure," he said like it wasn't a crazy query. "You become too obsessed, anything can, right?"

The answer was quick, obviously his honest opinion. Danny wouldn't put enough thought into anything to lie about it. What had she wanted him to say? If he'd said no, then she would just think her insanity level was rising. Yet agreeing with her didn't make her feel great.

The bed was warm, the man willing and sturdy… Tess had to move. The prospect of just letting herself be his junkyard whore was too tempting. Life in that trailer was as straightforward as any. With no one else's support, Tess faced the truth: she didn't want to be alone. Her mother had raised her to be strong and independent. She believed herself capable of handling anything. Maybe she was, but that didn't mean she wanted to do it alone.

Drawing in a long breath, Tess filled her lungs and held the oxygen inside while wriggling down the bed.

"Wrong answer?"

"No," she said, standing up again.

Her dress was on the floor near the dinette opposite the sink.

"You think different?"

That made her smile as she bent down to pick up her dress. This time, he didn't run after her or prevent her from guiding the straps to her shoulders.

"I don't know what I think, Danny," she said, picking up her beer as she muttered to herself. "I don't know what I think about anything anymore."

"I'm sorry you lost your mom," he said. "Fuck with your head?"

Propping a hip on the sink, she looked up the trailer to where he lay on the bed in the same position as before. "That's the understatement of the century," she said and shook her head. "I don't know. It was just the two of us… Never really occurred to me she wouldn't be around forever."

His head moved in a brief bob of understanding; nothing really registered on his expression. It was nice not to feel judged, but she should know better than to lose control of her mouth, especially so soon after losing control of her body.

"What 'bout your dad?"

She shrugged and picked at the label on her bottle. "Never knew him."

"Could be out there."

To a guy like Danny, the prospect of hunting the man

who'd sired her probably made sense. A sense of pity came over her. He might look capable, but he was so naïve.

"I wouldn't even know where to start, Danny."

"Someone's gotta know who he is. Hire like a detective or something, you know, like a private dick."

Naïve and juvenile, if his snickering was any measure. Still, he was sweet in his own way.

"I don't even know if he's alive," she said.

"Know where they met?"

She shook her head. "I'm not sure my mother knew who he was."

"Like mother like daughter."

The impact of offense opened her mouth, but her glare relaxed when she saw his smile. The guy was an idiot, not in a bad way, he was just trying to cheer her up. Pushing away from the sink, Tess moved toward him.

"My mom did not accost men with condoms."

"Sure," he said, adjusting his head on his fist when she stopped at the end of the bed. "Otherwise, no you."

Her focus descended to the label she'd picked at. "She had love once. I think."

"Not your dad?"

Frustrated, Tess tried not to let her annoyance rise again, but it wasn't easy. "I don't have a damn clue who he was or who she loved."

His brow creased in confusion. "I don't get it."

With her mouth closed, Tess inhaled through her nose. "I found love letters… I think they're love letters," she said, sinking down to the edge of the bed as he sat up. "Don't know who they're from, or even if they're to her… I found them in her room. I know she treasured them."

"This guy know she's dead?"

The simplicity of such a question hit her hard.

Tess whipped around to look at him. "Oh my God," she whispered.

"Guess that's a no," he said, slouching against the pillows. "Sucks for him, I guess… Wonder if you'll get another one."

Tess had no clue whether the letters were recent or

old. From her interpretation, they were written sometimes years apart. The guy, this H, could be out there. He would have no way to know the object of his love was dead… if her mom was that object.

"Oh my God," she whispered again and thrust the beer at him. "I've gotta go."

"Why?" he asked, taking the beer and hold of her wrist too. "Whoever he is, you're not gonna find him tonight."

"Do you have a Yellow Pages?"

She didn't blame his frowning recoil of surprise. "Heard of the internet?"

Tess shook her head. "I need an address… I don't use the internet, I can't."

Trying her best to ignore the twitch of curiosity in his brows, new determination inspired her.

"There's probably one in the office," he said, twisting to put the beer on the windowsill without letting go of her wrist. "We'll check in the morning."

"Morning?" she said, shaking her head when he got onto his knees and put one between hers. "No, I need one now."

"No," he said, easing her onto her back. "You need something else now… something I need too."

Lying on top of her, he slid a hand up her forearm to link their fingers and pressed the back of her hand into the bed.

"No," she said, shaking her head. "There's no time for sex. Sex makes me forget; it relaxes me. I don't need to be relaxed. I need…" He buried his face against her neck. The scent of his hair tickling her jaw was alluring. Safety. Oblivion. Companionship. "Danny…"

It wasn't possible to be annoyed with him or even frustrated with herself. The sensation of his tongue trailing along her collarbone and across her throat was impossible to ignore. Ecstasy triumphed. Everything became about every place his body touched hers.

"Forget," he murmured against her, taking a handful of her breast. "Forget everything and just be here, Little Red."

His mouth descended to her cleavage; her eyes

closed. No one had ever given her such a tempting invitation. That was exactly what Tess needed, and his permission pushed her over the edge. Fighting against temptation was too difficult. She wanted to feel. To forget and to feel only the physical.

Danny was offering her the simple life that she wanted, so for one night, she let herself give in.

SIX

"YOU'RE A STALKER," Tess said, striding down the sidewalk, trying to outpace the guy-who-wouldn't-quit next to her.

She was fast learning that her attempts to get away from Danny were pointless. His legs were longer; her hurry was his stroll.

"I'm taking you to breakfast," Danny said, hands in his pockets, moseying along.

"I don't want breakfast. I told you I don't need breakfast. Don't you have to go to work?"

A group of young women walking toward them noticed the man at her side. Admiring him, they pointed and whispered while giggling.

"Tomorrow," he answered her, then tipped an invisible cap at the gaggle. "Ladies."

More giggling and some flirtatious finger-waving. Yes, he was attractive. Tess knew that. Her libido had noticed when they first met. Stupid libido. While stoned he probably wasn't on his A-game, but even without the drugs, he came across as loose and unthreatening. Just a glance identified him as a guy who'd be a good time. Hot, beyond fit, and approachable, he was a potent mixture that equaled virile man.

"Take *them* to breakfast."

Still keeping the pace, he twisted and dipped down to speak in her ear. "They didn't suck my cock last night."

"Danny," Tess hissed, swatting his stomach, though he lurched back to avoid the blow. "I bet they would if you asked them."

"Didn't have to ask you," he said, flopping an arm around her shoulders. "You just knew."

"Stop stalking me, I'm going somewhere."

"Russell Figgs, PI," he said. "I remember."

In the Buckhorn office that morning, the idiot had retrieved the Yellow Pages and loitered next to her while she looked up the PI. The open door to the back had freed a cacophony of male voices and laughter, putting a fire under her to get out of there fast. The last thing she'd wanted to face was any of Danny's lewd tow-yard buddies. In her haste, Tess hadn't registered that Danny was paying attention to the directory as she searched.

"I'm going in alone," Tess said. "This is a private family matter."

"Your mom leaving the card in the car like that is weird."

Maintaining her pace, Tess closed her eyes to groan at herself. Last night had been as disastrous as it was incredible. The sex was mind-blowing. In the times in between, she'd talked and laughed more with him than with any other male she'd shared a bed with.

Though it was a unique experience, Tess hadn't worried too much, figuring they'd part and never see each other again. That false assumption led to her revealing much more than she should have. Drinking more alcohol than was smart and relaxing into the illusion was irresponsible of her too.

She'd referred to him as an idiot, but she was a bigger one. His easy smile and skilled hands awakened her stupidity. Tess never thought of herself as a bimbo or a ditz until proximity to Danny brought out the apparently dormant qualities in her.

Danny's arm was heavy on her shoulders; he thought

nothing of draping himself on her and ambling down the street with her pinned to his side. What did he think she belonged to him or something?

Shrugging his arm off, Tess tried to put some distance between them.

Of course he didn't let that go. Dipping down to scoop an arm around her waist, he spun them around to pin her back to the nearest wall. Surprise opened her mouth, which gave him the opportunity to slip his tongue between her lips.

Her mouth resisted… for a few seconds. Pushing hard against his tongue, she moaned when he fought back. The force of his kiss reminded her of the need of his body. Danny wasn't shy about persisting. Last night, in the dark, he'd been almost animalistic in his desire. There was something about experiencing his dominance while bathed in shadow.

His mouth left hers on a breath.

A long moment passed before Tess regained her senses. "Don't do that," she said, hitting his shoulder with the side of her fist. "I stop thinking when you do that."

"You're welcome," he said, pushing himself against her. "You need to relax. You always forget to breathe."

Maybe that was true; she didn't know. Tess had a plan, at least the beginnings of one, and Danny wasn't a part of it. Her mother had left her a clue, one that would hopefully lead to answers. She couldn't be thinking about a guy or a relationship.

"How do you feel about takeout?" she asked, spying a diner on the opposite corner. "Why don't you go grab us something to eat? This Figgs guy is just down the block. I'll talk to him and then we'll go back to your place…" Licking her lips, she made a point of eyeing him like her thoughts were slipping into the salacious. "We'll eat there."

"Naked?"

Tess smiled, catching her wrist in her opposite hand at the back of his neck to pull him down for a brief kiss. "Definitely."

"You got it."

He squeezed her waist then let her go to stride off across the street toward the diner.

Blowing out a breath, she tossed her hair from her face. "Okay."

Switching her mindset after a kiss like that was a big ask. Still, she didn't have any time to waste. Figgs was just down the block.

Tess strode into the glass fronted office and went to the secretary seated behind a low reception desk. "Hi," she declared, projecting her voice to the woman who hadn't even looked up from her computer. "I need to see Russell Figgs."

"You've gotta make an appointment."

"Okay," Tess said, though she didn't intend to leave without answers. "How's in thirty seconds sound?" The secretary blinked up at her, so she widened her smile. "Patience isn't my strong suit."

"I'm sorry, ma'am, we don't do same day appointments."

Tess pointed to the door behind the reception. "You could just hop back there and ask. There's an exception to every rule, right?"

Was she too pushy? Yeah, probably. But not rude pushy… a little rude pushy. Maybe it was Danny's kiss or her grief… or her intrigue about the letters. Could be anything, but she was amped and wanted forward movement. She had to make progress. Leaving with nothing, waiting another day for answers? She couldn't do it.

The secretary raised a brow. "He's with someone."

Ah, a client.

Tess smiled. "That's okay, I can wait."

Maybe sending Danny for food wouldn't work out so bad. If he tailed her to the PI's office, they could eat there, and she could kill two birds with one stone. Danny was laid back, but he'd eventually get bored sitting there waiting for who knew what. That meant Tess could get rid of him and get her mother's message both at the same time.

"I can give you an appointment," the secretary said. "If it's urgent."

"If it wasn't urgent, I wouldn't be so twitchy," Tess

said, figuring the woman should've reached that conclusion all on her own. "I need to see him. As soon as possible, which means I won't leave until I speak with him."

Her mother must have contacted the PI. If this Russell Figgs had a message for her or an item her mother wanted her to have, she couldn't afford any delays.

"I can't let you just sit out here cluttering up the place."

If their positions were reversed, Tess probably wouldn't want anyone sitting around, pacing, muttering, waiting, ready to go off any second either.

"Look…" Tess said, trying to calm herself while sort of wishing she'd brought Danny. He might not be one for hard work, but he could smile at the secretary long enough to let Tess sneak around into the PI's office. "He knows something I need to know. It's life or death."

Maybe not exactly life or death, but how did Tess know that for sure? She didn't. Her mom was dead, so it was about death. And life: her life.

The woman behind the desk wasn't impressed. "I doubt that, ma'am. What is it? Your husband screwing some floozy?"

If that was all Russell Figgs did, Tess was in trouble. Her mom wouldn't leave a message with someone who couldn't be trusted. If his business was frivolous or ridiculous, he may not understand the significance of whatever Anne told him.

Sealing her lips, Tess drew in a breath through her nose. "My mother is dead."

"You want the cops to investigate something like that," the secretary said, hazarding no emotion. "Call homicide."

"You know what…" Tess said, sidling down the length of the desk. "I think I'll just go back there myself and talk to him."

The secretary leaped to her feet. "You can't do that! You can't come back here."

At only five feet two inches tall, Tess couldn't delude herself that she could physically intimidate anyone. But determination had a lot to answer for.

"I think I can," Tess said, trying to dodge the woman who wasn't much taller than her but was doing her best to take up as much of the opening as possible. "I need to see him."

"No! No, I'll call the cops!"

"Go for it."

She didn't want the cops there, but in the time it took the woman to make the call, Tess could get to Figgs.

The door at the back of the room opened as the woman attempted to dodge and block. A tall, confused guy stepped out.

"What's going on out here?"

"She's a crazy person," the secretary called out.

That could be true; Tess was beyond caring. "Mr. Figgs," she said, keeping her attention on the panting secretary. "I need to see you."

"I said no!" the secretary yelped.

"It's important, Mr. Figgs."

"I don't see why—"

"My name is Tess Anderson and I—"

"Jesus," Figgs said, interrupting her as he strode forward. "Let her by, Mavis."

Figgs came over to sweep his secretary aside. He put a hand on Tess's shoulder, then stalled and froze. Lifting it off slowly, he showed her both hands and stepped back, almost treading on the bamboozled secretary.

Mavis wasn't the only one confused. What was up with this guy? Why was he suddenly wide-eyed and tense? Sweat beaded on his pale brow. The guy was nervous, scared maybe. Her resolve was firm, but the guy had height and a gut that could steamroll her if things got physical. No reason he should fear her… unless he thought she was armed. Except any weapon would have to be tiny to fit in the clutch she had looped around her wrist.

"Come," Figgs said, gesturing her past him like he was directing traffic.

Turning, he kept his secretary at his back, blocking her as Tess passed to go into the office. This Figgs guy was a weird one. Inside, he rushed past her to retrieve a key from the desk with shaking fingers. He unlocked the closet in the corner and produced a box from the top shelf.

"I didn't open it," he said, carrying what appeared to be little bigger than a shoebox over to a circular table in the corner. "You can check the seal, all the way round, I didn't open it."

Figgs put the box down and held up both hands in surrender as he backed away. Tess just stood there looking at him, confused, wondering if she should worry about what might be within the package.

"Uh… thank you?"

He nodded, but didn't make eye contact as he shuffled past her on his return to the door. "Take all the time you need. All the time. No one will disturb you."

He reversed out and closed the door. For a few seconds, she just stood there, wondering at the quick turnaround. Eventually, her focus settled on the box again. If Figgs had any reason to believe that the contents were dangerous, he wouldn't let her open it in his private office. She had extra reassurance. Her mother left the box; nothing inside would harm her.

Snagging a letter opener from the desk, she sliced through the tape and lifted the lid, eager to receive the message. Her anticipation dwindled to bewilderment. Money. Four rolls of bills. And a… gun? Why would she need a weapon? Two clips of ammunition were just above it. A gun? Money? Picking up one and then the other, she noticed the small white rectangle beneath.

Her lips parted to help her breathe. On the rectangle, right in the middle, was what appeared to be a single drop of blood. Something was written on top of it. After an anxious swallow, she put down the objects in the box again and slipped her fingertips under the card.

Blood. Why would her mother…? *Hades.* That was the word. Written in faint pencil, just like the word Pandora on the other card, though that one had been sans blood. Peering closer, she ran a nail across the edge of the bloodstain. Except it wasn't a stain, it was printed. A single drop of blood printed on the pristine white cardboard. Turning it over to see if it was on the other side, Tess found it was blank of blood. There was no faint pencil there either. Instead, she found a stream of numbers. Two rows. One long, uninterrupted number on the top. Beneath that was another number, separated by two punctuation marks: a comma and hyphen. Why? What did it mean?

So much for answers. Tess exhaled a long breath. Goddamnit. The mystery only got deeper. Maybe there was no end.

SEVEN

WITH HER WARES, TESS got the hell out of the area. Ditching Patrick and then Danny shaped a shameful pattern of behavior. Keeping people at a distance was necessary. For the protection of all parties.

Everyone was temporary.

Everyone except mother and daughter.

Now only daughter.

Tess returned home, got in the shower, and obsessed about the numbers. What did they mean? What did the names mean? Pandora, Hades, they were from Greek mythology. Everybody knew that. Were the names codes or keys to figuring out the numbers?

Her mind wouldn't stop working at a thousand miles an hour. Time was against her too. Her clients and the nightclub had been understanding about her loss. They wouldn't understand forever. At least, with regard to her own finances, the box money provided a cushion of time to figure everything out.

Determined to decode what her mom wanted her to know, Tess finished an alteration and gathered everything up. The intention was to stop at the stores to return the adjusted garments and tell them she wasn't accepting more work. Soon, she'd go back to pick up any remaining checks. Her bartending job would require notice anyway. She'd give it at her next shift the following night.

Whatever the next objective, Anne's warning loomed large. Soon. Her death didn't alter that directive. Tess would carry out her mother's last instruction. Though until she was sure there were no more clues in the area, she wouldn't go far.

After changing her clothes and slinging the hanging items over her shoulder, Tess grabbed her carpet bag and went into her mother's room for the letters. Her hand was outstretched, ready to pick up the cosmetics case from next to the bed. Except… it wasn't there.

She paused, frowning. The book was still there.

Retracing her steps, she'd sat on the floor reading the letters… put the letters in the case, closed it and put it on the book… Hadn't she?

Dumping everything on the floor, she rushed into her own bedroom. It wasn't there. The case wasn't anywhere. It wasn't downstairs, not in the kitchen or living room, not on her worktable… Where else could it be?

It hadn't left the house. Couldn't have. Not by her hand. That chilling idea didn't bear contemplating.

Going back upstairs, her mom's backpack was the next stop. Maybe she'd put it back. Unlike her to be so fastidious, but… No, the letters weren't there. As she shoved the backpack under the bed again, stretching to push it as close to the headboard as possible, a sudden sting of pain shot through her finger.

Blood on her pinkie. "Damn it," she said, rising on her knees to grab Kleenex from the nightstand.

Squeezing them against the cut, she lay down flat to seek the culprit and expected to see a loose board or nail or something. At first, nothing in the nightstand's shadow stood out. Still clutching the tissues to her wound, Tess reached out, slowly, searching for what had hurt her. Something cool and hard met her fingertips. What was it?

Kneeling up, she checked it out. An odd object. Metal, heavy for its size, it was the length of her hand. The flat circular piece that rested on the heel of her hand had something embossed on it, two curved shapes facing each other. From that was a short cylinder that split into two long prongs. What was she looking at? A symbol of something. Did it have a purpose?

Her gaze ascended to the book by the bed. The letters were gone. The only explanation… someone had taken them. A stranger. Mom was dead. No one else knew they existed. No, Patrick knew she'd found them, Danny too. The latter got a pass, she'd been with him since telling him.

Suspicion became paranoia. From childhood until that moment, the danger had been an abstract theory. Someone, a stranger, had been in her mother's bedroom going through her things… the idea made her shiver… it made her nauseous. Was this what her mother had lived with every day? The responsibility of it. The weight pushing her down, holding her back, stifling her.

Nothing else was out of place. As far as she could tell, nothing in her bedroom had been touched. The TV was still there, all the landlord's furniture. Her sewing machine too and that was an expensive piece of kit. It wasn't a random burglary.

One other person knew about the letters.

H.

Could it be him? Maybe the author had removed the evidence of his existence.

Whoever had been in the house had got what they wanted. If hurting her was on their agenda, they could've hung around and taken her out. If the thief knew about the letters, it stood to reason he could've been watching them for a while. He'd know she was a sitting duck.

The nightstand book taunted her. Her mother had been reading it. Tess had taken it from the sleeping woman's lap the night before she died. Anne wouldn't finish it. It would just lie there unfinished… sort of like her mother's life.

The injustice injured her. Anger was so much easier to hang onto than grief. Anne's life reduced to an illusion. Running away from whatever specter chased them, keeping her daughter safe. Why didn't her mother stand and fight or report the perpetrator to the authorities? Maybe her mom thought it was for the best, but Tess had seen how that kind of life ended.

Her desire to figure out her mother's message intensified. To leave town, she needed a destination in her sights. That meant deciphering the clues.

The setback wouldn't deter her. Guilt over losing the precious letters could easily give way to grief. Dwelling on those emotions would cripple her if she let them.

Stashing the money and gun in the back of her closet, she memorized the numbers on the second card while putting it with the first under the flatware tray in the kitchen. The library on her itinerary had metal detectors, so she put the weird metal prong thing under a bunch of utensils at the back of the drawer too.

Losing the letters was a blow, but Tess was going to stay on her path. She'd tour her workplaces, then head to the library to figure out what the hell Pandora and Hades had to do with the numbers on that damned new card.

***

AFTER AN ENTIRE DAY at the library, Tess was no further forward. She knew more about Greek mythology than she'd ever need. About Pandora and Hades, God of the underworld, what a great job. But the maddening numbers remained encoded.

Tired and fed up, she was still reading when the PA system announced the library was closing. By the time she got out into the cold, midnight had come and gone. Pulling her carpet bag higher on her forearm, she tucked it against her torso to keep in the heat.

Turned out following orders was all she was good for. Cryptography wasn't her specialty. Sure, it didn't help that she kept seeing the college kids traipsing in, spending ten minutes at a computer and disappearing again, presumably with exactly what they came for.

The temptation to sneak over and see what she could scare up was huge. Wouldn't help that she didn't have a damn clue about computers or the internet. Just thinking about flouting the rules was enough to heap more guilt onto her already ample hoard. Her mother would never have left a clue that required going online anyway, so it didn't really matter.

She felt alone and pathetic. Her mom wanted her to know something. Why was it so encrypted? Writing it out plain and simple might be dangerous, but something clearer would've been less infuriating. Obviously, Anne thought her daughter could figure it out. A hint. Was that too much to ask for? Something to put her on the right path.

The break-in was on her mind too. Sleeping in a house that had been violated by an intruder wasn't appealing. Everything had gone to shit. Since her mom died, life had been downhill. Losing her mom should've been rock bottom. But nope, Tess just kept on descending.

Her feet didn't take her toward home. By the time she realized that, Tess was crossing through the gate of Buckhorn Parts and Towing.

Why was she there? Who knew? Something about the oblivion of being under Danny made life more tolerable. The relief was short-lived, but she was weak enough to want it.

The chill of the dark night didn't seem as isolating when she raised her fist to knock on the trailer door.

"Yeah!" came the call from inside.

Her mind was still in a dozen places when she reached up to open the door. Noticing Danny wasn't alone, she froze. Three other guys sat around a folding table with him, a couple of them on folding chairs. Smoke hung thick in the air, its scent laced with that of the hundred or so beers they'd probably drunk.

Danny had his back to the far wall. Two guys sat on the recliners at the end of the table and another guy had his back to her. All of them took a good look at her though.

"Uh," she said, putting a foot on the first stair to boost herself a little higher. "Hi."

"Missed breakfast," Danny said around the cigar he was holding in his teeth. "This one needs GPS on her chassis."

His attention wasn't really on her. He was gathering chips from the center of the table, putting them into stacks.

"Yeah, sorry about that," she said, her eyes darting around the table, taking in the details. Poker chips, cards, ashtrays… "I didn't mean to interrupt."

"You can interrupt me," the guy closest to her said, checking her out. "Any time, Sugarlips."

All of them guffawed. Even Danny enjoyed the sentiment. Okay, that probably meant he'd clued the posse of guys in Buckhorn gear into exactly what they'd done the previous night… and no doubt how she'd seduced him with a rubber. Not her finest hour.

"What'd you need, Little Red? A ride?"

"It's fine," she said, deciding to retreat. "I can go."

"That means yes," Danny said to his buddies, taking the cigar from his mouth.

"No," she said, defending herself. "I didn't come here for that. I just wanted a place to crash."

Danny's attention met hers. Just the linking of their eyes increased her heart rate.

"You wanna crash here?" he asked. Tess nodded without even thinking about whether it was a smart plan. "Will you put out?"

Typical. Her head sank to the side. "If I have to."

"Make yourself at home, baby."

Given that she was there, and the guys started to talk about cashing out, Tess ascended and yanked the door closed behind her. She left Danny alone with his animated friends and went up the aisle to the bedroom. After dumping her bag in the corner, she closed the privacy curtain and stripped. A shower would be bliss. Her muscles ached from all the tension of the last few days.

She was rolling her head on her neck when the curtain opened behind her. Before she could turn around, his strong hands were squeezing her shoulders.

"I charge rent, you know," he mumbled, his deep voice just a breath from her ear.

"Mm?" she asked, her eyes closing.

His lips caressed her neck, creeping closer to her throat. "You've gotta cook and clean for me."

"I won't cook or clean."

"Then how you gonna pay your way?"

Turning around, her body met his as her chin rose.

"I'll think of something."

Her fingers were already working on his jeans, loosening his buttons one at a time.

"Always know whatcha want, Little Red."

"What I want is easy when I'm here," Tess said, slipping her hand into his jeans to curl her fingers around his shaft. "When I'm so close to this."

"Yeah?" he breathed, almost taunting behind his aroused smile.

Edging forward, he bumped her back, sending her down to the bed on her ass. That about brought her eye to eye with the serpent she'd unleashed.

Showing him a brief smile, she took him in both hands and opened her mouth. Danny was no slouch in the sack, despite slacking in just about every other area of his life. His hips moved in time with her advance and retreat. With her eyes aimed upward, Tess watched his drowsy desire grow to a vision of need that clenched his teeth. The strength of his jaw tightened; a groan tumbled from his throat. His head went back, and she sucked harder, pulling him deep into her throat, aching with a drive to satisfy him.

His open hand flattened on her head and he leaned back, giving more of himself to her. Skimming her palms up his legs, she brought them together beneath his dick, fondling and adoring him.

"Oh, fuck, baby," he said, suddenly bending forward, stealing his cock from her lips.

He scooped his hands under her ass, squeezing her tight as he loved to do, then tossed her to the middle of the bed.

"Danny…" she said.

Without taking his eyes from hers, he crawled onto the bed over her, reaching to the nightstand to snag the condom they'd left there the previous night, ready for their next session.

"Shh, baby," he said, stealing a kiss one way, then the other. As he put on the condom, he used his body to force her onto her back. "Damn that mouth."

There was no time to reply. He surged forward,

driving himself into her all the way to the hilt.

"Danny…"

"Temptress," he grumbled, his eyes closed tight.

Choosing to take that as a compliment, Tess wound her legs around his hips and yanked him back when he tried to retreat.

The sudden jerk opened his eyes on hers. "You invited this temptress into your trailer," she said, gathering up his tee-shirt.

He was polite enough to duck down so she could pull it off over his head and toss it away.

"I sure did."

With little effort, he pulled his hips back and held them there until she looked him in the eye. Only then did one side of his mouth tip up. He winked. His ease relaxed her. She had no clue how he did it, but he was an expert at imparting his calm.

Thanking him for that wasn't easy. Tess couldn't explain her need for that oblivion, so how could she voice her gratitude? Danny wouldn't quiz her. He accepted everything, and wouldn't even know how to judge.

Kissing her fingertips, she raised them to his mouth to offer the only kiss she could while on her back with him inside her.

The simple act did something to him. A new kind of determination darkened his gaze; he switched up one gear and then another. Pushing into her, moving fast, giving her what she needed.

Whatever he did was what she needed. The previous night and at that minute, Danny was a lover who wanted nothing. He had no expectation of her, and she none of him. That was what brought her back to him. Her body yielded to his, writhing and bucking in response to their merging.

Driving one fist into the mattress, he pushed himself onto a straight arm. Still pumping himself into her, he pinched her nipple, then dropped his fingers to where their bodies met.

Dampening his fingertips with her juices, he ran them up and around her clit. Heating and tormenting her, he sped up both of his caresses.

"Damnit, Danny," Tess whined, grabbing his braced arm.

Digging her nails in deep, she yelped and arched into the abyss of pure pleasure he fired through her. But he wasn't done, and kept up his caress until another orgasm consumed her. Only then did he slam his other fist into the bed and finish himself inside her.

In almost the same second that he climaxed, he left her alone. She didn't envy him the task of disposing of the condom. Lying there, staring at the ceiling, unable to catch her breath, Tess felt herself sink deeper.

Danny was oblivion. Easy, stable, safe oblivion. But he was something else too. The anchor she needed? No. He could never understand her nomadic life, and she had no right to steal his stability. No matter what, her time with Danny was limited. Yet when she went, a part of herself would stay with him. The possibility of what might have been would always be with her too.

EIGHT

THE NEXT DAY, WHILE Danny did his work thing, Tess stayed in the trailer trying to figure out the puzzle. Seated in the dinette with papers spread out in front of her, she didn't even look up when the door opened and bumped shut without the latch clicking in.

Danny passed the dinette to go to the fridge. "You been at that all day?" he asked, retrieving a beer. "Whatcha doing anyway?"

"Writing down everything I can remember from the letters."

Most of the information was committed to paper when she first sat down. Still, throughout the day, as anything came to mind, she quickly added it to the list.

"Why not go home and get 'em?"

"Someone took them from the house," she said, sitting back with her notebook in hand. "I can't remember reading anything about Greek mythology in the letters themselves, but…" Holding up a finger, she looked at him over the top of her notepad to see him crook a questioning brow. "I was thinking, what if H is Hades?"

He shrugged. "Could be." Danny took another mouthful of beer before frowning. "What's H again?"

Putting down the notebook, she pushed out of the dinette. "The writer of the letters. He's the guy who wrote the letters."

"How do you know he's a guy?"

"He talks about his dick."

"Good clue," Danny said, setting his beer on the dinette table.

Tess raised her arms when he gathered her top to take it off over her head. "Doesn't help me with who C is," she said, her mind working. Danny opened the snap of her jeans and lowered the zipper. "Can't help me with Pandora either. And the numbers are still a mystery. He mentioned Miami once… that was in the first letter I read." Pushing her jeans and underwear from her hips, Danny crouched to guide her feet out of the fabric one at a time. "But what would I do? Just show up in Miami?"

When he stood, he took her hips to pick her up and sit her on the counter between the stove and sink. "Miami's hot," he said, moving in close between her thighs.

In her pondering, she glanced up. "I'm going back to see Figgs tomorrow. I should've asked more questions. Like when my mom was there and if she said anything." Stinging pain joined the sudden pressure on her pussy, tensing her muscles. That's what he was doing? She hadn't been paying attention, but there he was, cock in hand, condom on, trying to push himself into her. "Geez, Danny, foreplay, baby."

"Right," he said and muttered, "foreplay."

Danny disappeared in a crouch again. This time, he wound his arms around her thighs and yanked her to the edge of the counter.

"It's fine," Tess said. "I don't even want sex right now, I—oh…"

His tongue slid through her, warming her clit with the heat of his breath and the slick, moist movement of his teasing.

Tess ran her fingers into his hair, holding it in her fist. "Right there, baby," she said, closing her eyes.

His lips caught her clit, holding it firm as his tongue flickered over her. Drawing in a long breath, she let it go in a moan and planted her other hand on the counter behind her to raise her hips closer to his intimate kiss.

It didn't take him long to get her going, not when he was so thorough in his skill. Lapping at her opening, he lubricated his route with the tip of his tongue, circling and pushing it into her, moving at the pace of her hips.

Close to the edge, Tess could feel the shimmers of climax quaking through her, ready to explode. Just before they did, he stood up and twined an arm around her to guide her body onto his waiting cock.

"Better," she said, relaxing her eyelids. His weren't much more open than hers. "You're so damn good at everything, Danny Boy."

One of his dimples appeared slowly, the same pace as the undulation of his body. In typical Danny style, he was in no rush, no hurry to get to the finish line. Pushing as far into her as he could, he paused there for a few seconds, then pulled back, leaving only half of himself inside her. He swayed in and out, playing with her, moving an inch back and forth.

Digging her teeth into her lip, the promise of orgasm was too close for her to ignore. "Faster, Danny."

"I've been thinking 'bout this all day," he said, skimming his hands around to unhook her bra.

It fell away and his rough hands closed around her breasts, fondling her, enjoying her, using her for his pleasure. He didn't want to go faster because he wanted that moment. That was what he'd been thinking about. The sex, sure, but she could read it in the way he drank her in. It wasn't just the orgasm; he wanted to savor her.

Tess had never been savored. The moment. She'd never lived in the now. Her life was running, always being aware, planning for what was next, suspecting every coincidence.

"Danny," she whispered, pushing off her hand to press her body to his.

"Not so bad havin' a willing woman waiting in my trailer at the end of the day."

Brushing her lips across his chest, she peeked up at him, squeezing her inner muscles to tease him a little. "I cooked for you too.”

His brows went up; she side-nodded at the stove. Tess held his ribs as he leaned to the side and took the lid from the pot to dip his finger into the sauce. As he sucked the digit into his mouth, his brow descended.

“No good?” she asked, worried his expression couldn’t mean anything positive.

It took another couple of seconds for his finger to slide free of his lips. His brow relaxed again, and he smiled down at her. “Don’t taste as good as you.”

On a laugh, she wrapped both arms around him. “That’s a good line.”

“Wonder if we’ve got any candles around.”

Dinner by candlelight. Nice idea that wouldn’t happen.

“I’m working tonight,” she said. “You’ll be stag.”

Leaning over her, he forced her back, his hips moving between her thighs. “Better make the most of you while I’ve got you then,” he mumbled, kissing her head and pulling his cock out to slam it into her again.

Once his mind was set on his goal, it didn’t take long for him to get there. His finesse took both of them over the precipice of orgasm. And, as usual, he withdrew to deal with the condom while she was left trying to figure out who she was and what planet they were on.

The mess of papers on the dinette table reminded her what she’d been doing before he arrived looking for action. Sliding from the counter, Tess snagged his beer and drank some while running an eye over her day’s work.

Without looking, she felt him coming down the center of the trailer. “I still can’t believe they’re gone,” she said.

Danny stopped behind her, reaching around to take the beer from her hand as he kissed the top of her head. “You call the cops?”

“No,” she said and breathed out. “I thought about it, but what are they going to do? It’s not like I have any evidence the letters were even there. Who would steal letters and leave the TV? Besides, it was sort of my mother’s philosophy to avoid official type agencies as much as possible."

"How come?" he asked, giving her the beer back and going down the trailer to drop into his recliner.

Turning to him, she had the bottle at her lips when she noticed his focus on her body. Jerking the bottle away, Tess glanced down at her naked form, comparing that to his clothed one. Next time she looked at his face, he was grinning.

"I should get some clothes from home."

"Don't bother me," he said, sliding into a slouch and propping the side of his wrist on the top of his head as he pressed the power button to extend the footrest of the chair. "Kinda works."

"Yeah, for you," she said, putting down the bottle and reversing up the trailer to open the closet next to the stove. "What if one of your buddies walk in? Not like you ever lock your door."

He frowned and glanced the way of the door like he'd never thought about it. Tess grabbed one of his tee-shirts to put it on. After scooping her hair out, she closed the closet and pointed at the stove.

"You want some food?"

"Later," he said and patted his thigh. "Take a seat."

"We just had sex," she said, retrieving another beer from the fridge. If Danny ever met a genie, his first wish would be for an endless supply. Of that she was sure. She opened the bottle and went to him. "We can't do it every minute."

"I've been working all day," he said, grabbing her wrist to tug her down onto his lap.

She laughed, relaxing against the high arm of the chair. Danny took the beer and gulped some down. "I've been working too and I'm working tonight."

"Okay," he said, putting the beer on the shelf behind the chairs. "Then you go first."

His hand snaked under her tee-shirt to slither up and over her breast.

"Danny," she said, scooping both hands around his jaw to make him look at her. "You know this stuff with my mom, trying to figure out her message, you know it's important to me, right?"

He nodded, his head heavy in her grasp, and his hand still playing with her breast. "Sure. Important. Got it."

Ducking forward, he freed his head from her hands and pushed her head aside to kiss her neck.

Either he didn't understand, or he didn't care. A smile warmed her lips. Danny was just Danny. Nothing deep there. No complex man with far-reaching ambitions. All he wanted was his trailer, his beer, and sex while she was there to give it up.

"I have to shower," she said, fighting her urge to relax into the promise of what he offered: instant carnal gratification.

Wriggling out of his hold, Tess found her feet in sync with his disappointed groan.

"What's the point of having a gal roommate if I can't get laid?"

Shaking her head, Tess didn't subdue her smile as she addressed him over her shoulder. "You just did get laid… I'll come back after my shift and we'll do it again… You should probably buy more condoms."

Opening the shower door, she turned on the water and shirked the tee-shirt.

"Nah, I'll just wait here, smoke some weed, play my guitar… Earl's cable's out."

"Earl?"

"Buckhorn," he said. "Guy who owns the joint."

In the shower, there was no shampoo or conditioner or separate soap, only some white bottle with green writing that claimed the contents were three in one. Typical Danny to go for the easiest option. Wearing a smile, she shampooed her hair and washed her body.

When Tess turned off the water and opened the door, Danny was standing there holding a towel, waiting for her. She hadn't expected to see him right there, but took the towel to dry her face. Even before he opened his mouth, she knew what he wanted.

"No," Tess said. "I can't go to work with you all over me."

"You just used my soap."

Good point. So, no matter what, she was doomed to carry him with her for the rest of the night, which would drive her crazy.

"If you're that bored, come to the club, have a drink."

"Bad idea," he said, shaking his head.

Tess went to retrieve her clothes. Leaving the panties, she put everything else on. "Why? Just sit there at the bar and I'll ply you with alcohol."

"Yeah," he said, slipping his hands into his pockets as he slumped back to lean on the closet. "But I'm in a gettin' busy kinda mood. Places like that are prime pickings with so many liquored up women."

"What a gentleman," she said, using the towel to dry her hair as best she could. "Is my bag still in the bedroom?"

Raising his brows, he went to look and came back a few seconds later with her carpet bag. Tess put it on the counter to retrieve her comb from a side pocket. Standing just behind her, Danny ran an eye over her mess on the table.

"You remember a lot from those letters."

"Huh?" she asked, still combing her hair, moving around to his side to see what he was looking at. It was nothing specific, though her notebook was there on top of everything else. "I read them a bunch of times. And I know there's a lot I missed... What I really remember are the questions they raised."

"Questions?"

"Yeah," she said as he finished his beer and went to get another. "Whoever this H was or is, he's angry about something. I don't know what. My mom told me there was something behind us, you know? Something we should be afraid of."

"Maybe it was him," Danny said, propping a shoulder on the fridge.

"Maybe," she said, her focus drifting back to the notes and Xeroxes she'd taken from the library. "But he loved her... For as long as I can remember, every time we moved to a new city, we got a new last name. I've had so many that I can hardly keep track. I'm wondering if maybe when I was little, or maybe before she had me, if my mom changed her first name too… Maybe that's why he calls her C."

"And you think H is Hades."

She shrugged and turned to him. "I don't know, Danny." Tess sighed. "If it is, then my mother was telling me to go to him or warning me to stay away from him."

If that deduction was true, she had a hell of a choice. It was one extreme or the other. H would save her or kill her.

"What do you think?" Danny asked.

"I don't know. I'm going back to see Figgs tomorrow. Hopefully, he'll remember something my mom said, something useful. After that I'll go around the places she worked. She did cleaning jobs for a bunch of places and worked in a nursery. She knew so much about plants…" Referring to her in the past tense stung. "I've searched the house and there's nothing there, but she could've left something at work."

"Woman with a plan," Danny said, opening the closet to reach into the back. When he pulled out the guitar case, his proud smile made her laugh. "You've got it covered, baby."

As he passed her on his way to the recliner, he kissed her head. He put the case down and opened it up to produce a guitar from inside and his smile grew again. Simple pleasures.

NINE

THAT FRIDAY, DANNY made himself known the moment he entered the trailer. "Where's my dinner, woman!"

After finishing with the buckle of her sandal, Tess sprang to her feet. "Make it yourself, hick," she said, striding down the trailer.

When he noticed her outfit, his head tilted. Throughout the week, of the two of them, he'd cooked most often. Always something quick and easy, which was just fine. Her priorities lay elsewhere.

Each day, she buried herself in her notes and lost track of time. The infuriating mystery remained unsolved. Her mother's workplaces had yielded no results. Russell Figgs had disappeared. Snap. Just like that. Gone. Every day that week, his office was locked up. Empty. Abandoned. She'd tried to trace his home address, only to find he was unlisted.

Her mess on and around the dinette was just part of the trailer's décor now. She'd stuck anything significant on the day shades. Danny hadn't complained. He never complained about anything. The only thing on the other side of those windows was the concrete wall of the office building. It wasn't like she'd blocked out any exciting vista.

Her intention was to go past him, but he stepped into

her path and reached up to press play on the music system. The Pointer Sisters track that vibrated through the air was his way of letting her know what was on his mind. Like she needed a hint. Sex was always on his mind.

The familiar tune complemented the curl of seduction on his lips and the light in his heavy eyes. Though the latter was probably less related to being horny and more to the lingering scent of weed in his aura. Seemed that was how he got through most days in the junkyard. She didn't blame him. Being stuck in the office couldn't be riveting work.

Tess put a hand on his chest as he bent his knees to curve an arm around her. "No," she said, but he took her hand and moved them to the music. "I'm going out."

"I got everything you need right here," he said above her ear, dipping lower to kiss her neck.

The guy was insatiable. How had he ever survived without a woman on hand twenty-four seven? Not that she was complaining. Being wanted so much was a novelty, she'd never felt so desired or welcome anywhere. And their intimacy did ease her worries. Whenever they were screwing, Tess could forget and just be with him.

"Danny," she whined.

Time was running short. But if he kept kissing her like that… His splayed hand slid down to gather her dress up out of the way of her ass so he could squeeze and stroke her.

"I can be quick," he mumbled in her ear.

Raising her hand to look at her watch over his shoulder, Tess exhaled. "Okay."

Spinning her around, Danny tossed her dress out of the way as she bent over to grab the sink. He pulled her panties down to her knees and rubbed her clit a few times. To speed things along, she opened the cabinet above to retrieve a condom and offered it to him over her shoulder. After Danny grabbed it, she heard him spit out the pack he'd probably torn with his teeth, then his fingers were slipping into her, testing if she was ready for him.

"Love the heels, babe," he said, but still had to bend his knees to line up their bodies.

It couldn't be comfortable for him, always making

allowances for their height difference.

The moment he slid into her, a familiar internal hum of completion agitated her hormones. Both of them exhaled in the same tone of bliss. Her lips curled, but her laugh didn't linger when he began to do his thing.

Saying his name, Tess pushed back, working to get them where they were going. Instinct moved her fingers to the center of her body. Before she could think to stimulate herself, Danny's hand overtook hers, shoving it aside to massage her clit. The guy already had one powerful forearm supporting her hips, holding her up so her toes were barely touching the floor. He was a guy who liked to be in control.

The longer Tess stayed with him, the more she got to know the person behind the lazy first impression. He could cook, play guitar better than anyone she'd ever heard in real life, and liked to be in control. When it came to sex anyway.

He filled her with his need, driving in fast and hard, doing his bit to keep the promise of haste. Tess yelped and grabbed for his hand between her legs to stall it. Holding him tight, she panted out short breaths charged with her desperate agreement.

He surged into her, shunting her against the sink, dropping her hands and her hips at the same time.

Accomplishing anything after they were done was impossible. No point in trying. Bent over the sink, her forehead on her forearm, her eyes closed. She'd thought it was his eyes, being under his intense focus that immobilized her after they got off. But it wasn't. They'd done it in various positions, all around the trailer, even in the office during work hours. Every time, afterwards, she felt weak, inside and out, like each time he was stealing something that she needed to exist.

The hard smack of his hand on her ass snapped her out of her daze. "Thought you were in a hurry."

"Right," she said, doing nothing as he pulled her panties up. "Hurry. Yeah."

The cable was working again, so he went to his recliner, the one closest to the door that he always favored, and turned on the TV. Tess washed her hands and took her compact from the clutch she'd put on the counter earlier. Checking her makeup and flushed cheeks, nothing was too out of place. Not on the outside anyway. Inside she was still dizzy.

"Bring beer home," he said, popping out the footrest of the recliner as he slouched into his familiar position with his forearm on his head.

"Beer?" she asked, putting her compact away.

"We're almost out," he said, slipping a hand down the front of his sweats.

"Sure," she said, tucking her clutch under her arm. "Anything else?"

"Nah, I'll order pizza… We're outta that breakfast milk you like too."

Coconut milk wasn't urgent. It wasn't exactly breakfast milk either, that's just when she tended to enjoy it.

Bending over him, she put a hand on the arm of the chair, and he tipped his mouth her way to accept her quick kiss. Before she could stand up, he hooked a finger into the neckline of her dress and curled it to pull her close for a longer, slower kiss.

"Mm," Tess said, drifting on the awakening of his kiss.

Moves like that were usually reserved for their bedroom. Memories of what had followed kisses like that in the past heated her mind's eye.

"Shower the other guy off before you come home though, baby, huh?"

Surprised by his request, her eyes opened to find he was already looking past her at the television on the wall beyond the dinette.

Standing up straight, Tess didn't know whether to be offended or reassure him she didn't intend on sleeping with anyone else. From his obvious indifference, it didn't seem that he wanted any guarantees. They'd slipped into living together with no major hitches. That was probably because they did their best not to step in on each other's business.

Backing off, Tess said nothing else as she exited the trailer. Danny knew she was ensconced in her mystery, but never asked much about it. Never more than was necessary to prove he was paying attention to the fact she was talking. Tess didn't mind dealing with it by herself. Explaining her history would take too long. And, in truth, there was too much she didn't understand about the "*why?*" to convey it to anyone.

Danny wanted nothing from her. They didn't get gooey and mushy. Their interactions were friendly, but it wasn't like either of them had asked for or made promises.

Their relationship, if it could be dubbed that… association was a better description. Their association fit her. It gave her what she needed: a companion. Someone to stop her feeling alone. There was no jealousy or arguing. He wasn't attached to her, as he'd proved by referencing her being with another man. With Danny, everything was uncomplicated.

Switching out of the relaxed mindset in the cab on the way to the bar, it was important to be vigilant. When engrossed in her work, her purpose was sure. The aim of going to meet Patrick wasn't so clear.

She'd walked out on him the previous week. There was a chance he wouldn't be waiting for her at all. If it wasn't for her suspicions, maybe she wouldn't have kept the date. She just had to know.

Tess and her mother had run from their lives dozens of times. So far, she'd been lucky that they hadn't had to run from physical danger. None that she knew about anyway.

When the cab dropped her off, she experienced her first real dose of fear. It was a crowded bar; nothing could happen to her. People would see. People would hear if she screamed.

Tess wasn't afraid of Patrick because she'd walked out on him. That he might be the person who'd gone into her mother's bedroom and taken something of hers? Yeah, that guy was scary.

Deciding to stand up to whatever her mom was running from was going to mean doing things far scarier than meeting a man in a bar. She wasn't alone. Danny would notice if she dropped off the face of the Earth. If for no other reason than there was no one around to suck his cock, he'd notice.

Pushing her shoulders back and her chest out, Tess

strode on, opening the door and going inside. The background music and conversations of others gave some comfort. The bar was the same as always. Turning to check their table, she ignored the part of her that wanted to find it empty.

It wasn't.

Raising his hand in a static wave, Patrick rose out of his chair to sweep a hand toward their table, showing he'd already got drinks. Forcing herself to smile, Tess went to him. He often bought drinks before she got there. Even when she offered to buy them, he would say he was happy to pay. That night, the paying part was less her concern than the drink being exposed to the air, vulnerable to anything anyone might slip into it.

"Hi," Patrick said, leaning over to kiss her cheek as she slipped in at her side of the table. "I wasn't sure you'd come."

"I wasn't sure either," she said, sitting down just before he did.

No matter how she tried to play it in her mind, she couldn't pick the right course. Confronting him with her suspicion could just scare him back into his hole or force him to take drastic direct action. Strategy wasn't her strong suit.

And there, in that minute, her stupidity was blinding. Another warm body to fill the void left by her mother wasn't what she wanted. She wanted someone to care. That was what her mother did. Anne loved her… and that was why she'd run from the Big Bad.

Damnit.

Why hadn't she seen it sooner? They'd been running her entire life. They were running because of her, because her mother wouldn't risk the life of her child for any reason.

Patrick reached over to touch her wrist. "Are you okay?"

Taking her arm from beneath his grip, she sat back. "Yes, sorry," Tess said, still not sure how she'd get to the truth. "It's been a long week."

"I was worried about you. You disappeared and then… I didn't know what to do."

Because she didn't have a phone number and had never given him her address. If he was genuine in his identity, her behavior would seem odd. If not, she wasn't in any rush to give him personal information.

"I know, I just… You know, with my mom and…"

"Sure," he said, nodding. "You've been through a lot recently. Did you find out more about your mom's letters?"

She shook her head, keeping her focus from his, deciding then that she wouldn't reveal the truth. "No. I couldn't face it. I wouldn't know where to begin and I don't even know if they're hers."

"Yeah, you said that," he said, sipping his drink. An awkward silence descended. The rest of the bar was happy and busy; their little corner by the window was neither. Patrick cleared his throat. "I guess the place to start is with how they were exchanged."

That took her gaze to his. "Exchanged?"

"Didn't you say there were no envelopes or that you couldn't find them? Do you think whoever he was writing to wrote back?"

The subject was sensitive. Still, as long as he was putting useful ideas in her head, she wouldn't stop it. Already her mind was working. In what she'd read, there were references to received letters. So, yes, they had been writing to each other back and forth.

"I… I don't know," she said, pushing up to sit straighter. Moving her purse in time with the adjustment, she used it to knock over the drink, making it seem accidental. Liquid cascaded across the table; both of them shoved their chairs back to avoid the stream. "Damnit, I'm sorry."

Apparently Patrick hadn't been fast enough. "That's okay," he said, swiping at his pants. "I should go to the restroom to clean up."

"Sure," Tess said, offering him a tight smile.

He started to rise, but paused to look her in the eye. "You will be here when I get back, won't you?"

"Of course," she said, widening her smile. With a nod, he got up to head for the men's room. Tess watched his progress until he was out of sight. "Just don't expect me to drink anything you put in front of me."

Leaving the table, Tess went to buy a bottle of wine. That would sustain her and prevent the necessity of skirting drink offers. She'd stay a while, see if she could read any cracks in his persona while they discussed the week. Avoiding talk about herself, she'd see if he tried to divert conversation her way or raised the letters again. If he had an obvious interest, her suspicions about him could be valid.

Coming to meet him had been worth it already. The exchange of the letters had niggled at her. Why hadn't she focused more on that detail? Now she would. How would two people correspond when at least one of them was moving all the time?

TEN

HER DATE LASTED AROUND three hours. Despite that, when she got back, Danny was in basically the same position she'd left him in.

"Ran outta beer two hours ago," he said, his attention trained on the TV.

As asked, she'd bought beer. Stashing most of it in the fridge, she kept two and opened them. Neither was for her; an entire bottle of wine at the bar was her limit. She took both to him and handed one over. He sealed his lips around the top and tipped his head back to empty it into his throat. Because she was blocking his view of the TV, he used an arm to edge her over a few inches.

"Let's say you want to send me a letter," she said.

He finished downing the first beer and tossed the bottle toward the kitchen sink. It clattered against the metal, then slowed to roll back and forth by the drain. Tess handed him the second as she pushed up the table section between the two recliners and kneeled on the fixed central portion facing him.

Drinking beer and focused on the TV, Danny didn't acknowledge her with more than a grunt. He was more interested in taking his hand out of his pants to switch it out with hers. Without disconnecting his eyes from the game, he slipped her hand beneath the waistband of his sweats. He was only semi-erect, but she gave him a squeeze and started to stroke him. It didn't matter to Danny that her mind was elsewhere, not while she was taking care of his business for him.

"You want to write me a letter," she said again. "Except I keep moving and you don't have my address. How would you get it to me?"

Relaxing his hips to slouch more, his hand went to the back of his head. "Depends if I know where you go."

"Where I go?"

He slurped more beer. "I want you to have something and can't send it, I put it somewhere I know you'll be. That's how one of my weed guys transacts."

Made sense. Except Tess and her mother didn't frequent the same cities, let alone the same places.

"You'd just leave it out in public?" she asked. "Anyone could pick it up."

"No, you hide it under something or in something… You've gotta talk to figure it out, so you know where to look."

"What if you couldn't talk to figure it out?"

"I don't know," he mumbled, probably irritated that she was interrupting his sports-fest. "Why would I know something like that?"

Tess intercepted his bottle on its way to his lips. "You watch those crime shows," she said, taking a mouthful of beer. "You like mysteries."

"You're no mystery," he said, snagging the bottle when she lowered it. "Suck it for me, baby."

He raised his hips to push himself deeper into her fist.

Leaning closer, Tess rested an elbow on his shoulder and relaxed her forearm on his chest. "You don't help me with my mystery, I won't help with your cock." Pushing a little closer, she took her lips to his ear. "Ever again."

"I got 'em lined up for your job, Little Red."

"Yeah, 'cept you'd actually have to go out to the street to trap one and haul her back."

"Too much effort."

"Exactly," she said, sliding her hand out of his pants to climb over and straddle him. "Too much effort."

Leaning back, curling her fingers around his knees for support, she rolled her hips, using her body to arouse his.

Her position didn't block his view of the TV; he just kept on watching and slurping his beer.

"You shower after your guy?"

"I didn't have sex with him," she said, pushing herself flush against him.

"Cool. You wearing panties?"

"No action until you talk this out with me. Toss ideas at me."

He shrugged, switching his focus to the TV at the same time as he slipped a hand under her dress and into her panties to play with her clit.

Gritting her teeth, Tess hissed in a breath. "You think if you turn me on enough, I'll forget my question?"

One side of his mouth sloped up, and he winked, still fixated on the TV.

Boosting her hands from his knees, she fell forward to grab his shoulders. "I'll suck it," she purred, holding her lips just away from his.

His finger slithered south to push into her. Try as she might to ignore his tormenting, her hips moved like his brain was the one in control of her body.

He tipped his head back to gulp down the last of the beer, then slammed the bottle onto the shelf behind the chairs.

"Got a better idea."

Wrapping both arms around her, he put the chair down, dropped to his knees, and laid her on the floor. He didn't even bother to ask. He just pushed up her skirt, yanked his pants down, and sank himself into her.

Tess wanted an answer to her question for about as long as she remembered she had one. Sliding her hands up and down his body, she gave herself to him and appreciated what he gave her. She didn't even realize anything was different until in the scorching midst of her orgasm, Danny rose higher and released a long feral call of what could only be described as rage.

The depth of that primal exclamation stalled her own pleasure. When she looked up at him, he wasn't looking at her. Judging by the fierce scowl on his face, his mind was somewhere else completely. His mouth only closed for a fraction of a second after his shout silenced. Just as quickly as it came, it became a curse. He shoved off the floor to stalk up the trailer.

Confused, she rose to her elbows. Tess had never been so with it after sex with him, but he'd never been so expressive. Ever. Literally ever, in all the time she'd known him. Something could be wrong. Had she broken him?

Pushing her dress down, she clambered to her feet. "Danny," she called after him.

The moment she passed the restroom door, he shoved it open, blocking the hallway. Instead of reassuring her or laughing off his odd behavior, he grabbed her wrist and stepped forward, forcing her backwards. He raised her arm to slam it against the frame of the shower.

"Is that good?" he barked.

Danny didn't bark. He never got angry. Yeah, sometimes there was the odd grumpy word but never fury.

"Wh… what?"

He pointed at the scar on her arm. "The implant. You've got the implant, right?"

Her jaw moved, though it took her a few seconds to figure out why he was asking. "Oh my God, we didn't use a condom." His grip on her wrist tightened, which was enough to remind her of his question. "Yes! It's good. Less than a year old."

He breathed out. "Okay."

His scowl relaxed as the rest of his muscles did; relief washed over him. His fingers loosened from around her wrist, and he closed his eyes.

Just as she'd thought earlier, before her date, they'd never promised themselves to each other. Although she was pretty sure he hadn't been with another woman in the last week while they'd been living together, that didn't mean he was clean as a whistle.

Rather than question him about his sexual history,

Tess decided it would be a good idea to get herself to a clinic as soon as possible.

"I did buy more," she said, watching him run a weary hand through his hair. "They're in my purse."

"I'll get a whole bunch tomorrow," he said, walking away from her to open the fridge. "Put 'em everywhere. We can't let that happen again."

"No," she said, taking the beer he offered.

He held his toward hers, she raised it up to touch the bottles to each other. Like that gesture was enough to erase the moment, he left her there by the shower to go back to his recliner.

That was his happy place. The place he sat when he wanted to relax and just be Danny. A happy place seemed like a damn fine prospect. Tess had been nowhere that could...

"The glitter," she whispered. Something from the letter came back to her. "The glitter... you know our code."

It was so obvious she wanted to kick her own ass. Striding Danny's way, she put the beer on the counter by the sink.

"Can you get me a vehicle?" His mouth was on the lip of the beer bottle, but he tipped his eyes her way. "You and the guys fix up cars here, right?"

Propping his beer on the arm of his chair, Danny moved to get more comfortable. "My truck's good enough to pull this hunk of junk. You can take that. When'll you be back?"

"I won't," she said, grabbing her clutch from the counter behind the beer. Opening it up, she showed him the box of condoms, then put them beside her bottle. "To replenish your supplies."

She wouldn't need them for the foreseeable future. Their slip was enough to remind her how dangerous distractions could be. What happened to being a woman on a mission? Sex and the simple life shouldn't distract that woman.

Her carpet bag was still in the bedroom, so she went to grab it and fill it with the clothes she'd brought from home earlier in the week.

"You're leaving?" Danny asked when she went to the closet to get the last of her things.

"Yeah," she said, flashing him a smile. "You've been a real star, baby. Thank you."

If it wasn't for him, she may never have thought about her mom's happy place. As a child, she'd never understood why the shabby old building was so important. She hadn't minded, because whatever incarnation the building took, she usually got to play. Laser tag hadn't been fun, the trampolines were, as was the bowling alley; that had probably been her favorite.

Once the closet was empty of her things, she scooped her mess of work up from the dinette. Pulling everything from the walls, it didn't take long to stow the papers. Danny could have his bachelor trailer back. Almost like she'd never been there at all.

"Anytime, Little Red." She fastened her bag. "You going right now?"

"I have to pack up the house." Which could take hours. Her neighbors might complain about the noise of the washer and dryer, but they wouldn't have to worry about her much longer. "I'll stop by in the morning to pick up the car, just whatever you can figure out would be great. I can pay."

The money from the box Figgs gave her was at the house. At least it should be.

Danny obviously wasn't the type for the big emotional goodbye. She'd miss him. But there was something comforting about knowing he'd be there, just being himself, ticking days off the calendar.

Leaving her bag by the door, Tess kneeled on the floor at his feet. His attention slid from the TV to her once and then again.

"Gonna suck it before you go?"

Just like him to think there would only be one reason for a woman to kneel in front of a man.

Laying her hands on his thighs, Tess slid them higher as she pushed up on her knees. "I'm saying goodbye," she said, sliding her palms up under his tee-shirt. "You're a good guy, Danny. You did this woman a favor in a dark time. I won't forget that."

On a slow blink, one corner of his mouth rose. "No sweat, Little Red. Anytime."

"Come here," she said, putting a hand on each side of his face to guide their mouths together.

The sweet sensation of his kiss always spoke to the deepest part of her. He never hesitated to reciprocate. Their kiss, this last kiss, was their final gift to each other. Tess was saying goodbye. Of all the people she'd walked away from in all of her many lives, she'd would miss Danny the most.

Finding him at just the right time, he had been exactly what she needed to absorb the blow of loneliness brought on by her mother's death. From then on, Tess would be alone, but her memories of Buckhorn's Danny would still warm her when she needed comfort.

ELEVEN

SANITIZING A HOME TOOK time. Tess hadn't appreciated how much more it would take without her mother's help.

She almost forgot about the weird metal thing she'd stashed in the kitchen drawer. Was it important or irrelevant? Given that someone had gone to the trouble of breaking in to steal her mom's letters, it would be best to keep the metal object somewhere secret.

The base of her mom's urn unscrewed, just like the lid. After wrapping the prongy thing in a bunch of duct tape to prevent rattling, she taped it into the urn base before screwing it back on. Job done.

By morning, the process was complete. The landlord had their security deposit. The place was sparkling clean, and she left a letter telling him to keep the deposit to cover her notice.

Closing up the house was difficult. It was the last place her mom lived; the last place they'd lived together. They'd never be anywhere together again.

Errands distracted her. Somewhat. First was the post office to set up a PO Box. Next, she did a quick run around all the stores that still had her inventory to tell them where to mail her checks.

Most of her mom's clothes were left at a charity place. Walking away wasn't easy. All she kept thinking about was how her mom would insist they carried nothing unnecessary. Sentimental items stayed, but the clothes that didn't fit or weren't her style had to go.

Finished with her tasks, Tess hailed a cab and bundled everything inside, keeping the urn with her mother's ashes in her lap for the ride. As they approached Buckhorn, something long and gleaming parked in front of the yard brought her to the edge of her seat. Stunned, she raised her sunglasses to the top of her head and blinked at the sight up ahead.

"Just here's fine," she said.

The cab driver stopped. Once she'd paid the fare, he helped her take her things from the trunk.

Her sewing machine was in its box, strapped to the extended handle of the suitcase. With a backpack on each shoulder, she hooked her carpet bag on one forearm and held her mom's urn to her body with the other.

Striding up the block, it was difficult to believe the sight. His damn trailer and a huge black truck in front of it. His truck, obviously.

Danny leaped out the driver's side and opened his arms. "We said early."

"We?" Tess asked, pausing, standing up her suitcase.

He didn't get that she'd stopped ten feet away to show her displeasure because he jumped to action and narrowed the space between them to nothing. After first taking her carpet bag, he squeezed his fingers under hers to curl them around the handle of the suitcase. She tightened her grip.

"Gotta get on the road, baby," Danny said.

"I said a vehicle," she said. "I don't want your trailer and I do not want a travel buddy."

Despite always having one in the past. That path of thoughts had the potential to be dangerous. Just like her future. Avenging her mom, taking down the threat that plagued their lives, whatever was ahead of her, no way should it or her actions endanger the innocent Danny.

His gaze settled on the urn tucked under her breast. "What's that?"

"My mom," she said. The look in his eye raised her defenses. Tess let go of the case and wrapped her other forearm around the urn. "Quit looking at her like that."

"Her?"

"Danny!"

He shrugged. "Okay, cool. If she wants to tag along, that's fine by me."

He spun to stride away, taking her bag, suitcase, and sewing machine with him. Snapping to attention, she hurried after him, but he'd already loaded her suitcase into the back of the truck.

"That's my stuff!"

"I know, baby," he said, unthreading the other backpack from her shoulder to toss it in too. He looked at her mom again. "Don't think I should put her back here."

"No, I don't think you should," she said. He closed the tailgate and snagged her pinkie with his own. "What are you doing?"

His plan became apparent when he guided her around the hood and opened the front passenger door.

"You don't wanna drive," he said when she made no move to get in.

"Who says I don't want to drive?" she asked, though that hadn't been her objection.

"You ever hauled an Airstream?"

Growling in frustration, Tess didn't want to argue with him. He picked her up to toss her into the vehicle.

Once the door was closed, he hurried around to the driver's side and got in. After sticking the key in the ignition with less finesse than he usually showed, Danny put on his seatbelt, then waited.

When nothing happened, he nodded beyond her shoulder. "Seatbelt, babe."

It would've been insensitive to forget given her mother had died in a car wreck. Except Tess hadn't forgotten. Putting on her seatbelt would be a signal that she intended to go with him.

Now that they were alone in the quiet, it was a good time to make him see sense.

"Danny," she said, looking at him. "I really appreciate what you're trying to do. I do. But... I don't want a boyfriend."

His tongue moved to the corner of his mouth. Waiting for his response, she hoped being blunt hadn't offended him.

"Fuck buddy," he said, startling her. "That's what I'll be... or friends with benefits. I don't know the difference... I think it's something to do with ice-cream."

What the hell was he talking about? It didn't matter. His motivation was more relevant.

"You're coming with me for sex?"

Releasing his own seatbelt, he reached over the cab for hers, pulling it across her body before clicking it into the slot.

"Sex is as good a reason as any to hit the road," he said, putting on his own seatbelt again, then starting the engine. "Not so bad having a base on wheels, baby, you'll see. No motel bills, just gas and rubbers... We go where we like, stop when we like, screw when we like."

When he was being so him, it was difficult to remember her point. "This isn't a vacation, Danny. I have a purpose and I don't have time for fooling around."

"Right, no fooling around," he said. "I'll just give it to you hard and fast when we stop for gas."

"Danny," she groaned. "Sex isn't a reason to leave your life."

"Time to get outta town anyway. Earl got on my case; we had a blowout. I'm done with Buckhorn."

"You fought with your boss?" she asked, not paying much attention to the fact they were moving. "You can't leave after one fight."

Danny's focus had been on the windshield a while. His certainty was enviable. He didn't know where they were going; he couldn't when she didn't even know. Yet he didn't break a sweat, not even an eyelash twitched in hesitation.

"Already quit," he said, sliding a hand up the steering wheel to rest his wrist on top. "Bored there anyway."

The amount of time he spent getting stoned at work was no doubt a problem for his boss. From Danny's perspective, Tess had assumed being out of it all the time would alleviate any boredom he felt while manning the office.

"Bored? Okay," she said, tightening her hold on her mother's urn. "That doesn't mean you should leave town. This is your home."

His lips quirked. His dimple gave her a glimpse of his amusement. "Why you think that? You think a guy who lives in a trailer on wheels ever sticks anywhere for long?"

Now that he said it out loud like that… The trailer was modern, inside and out. Clean, well-maintained, easy for a guy who was a mechanic by trade. But he was right. Just the fact that he had it, and that he took care of it, implied he wasn't one for putting down roots. It actually made her wonder why she and her mother had never thought of hauling their home with them wherever they went.

Her head relaxed to the side, coming to rest on the seat. "You never talk about your family," she said. "About where you're from."

"You never asked."

No, she hadn't and didn't like what that said about her as a person. "Can I ask now?"

"Ask later," he said, nodding toward the stereo. "Road trip needs music."

Glancing at the stereo, it didn't surprise her he wanted music, but *was* surprised to see a tape deck in such a modern truck. "My God, where did you get that thing?"

"Had to put it in myself," he said. "There're tapes in the glovebox."

Opening the hatch between the seats, Tess nestled her mom's urn inside. Perfect fit. Once she was happy it was secure and wouldn't be bouncing around, she flipped her focus to the glove box. Digging around inside, she saw there were a few CDs at the back, but mostly it was filled with cassette tapes.

She laughed, picking them out. "I can't even

remember the last time I saw cassettes.”

They weren’t descriptive, no names or listings of what was on them, just identified by a number. Every cassette appeared to be a homemade mixtape, and they were loose rather than in their cases.

“Look for mix five.”

“Okay,” she said, searching until she found number five.

Holding it up, she gave him the eye, but he just smiled and nodded at the stereo again. “Go for it.”

Pushing it in, Tess didn’t know what to expect. “If *Slow Hand* comes on, you’re on your own,” she said as the music started and Gloria Gaynor’s voice filled the cab. If she’d had to put money on it, the camp track would’ve been way down the list of possibilities. Tess laughed. “Are you kidding me?” But there he was, mouthing the words without shame. “Are you secretly gay?”

He took a breather from his lip syncing. “They say the wife is always the last to know.” Shaking her head, she couldn’t stop smiling at him. “There’s an epic Abba medley on the other side.”

“Can’t wait,” she said, propping a shoulder on the back of her chair to support her temple on the heel of her hand. “You do have some surprising traits, Danny…” She frowned. “I don’t know your last name.”

“Winger,” he said, reaching over to take her hand from her leg. “Come on, everyone knows the words to this one.”

“No,” she said, freeing her hand from his. “I can’t sing.”

“Oh, right, yeah, that’ll lose us the respect of the audience.” His easy sarcasm tempted her to laugh again. “You can’t be embarrassed with me, baby. I’ve seen you naked.”

Still smiling, Tess squawked and sat up. “Are you saying that’s embarrassing?”

“No, I’m saying I’ve seen you exposed and vulnerable…” A breath later, he lowered his volume to mutter, “Seen you come more times than I could count too.”

“You can’t judge me for something you do to me.”

"Nobody's judging," he said, his arms loosening in a shrug. "You're safe with me, baby. Is what I'm saying. Always safe."

Taking her hand in his again, he raised it to his lips to kiss her palm, then laid it on his thigh, twining their pinkie fingers again. He'd done that a few times this week. Such a simple gesture. Somehow it was more intimate than just holding hands.

Bringing Danny along on her adventure hadn't been the plan. Eventually, they'd have to part ways. Still, while they were together, she didn't think there was anything wrong with enjoying him.

TWELVE

BEING ON THE ROAD WITH Danny was easy. He made everything so easy. The rocking of the truck had been responsible for her drifting off more than once over the last three days. Apparently, she'd been lulled to sleep again. Music floated into her consciousness before anything else. It wasn't loud, which was sweet, he'd probably worried about disturbing her. When his muttering of the song lyrics met her ears, she smiled.

On her side, tucked against the semi-reclined seat, waking up to the sight of his profile was a gift. The darkness outside didn't worry her, though it did mean she'd been asleep for a while. Last she remembered they'd just finished lunch and got back on the road.

For three days, they'd been driving, rather Danny had. Parking at truck stops whenever he wanted to rest, they'd fill up with gas, pack snacks, and then get moving again.

"Got another hour in me, then you're up at bat," he said.

Tess smiled. "How did you know I was awake?"

"You stopped snoring."

When she laughed, he caught a glance her way for a quick second to show his dimple. "I do not snore."

"Maybe you do; can only take my word for it."

Despite her increase of awareness, it took about a minute for her to sit up and stretch. When she did, her extended arm blocked Danny's view. Teasing wasn't usually part of the routine when fleeing her life. A lot of things were different with Danny. They played with each other. Had fun. Danger seemed a million miles away.

As soon as her arm got in his way, he pushed it down to his lap, which gave her an excuse to rub him through his jeans.

"In an hour," he said, hooking her pinkie with his to drag her hand from his groin.

That was what he'd meant by up at bat. With him driving all day, it was fair that she do the majority of the work in bed. In the foreplay arena anyway, he still preferred being the driver once they got up to speed.

Figuring it best to let him get through the hour without distractions, Tess unhooked her arm from her seatbelt to reach over her mom, squeezing between the seats to search her carpet bag in the back. Retrieving her notebook was easy, the hunt for a pen took a little longer. Once she had both, Tess flopped back into her seat and put her arm beneath her seatbelt again.

No matter how many times she looked at the cards clipped to the cover of her notebook, deciphering them was impossible.

"They have to mean something."

"You've been staring at those for days," he said.

Because they plagued her. "They have to mean something," she said again, her voice stronger. "How do you break a code without a key? What would she be trying to tell me? Is it a name? An address? I looked up a bunch of zip codes in the library, I covered every combination. I'm sure I did... Maybe I missed something."

"You check on the computer?"

She glanced at him, the end of the pen on her lip. "I don't use computers, you know that."

"Internet's a wonder, you should catch up with the cool kids."

"Cool kids can keep their death trap," she said, her attention descending to the cards again.

The tip of the pen slipped between her lips.

"You know they put the hole in the lid so you can't kill yourself."

Random wasn't unusual for Danny.

Her eyes went up on a blink. "Baby, I—"

"The lid," he said, bobbing his chin toward her, still watching the road. "Of the pen." She took it from her mouth to look at it. "They put that hole in there, so if you swallow the lid while you're chewing it, you can't choke on it... I say you could still choke, but, you know, who's gonna test that theory?"

"That's interesting," she said, not really sure why he'd felt the need to share the trivia.

"You think the internet will kill you, but you'll put the pen in your mouth."

Okay, so that was why.

She couldn't equate the two. "The pen company don't want to be sued," she said. "They want to prove they did everything any reasonable person could do to protect those using the product. You can't sue the internet."

"The internet's not trying to protect you?"

"It's our job to protect ourselves," she said, admiring the gleam of artificial light on the lid of her mother's urn. "And the people we care about."

"You won't use the internet because you're protecting yourself," he said, like he wasn't sure. "From what? What are you protecting yourself from?"

"What?"

"You think the internet is evil?"

"My mom didn't trust it."

"What did she think would happen? Something would jump out and grab ya?"

He gave her leg a sudden squeeze.

"You're mocking my dead mother?" Tess said, sliding her ass down while bringing her feet up to the front edge of the seat, propping the notepad on her thighs and the end of the pen on her lip.

"Feet down."

Tess groaned and let her heels slither back to the floor. "I think you should give up towing," she said, pushing up to sit straighter. "It's affecting your head."

"I've seen a lot of car wrecks, Little Red."

"Yeah," she said, leaning toward him. "But those people didn't have such a strong, careful, sexy driver, did they?"

One side of his mouth responded to her teasing, which was enough for her. Danny was a good driver, as far as she'd seen anyway. But his attention to her positioning was a surprise. He didn't let her put her feet on the dash or on the seat. He allowed her to sleep twisted toward him, but that was about as much of a concession as he gave.

Righting the back of her chair that had been reclined while she was sleeping, obviously by her driver, Tess concentrated on the cards again.

"We have to stop at a library," she said after a few minutes of pondering. "I must have missed something."

"I can use the internet," he said. "I can check it out for you, if you want."

"Thanks, but no thanks."

He snickered. "What do you think's gonna happen to me? It's a keyboard and a screen."

"And a connection to the world," she said. "Everything on the internet can be tracked, traced, followed."

"That's what you think?" he asked like it was the most ridiculous thing he'd ever heard. "You think we're being followed?"

"I'm saying it's possible."

"I'll take that risk for you, babe."

Except she didn't appreciate his amusement. "Every time we talk about this, you do that, you laugh at me. This is serious. It's a serious thing. The danger is real. I know it's real."

He frowned. "How do you know it's real?"

"The letters said so," she said, tapping the pen on her cheek.

"You just found the letters after your mom died. Why

did your mom tell you to fear the internet before there was danger?"

Sometimes his lack of interest was frustrating, more because it meant she had to repeat herself than anything.

"Danny, just trust me, please," Tess said. "The danger has been real for a long time."

Her only concrete confirmation of it came in the letters. Tess wished her mom had been honest before she lost her life. Just like her, Anne must have believed there was time or her mom hoped the danger would go away on its own.

"Anyone ever hurt you?"

His frown would be sweet, if she wasn't sure it was incredulous in addition to being confused.

"You can't understand, baby, okay?" she said. "It's not about being hurt. We're trying to stop the hurt."

"We are?"

Exhaling, she rid herself of the frustration. He was so… Danny. Staying mad at him while he was providing a shining example of his simple outlook was impossible. As she sat there, scrutinizing his profile, Tess experienced a new kind of negative emotion. Beyond guilt, the weight of her worry for him exceeded anything she'd felt before.

Anne knew what she was running from and her focus had been keeping her child safe. Tess had been safe. But now it was her responsibility to look after someone else and she was at a disadvantage. With no clue as to what the danger wanted, she couldn't be sure to avoid it or keep it from hurting Danny.

"Do you have a gun?"

His attention flew from the road to her and back again. "Why do I need a gun?"

"For protection," she said. "I don't know what this thing is. I don't know what wants to hurt me… I don't want you to get hurt because of me."

Though her concern was real, he once again showed little awareness of how genuine the threat could be.

"Don't you worry 'bout that, Little Red. I got all the guns I need right here." Taking a hand from the steering wheel, he squeezed his fist to showcase his bulging bicep.

"Check that out."

Scaring him wouldn't achieve anything. Giving up, at least for that moment, Tess let him keep his innocence.

"Amazing, baby," she said, earning herself a grin.

Danny was proud of his physique with good reason. It wouldn't hold up in the face of gunfire, no defense would. Not any they had at their disposal. Her mother had to think there was a chance of weapons being used against them, she wouldn't have left a gun with Figgs otherwise.

"You ready to tell me where we're going yet?" he asked, breaking her trance.

Tess had been staring at nothing, thinking about nothing for God only knew how long. "I told you."

"A state," he said. "Don't know more than that."

"I'll tell you when we get there."

It didn't help that she hadn't been to the building for years and didn't actually know the nature of its current form. Tess hoped she'd recall its exact location when they got to the area. Figuring something would be familiar, she would pick out landmarks and streets that she did recognize. The building was easy to visualize, how they'd got there wasn't so simple.

"The truck stop up ahead has a grocery store, it's small, but I'll get something good," Danny said. "Cook you up something special."

As always, he didn't fight her. Danny always accepted her. Even when he teased or questioned her, he never gave any hint that there was anything she could ever do that would anger or upset him.

She smiled. What Tess really wanted to do was climb on top of him and lose herself in his kiss.

"You've been driving all day," she said. "We can just grab takeout."

Scowling, he shook his head. "Want something without all the grease."

"Okay, I'll make something."

"I don't mind cooking, honey."

Honey? Her smile widened. Was it possible they were becoming some old married couple already? They'd known each other just less than two weeks, yet they spent so much time together, and in close quarters, that they'd learned each other fast.

Danny could probably live with anyone. Nothing ever fazed him. Tossing her notepad to the dashboard, she freed her arm from her seatbelt and sprang up to hook an arm around his neck to pull him close. She planted a long kiss on his cheek and followed it with shorter ones, nuzzling her mouth against him.

"I'm so happy you're here," Tess said, slipping her fingertips under the neck of his tee-shirt.

"You tried to ditch me," he said, stroking her forearm.

"I did, but you didn't take no for an answer. Thank you, baby." Kissing her way toward his mouth, she took what she could until he tipped his head her way, allowing their lips to meet. "Does this thing go any faster?"

"Does if you sit right in your seat."

Dropping back, Tess hooked her arm back into the seatbelt while he put the pedal to the floor, getting them to where they were going as fast as physics would allow. Danny was exactly as he presented himself. Honest, down-to-earth, what you saw was what you got, and Tess wanted to get it. All of it. As soon as possible.

THIRTEEN

WITH THEIR HUNGERS for food and sex sated, they lay in bed together in the dark. Pressed tight to his side, her head tucked under Danny's chin, he slept with both arms around her. She didn't know why he liked to hold her so close. For her, at first, it was strange. As was spending so many nights with the same man. But after living with Danny, she wasn't sure she'd know how to sleep any other way. Certainly not in the trailer.

Sometimes she'd wake in the night and he wouldn't be in bed with her. For such an easygoing guy, his insomnia was a surprise. He'd always come back to bed if she asked him to, even if it was just to hold her until she was out again.

That night, Tess was having her own trouble falling asleep.

"Danny," she murmured, pointing a fingertip up on his clavicle.

"Mm?"

If he hadn't responded, she wouldn't have woken him. It had only been a few minutes since they'd lain down together. Hearing his voice took some of the weight from her worries.

"Tell me about your family."

He shifted to press a kiss to her head. "Just sleep, baby."

Since it came up on their first day in the truck, Tess had tried to bring up his relatives a few times. He always pivoted to something else. In typical Danny fashion, he didn't make a big deal of it, just asked her to change the cassette or for sex, depending on where they were.

Resting a hand on his chest, she pushed up to look down at him. "I want to know something. Please."

His eyes opened just long enough to meet hers, then they were closing again. "What you want to know?"

"Anything. Everything. Where are your parents? Do you visit them? I've never seen you speak to them. You don't call or anything."

"Mom's dead. Haven't seen my father for about a year."

"Why not?" she asked. Laying the underside of her upper arm against him, she rested her hand on her cheek. "Did you fight? What's he like?"

"Strict," he said, his eyes still closed, his body loose.

She smiled and touched her fingertips to his lips. "Is that why you're so not?"

The groove between his brows seemed more amused than affronted. "I'm strict."

"About having regular sex and beer in the fridge isn't the same thing," she said. "Do you miss him?"

"No," he said so fast her fingers bounced to his chin. "Yes."

That quick turnaround was revealing. He wanted the answer to be the first, but the truth existed in the second.

"You don't want to miss him," Tess said. The tension in his jaw under her touch bunched tighter. "You did fight, didn't you?"

"No. He wouldn't give a damn about my opinion even if I screamed myself hoarse. No point arguing with someone like that."

"I can't believe he doesn't care about you," she said. "Maybe you should call him, see if you can talk it out."

He wrapped his fingers around hers to move her

hand to his chest. "We don't talk."

"Never? How do you let each other know what you're feeling?"

He rolled his fingers into a fist and bumped it against her hand. "If we've got a problem, we slug it out."

"Physically?" she asked. "You fight each other… physically?" Tess sat up in the middle of the bed. "Did he hurt you when you were a child?"

Danny sucked in a breath and opened his arms wide. After a long, loud, exaggerated yawn, he raised his arms up, only to let his hands flop onto his chest.

"You normally sleep like a babe," he said, opening his eyes wide then letting them relax. "Usually you're out like a light. You've got something on your mind… or you want another round… I've got a helluva bedtime story for you." He patted his upper chest. "Come sit here, baby. I'll tell it real slow."

"Danny," she said. "Please answer me."

He groaned. "Babe, it's fathers and sons," he said, crunching his abs to rise just enough to snag her hand. Yanking her down against him, he wound both arms around her. "They've gotta teach us to be tough."

"No," she said, laying her fingers on his temple to stroke them down to his chin around the perimeter of his face. "It's no one's job to be violent with anyone, not for any reason."

His dimples were probably meant to alleviate her concern. "I gave as good as I got, babe. Don't you worry about this guy holding his own."

She kept stroking his face, admiring every inch of him. "I can't imagine it… I can't imagine you hurting anyone… I can't imagine you that angry."

"It's not about anger," he said. "Not always… Frustration? Sure, but beating something helps… We've got to know how to defend ourselves… and those we care about."

She'd said something like that in the truck, about protecting people. "When I was young, sometimes I'd pretend…"

"Pretend what?"

"Since I was little, my mom always taught me it was important to be strong. Strength comes from inside us. She used to say that every time we think we have nothing left to give, no fight left, our strength is tested."

"She wasn't wrong."

"I used to pretend that I could stop it. When I was a kid, young, you know, I used to lie in the dark imagining I was strong enough to stop it."

"Stop… what?"

"Whatever my mom was afraid of," she said. He scooped his fingers up through her hair, pushing it from her face. "I didn't know about it then." Tess exhaled a quiet scoff of truth. "I know nothing about it now. But I've always known my mom believed in it. She believed something wanted to hurt her, hurt us. I don't know… I don't remember thinking about the danger. I don't remember being afraid. I just remember wishing I was strong enough to take her fear away. That was what made me angry, that something scared her so much. I wanted to make it better. To help her."

"You were a kid."

"Yeah," she said, giving herself another few seconds of reflection before seeking his gaze again. "So were you. When your father was hurting you. It wasn't a lesson. You shouldn't have needed to defend yourself, he should've defended you."

"It's complicated."

"No, it isn't," she said, an odd anger warming her words. "It was his job to care for you."

"It was his job to keep me alive and he did. Just like your mom did for you."

She shook her head. Could he really believe that? Could he…? Danny, her Danny, the guy who freed the bugs they found in the trailer rather than squishing them, he valued life. But there was more than just existing. The thrilling, carefree side of life had passed her by. Still, she had to believe it existed and couldn't believe that Danny might doubt it.

"My mom loved me," she said. "She cared for me. She talked to me."

"Mothers and daughters are different, I guess. It's

picnics and rainbows for them.”

“We fought too,” she said. “Argued. I was a hellion of a teen. As soon as I hit sixteen, I ran away. Again and again, I didn’t give her a break. I wanted a life she couldn’t provide. I wanted freedom… It was stupid. She wanted that as much as I did. I know she did. I know it now anyway. She couldn’t let me see her frustration with our existence, not when I was being a nightmare. She couldn’t cut me a break because it would mean one, or both of us, being hurt.”

“Same for me and my dad,” he said.

Sliding a leg over his torso, Tess sat up, stroking her hands up and down his body. “You rebelled?”

He snorted. “Yeah, right,” he said. “Rebel? Maybe if I was suicidal.”

“Danny,” she said, curling her fingers around his jaw. “My God, baby, you were raised in horror.”

To her surprise, his lips curled, and he shook his head that was still deep in the pillow. “No. I had everything I ever needed.”

“Material possessions don’t—”

“His time. He was there for me. Taught me lessons I didn’t even know I needed to learn,” Danny said. “He’d drop everything for me. Go to war with me… when I was a kid… Doubt that’s true these days.”

Running her fingertips around the edge of his face, she brought his attention back to her. “What happened? What changed?”

“It’s complicated.”

Experiencing a Danny with barriers was new.

“But you said you miss him,” she said. “You shouldn’t miss him.” As her mom’s death proved, life could be stolen in a snap. “How about when I’m done with my crazy crusade, I help you fix things with your dad?”

He surged up to wrap his arms around her. “I have a better plan,” he said, flipping her onto her back, merging his mouth with hers.

Sex was a distraction. Even though talking about his father hadn’t been easy, Tess was glad she knew more about the man sharing her bed. His relationship with his father was obviously complex, but it meant something to him. Just as it meant something that he'd trusted her with the truth. Some of it anyway.

Judging by how much distance they'd covered over the last three days, they were about halfway to their destination. Eager to find out if her guess was right, Tess wanted to get there while simultaneously fearing it could be a dead-end. If there were no clues on where to go next, her predicament would be the same as before: trying to figure out the damn numbers.

"Danny," she murmured, clutching his head to take his mouth away from its trek down her neck.

He looked into her, desire hot in his drowsy eyes. Searching beyond his need, she wanted to see something in him, some sign that he understood. Everything was a mess. The only thing she'd ever been able to rely on was gone. In a few days, she could come face to face with whatever had been trying to track them down her whole life. If that happened, *when* that happened, the outcome would be… who even knew? Another mystery.

"It's okay, Tess," he said without her uttering more than his name. "Stop concentrating… You're allowed to stop thinking. To turn everything off…" He smiled and brushed his lips over hers. "Everything except me."

Her mind did work too hard, which was probably why sleep had eluded her. So much was riding on her being right. Just like so much was riding on her deciphering the numbers that, so far, meant exactly nothing.

She wanted to do more than hear his voice. "When I'm with you, I…"

Silencing herself, Tess swallowed. For the first time, she felt nervous in his arms.

"I know, baby," he murmured, his breath warm as it passed her lips. "Nothing's too broken to fix."

She didn't know exactly what that meant, but it didn't matter. He'd said exactly what she needed to hear. Once again, he proved his worth. His value grew all the time. On the trip, he'd been her constant, keeping her fed and rested. Been by her side. Relying on him too much would be dangerous.

Crashing in the trailer was a temporary solution. All she'd wanted was another warm body, and somewhere that hadn't been violated by a thief. Danny had become so much more. Her only friend in a vast world filled with strangers.

Danny wouldn't hurt her, couldn't hurt her. Danny was everything she needed. The epitome of safe. Explaining she'd have to leave him behind would be difficult. If she was smart, she'd do it soon, wake up before him and split.

If she was smart.

Closing her eyes when his kiss deepened again, Tess was already making excuses to herself about keeping him longer. Safety, comfort, who'd have thought such simple qualities would be so seductive?

FOURTEEN

"I GOT IT. I KNOW WHAT I'm doing," Tess said, trying to figure out the fold in the map.

They stopped at six different gas stations just to find one. Everywhere tried to sell her a GPS thingy. No one seemed to understand that a good old-fashioned map was just as good.

"You've got a helluva stubborn streak, babe," Danny said, ejecting the tape to flip it over and push it back in. "What do you say we sack the big drama mission for a while? Plenty of beauty spots to park up the Beast." As they'd taken to calling the Airstream. "We'll do a supply run first, get some good green, snacks, beer… plenty of beer. The essentials, you know? We kick back in the middle of nowhere. Nothing but green trees and blue sky for miles. I know some real good middle of nowhere spots."

"I'm sure you do, honey," she said, frowning at the map, trying to figure out exactly where they were.

"That thing's probably out of date," he said. "Check what year it was printed."

Tess was having enough trouble trying to find the right road; she didn't want to waste time looking for printing details. "It'll be here. The building is old, the twenties, I think… maybe the fifties."

He laughed. "Not much difference there." Jerking her hands toward each other, she showed him a glare before snapping the map open again to return to her searching. "So we stock up for a few days… few weeks maybe. Buy a shit ton of rubbers. We go skinny-dipping, count stars. Just you, me, and nature… We sleep all day, fuck all night… Can't think of anything better, can you?"

"Sounds perfect," she said, lowering the map to scan outside, seeking landmarks.

"So we're going?"

"After my big drama mission… and after we've fixed things with your dad."

Danny groaned. "Shouldn't have opened my mouth. Forget the old man."

"No," Tess said, glancing back and forth between the map and the streets they were driving through. "I'm glad you told me. I want to help."

"We don't need any help," he said.

It had been four days since he'd told her about his father issues. Tess didn't bring it up often, just enough to let him know she hadn't forgotten.

They were in the Rotunda building's vicinity; the only place mother and daughter had visited more than once. Anne's happy place. At the time, she had thought little about why her mom dubbed it that. Whether they were bowling, or she was rolling around in ball pools, it was an exciting place for a child.

But the glitter.

It had to be; she had to be right.

"You've got a great incentive now," she said, close to figuring out where they were.

"Incentive?"

"Sure," she said. "You have to fix things with your dad before we can lose ourselves in nowhere. You'll patch things up much faster if you know a mountain of weed and unlimited pussy is on the other side of the finish line."

"I have unlimited pussy now," he muttered. "I can buy weed anywhere."

"You'll have peace of mind when you fix things with him—left! Left! Go left!"

At the last second, he took the turn, going faster than he should while hauling a trailer. Horns blared from at least three different directions. Once they were on the straight again, he turned his frown to her. Wearing a broad smile, Tess kissed her fingertips, then touched them to his lips.

He drew his attention around to the windshield again. "She sucks your cock, Danny," he murmured. "She's hot and sucks your cock."

"What are you doing?"

"Reminding myself."

Of reasons not to yell or throttle her? Probably best not to comment on his private discussion, so she reassured him instead.

"It's good," she said. "I know where we are now… I think."

"Love the confidence, babe."

"Come on, baby, where's your optimism?" she asked, reaching over to curl her pinkie around his, taking it off the wheel and over to her lap. "This is exciting."

"Mm hmm," was all he said as his fingertips glided up under the hem of her dress.

"Well, I'm excited," she said, pushing her shoulders back and relaxing her legs to let his fingertips play on her inner thigh.

Excited and flat-out terrified. The heat of anticipation bounced back and forth from positive to negative. Her mood was erratic. Some part of her regressed to being six years old at Christmas. Another part was dark and heavy, obsessing about all that could go wrong. For all she knew, the Rotunda wouldn't give up its secrets. The alternative was a team of trigger-ready snipers waiting to blast her apart as soon as she set foot in the parking lot.

"Excited enough to pull over and park?"

"I don't know how you do it," she said, following the route on the map with a fingertip. "How you drive all day long and still think about sex so much… I've lost weight since I got with you, I'm exerting so much energy."

That was quite an accomplishment given their awful diet on the cross-country drive. Whenever they could, they stopped for proper food and bought groceries to cook for themselves. Still, she'd eaten more candy and diner food in the last week than she probably had in the entire year up to that point.

"It's a skill," he said. "I use the drive to do the thinking, so I can get right to it when we stop."

And usually they did. On many nights, they ended up having sex before even deciding where to eat or exploring the truck stop. It had been fun. Danny speed wasn't regular person speed. Nothing was rushed. They didn't set alarms, so woke up whenever they felt like it. They'd enjoy each other for a while until Danny felt like getting out of bed. Then they'd use whatever facilities they could wherever they stopped, grab supplies and gas before hitting the road.

Most of the time, breakfast was an on-the-go job, but if there was a pancake place, Danny had learned to take her inside to sit down for breakfast. She loved pancakes, had since she was a kid, which was funny because Danny's favorite part was pouring the syrup for her. Tess let him amuse himself trying to get the perfect spiral before the syrup ran into itself.

"I know it's been tough on you," she said, pointing to an intersection. "Turn there."

"It's not been so bad. I live life on the road anyway."

Something they had in common.

Tess finished with the directions, and Danny guided them into the lot of the grand circular building. He stopped facing the entrance, though a good fifty feet away. He killed the engine and then they both sat there, staring out the windshield.

"Need me to go in for you?" he asked, probably confused about why they'd driven over three thousand miles to get to a place she was just going to sit and stare at.

"No," she said, her skin prickling. "No, I got it."

Danny didn't know they'd arrived at their ultimate destination. He'd just accepted directions as she gave them, and there they were. Outside the building her mother loved. The building Tess had played in as a child. Whoever H was, if she was right, he'd been there. Just like them, he'd have a connection to the place.

All her life she'd been ignorant to its significance. Sure, she'd had fun times with her mom, but Tess hadn't known it was their connection to another person. Still, she doubted herself. Maybe H wasn't Hades. Maybe C wasn't her mom.

She couldn't even look at her mother's urn. Second guessing herself after completing the journey would be ridiculous. If she focused on her mom, thought too much about what she'd endured, maybe she wouldn't have the strength to do what was necessary.

"Babe?"

"I'm okay," she said, forcing her focus away from the building to smile at him. "I'm just going to go in and…" She pressed the button to release her seatbelt. "It won't take long. You should stay here."

Opening the door, she got out and started across the parking lot before Danny could say anything else.

It was a building. No big deal. Just a building.

Getting closer, the sign under the covered portico became clearer. It declared the prices of admission for the roller disco. Spinning around, losing none of her momentum, she hurried back to the truck, approaching Danny's side instead of her own.

His window went down.

"I need money," she said.

He closed the lid over the urn. Dumb as it was, she liked to keep it uncovered while they were driving. Above it, in a shallower panel of the lid, was a tray where they kept their cash.

Danny passed her the stack of bills, but she just peeled off a couple and gave the rest back to him.

"That enough?" he asked. A furious nod was her only reply. "Hey…" Danny snagged her hand to pull her back as she turned. He smiled. "You've got this, Little Red. You've got it. Don't stress your pretty head."

His support, and the gorgeous dimples, relaxed some of the tension from her tight muscles.

Hooking a hand around the back of his neck, she tugged him close to steal a kiss. "Thank you, baby," Tess said and pounced away to start her trek over again.

Whatever happened was going to happen. No point worrying about something that hadn't happened. And if she got killed, hey, then she couldn't worry about anything.

Pulling the heavy door to get inside, she went across the entryway and through another door. The retro booths inside looked like old movie theatre ticket stands. Being polite, Tess was too preoccupied to pay attention to what the person inside said. They put a wristband around her arm, then allowed her through the turnstile.

The music was right in Danny's wheelhouse. Shame she'd told him to stay outside. He might actually have fun in there.

Ascending the stairs, she appreciated the new pink carpet and the gleam of the brass banister. Her head tipped back, waiting for the revelation of the domed ceiling. One gradual slice at a time, it came into view. Lights flashed across it in wild arcs of neon joy, scattering sparkles from the glass mosaic in a dozen directions.

"The glitter," she whispered when she got to the top, her focus glued to the towering view above.

When she was little, she'd lie on the carpet and look up at the tiny glass beads that made beautiful patterns with their reflections. Her mother called it The Glitter. It looked like a patchwork of what happy would be.

Laying her hands on her stomach, Tess hadn't expected to be so emotional at seeing it again. All she wanted to do was lie on the carpet and pretend to be five years old. If she could trade that moment, trade everything she'd gone through, she would do it if it meant having another minute of happiness like that.

Her memories of the place gained a new hue. Her mother loved the building. Not because of the architecture or the décor, but for a secret she'd kept all her life.

Tess hoped anyway.

Gathering her emotions, she stomped them deep down and closed the lid over them. It wasn't the time to give into feelings. Tearing her attention away from the ceiling, Tess scanned the vast room. No alleys, signs of a pin or bowling ball anywhere. The central roller rink took up most of the room. It was filled with people going round and round.

Everyone was having a good time. All around the room were people in booths or at tall tables that circled the main roller rink. She could see a cotton candy stand, an ice-cream parlor, and a long milkshake bar.

To the left was the desk to claim your skates. Tess needed what was built into the wall beyond that desk: the lockers.

Striding that way, she showed her wristband to receive a pair of lace-up roller skates. Keeping her smile in place, Tess didn't want to draw attention to herself. The huge cavern of a room provided plenty of opportunities for anyone to see what she was doing.

Luckily, the skates desk had a central broad shelving unit that housed dozens of skates. That gave her some cover. Passing the end of the square counter area, Tess went by one long bench to round another.

The lockers had always been there. For as long as she could remember. Stopping in front of the bench, just a few feet from the lockers, she counted from the top left corner.

"One, two, three, four…" Her skates were tied together by their laces. Without looking, she lowered them to the padded bench behind her legs. "Five…" She slowed her counting. "Six… Seven." Settling on that locker, she swallowed, her trepidation rising as she switched to count the vertical axis. "One… Two…"

Three.

FIFTEEN

SEVEN ACROSS, THREE down. Tess didn't remember where it had come from or even when she'd been told it was their code. It always just… was.

The lockers that weren't in use still had keys in the locks, a wristband attached. Seven across, three down didn't have a key.

"Fuck," she said to herself, catching the eye of a couple who were tying the laces of their young twins' skates. Smiling, she held up an apologetic hand. "Sorry."

What to do? Wait? Was that the plan? Wait until whoever was using the locker came back to retrieve their things? Except, if that was the place H and C exchanged their letters, others shouldn't be able to use it. Otherwise letters could be intercepted before the recipient retrieved them. They'd take it or hand it to management.

Wandering to the end of the bench, Tess glanced around. Something… What was she missing? Something. Behind her was another bench with lockers that were obviously newer. They were set out of the wall. It couldn't be them. Couldn't be there. Seven along, three down was vacant, so she checked it just in case, but there was nothing there.

The couple with the twins guided their kids toward

the roller rink. They were just… leaning forward, she watched until, yep, out of sight. Shooting to her feet, she took advantage of the opportunity to check out the locker in the central section. Definitely built into the wall. Definitely seven across, three down. She tried pressing the door and prying it open with her nails. Locked.

Well, duh, every other vacant locker had the wristband key and was ajar. Spinning around, she fell back against the lockers, cursing the futility. She'd got it wrong. Going to the stupid building was a stupid idea. Stupid.

Tess didn't like to be defeated. She wouldn't be defeated. The Corvette hadn't beaten her. After driving across the country, she wouldn't give up easy.

With renewed purpose, she strode around the service counter, her attention darting all over the place. How to get it open? She couldn't make noise or be too violent with so many people around. There had to be a way and she'd find it, even if it meant breaking in after hours to rip the damn thing out of the wall with her bare hands.

Someone had the key. Could she locate it by checking the numbered wristbands worn by the skaters? Damn, she should've picked up her skates from the bench. Without them, she couldn't go onto the rink. Not that it mattered. As a newbie, she'd only end up on her ass. There had to be something…

Her attention snagged on the milkshake bar. More specifically, on a guy seated on one of the red and chrome stools talking to the long-legged blonde perched next to him.

Moving again, it didn't even occur to her not to approach as she strode over, winding around the happy revelers. Everything was open plan. Slightly different décor distinguished different areas. Just like walking through a food court in the mall.

Even over the music, the blonde's laugh illuminated the air.

Determined, Tess slipped between the pair, putting her back to the beauty to block her out. "Can you pick locks?"

"Hey!" Danny said, curving an arm around her hips to ease her back, so she faced the bar between him and the blonde. "Tess, this is Carly. Carly, Tess."

Tess wasn't sure why the blonde's lip was curled with such disdain. "Nice," Tess said with a nod. "Pleasure." She slapped a hand on Danny's shoulder to get his attention again. "Did you hear me? That's a 'mechanicy' type thing, isn't it?"

"I ordered a milkshake," he said, jabbing his thumb over his shoulder just as a woman trussed up like a fifties waitress came over on skates with two milkshakes and a basket of fries. "See." The server put the milkshakes down in front of Danny and the blonde, sliding the fries between them. "Know what else? Luz, she's the manager, she says we can park in the lot overnight."

"Okay," Tess said. Depending on how things went after getting into the locker, that may not be a good idea. "Remember I had a question?"

"Uh huh," he said, stuffing fries in his mouth and picking the cherry off his shake by the stem. "This place is great."

He sucked the whipped cream from the underside of the shiny red cherry. Whipped cream and fries couldn't complement each other, but he registered nothing negative as he offered the cherry to her mouth.

Taking the fruit between her lips, Tess held it while Danny pulled off the stem. He tossed it onto the counter on his return to the fries. He crammed a few in his mouth before plucking the naked cherry stone from her pursed lips.

"Danny?"

"Yeah, I'm listening," he said around the fries. "I heard you. Can I finish my shake?"

He picked up the damp glass, ignoring the straw in favor of gulping from the side.

"Are you two a thing?" Carly asked.

Danny tipped his head back, catching a slurp of milkshake before it could escape his lips. "We're not that specific," he said. Impatient, Tess pinched his arm. "Okay, fuck, give me a minute, woman. Whatever it is, it's not going anywhere."

"Three thousand miles, Danny," she said, reminding him of their journey. "Dead woman in the truck."

"Oh my God," Carly exclaimed.

"She was already dead when we put her in there," Danny said, then frowned at himself. "That doesn't sound better, does it?"

"We were having a conversation, Danny," Carly said, her shoulders moving to better showcase her breasts. "I'd love to talk some more."

Ah, that was this Carly's interest? Sex?

"Oh, for the love of…" Tess muttered, reaching past Danny to pick up his shake. Slipping the straw between her lips to suck it down hard and fast, it didn't take more than half a dozen long drags to finish the whole thing. After slamming the glass down, Tess grabbed Danny's face and stuck her tongue in his mouth, showing without words that there was no way the blonde was getting lucky. Pushing him back just moments after he got with it enough to respond, Tess switched her attention to the blonde. "Not gonna happen for you. Not with this one. Not today."

Exhaling her annoyance, Carly grabbed her purse and leaped from the stool to strut away.

Danny's hand slithered under her skirt. "Little Red on a mission is hot," he said.

She snaked her arm around to remove his hand from her ass. "The shake is done. Can you help me now?"

"Sure," he said, scooping up a bunch more fries as he bounced off his stool. "Where we going?"

"This way," she said, going back the way she'd come.

"What kind of lock is it?" he asked around the fries in his mouth.

She tossed her hair out of the way to glance at him over her shoulder. "Locker."

"Ah, that's easy. Thought you might have a challenge for me."

As Tess was about to lead him beyond the service desk, he diverted to go straight there. One assistant was on a phone, the other was talking to a group of teens who'd just arrived ready to take over the rink.

It didn't matter though, Danny didn't want to speak to anyone. In fact, when he let go of her hand to boost himself up to peer over the counter, she got the impression he'd chosen his moment carefully.

In one slick move, he swiped something from the lower side of the counter, then landed back on his feet to continue walking without missing a beat.

Tess hurried to catch up and watched him take apart a pen until all he had left was the long clip. He slipped everything else in a trash can at the other corner of the counter.

"What are you doing?" she asked as he unfolded the clip, which had been folded back on itself.

"Nothing," he said, glancing around as he straightened out a paperclip that she hadn't seen until that second. "What are you doing? Which one we want?"

"Seven across, three down."

Tess didn't see him count, but he went to exactly the right place. She expected to keep look out or something. Danny had a different idea. With the pen-clip he'd unfolded hidden in one hand and the straightened paperclip in the other, he scooped an arm around her to put her in front of him.

"Pull your hair over your shoulder," he said, crouching to kiss her.

"What are you doing?"

"Concentrating," he said, both hands at the back of her neck, though he wasn't holding her.

Surprised when he kissed her again and dipped his tongue between her lips, Tess pulled away, which gave his hands less space to work with. Her eyes ascended to his. What was he doing? He was… using the kiss as cover. Her lips curved as his did the same. Tess's role was to sell this while he was concentrating on something else.

Coiling both arms around his neck, Tess pulled him close and surrendered herself to the kiss.

Prepared to put on a performance, she expected it would take a while. Except, almost before it started, the metal door popped open.

Breaking the kiss, she met his eye again. "You weren't even looking."

"You better be quick," he said, turning her on the spot, crowding in close to give her some cover.

Yes, the teens would get their skates and then pour into the locker area. Putting both hands inside, Tess lifted the sneakers and pushed aside the glasses, running her hands all over the bottom and up the side walls, in a desperate hope that she'd feel paper.

Nothing.

Breathing out, she sagged against him. "Damnit."

"Give me your hand," he said, presenting his palm over her shoulder.

She did, and he turned her palm upward. Guiding her hand forward, he separated her fingers so his could feel the ceiling of the locker in sync with hers. The one place she hadn't touched. Missing that one section was dumb, but she didn't think it would make the slightest bit of—

Just as she registered the seam under her fingertips, Danny's hand stopped. He must have felt it too.

"Oh my God," she whispered. "What is that?"

He applied pressure, maybe thinking it was on a spring, it wasn't. He crouched lower until his breath warmed her ear. "Use your fingernail."

Yes. Slipping her nail into the line in the metal, she tried to pry it open. At first nothing happened, but she could feel movement, like maybe it wanted to give.

"Don't fucking test me," she murmured her magic words.

They'd worked with the trunk of her Corvette. Just like that day, the metal gave and dropped at an angle, just a tiny amount, less than an inch, but it was enough to let an envelope slide out.

When it was on her palm, Tess stopped breathing. It worked. She'd been right.

"Make out time," Danny whispered in her hair, closing the panel and turning her around. Still in a daze, the paper mesmerized her. "Babe, come on."

Right. Yeah. They had to cover their asses. Sliding both hands around him, she skimmed them down to his ass to tuck the letter into his back pocket. His hands were working behind her again. The kiss wasn't as intense as their usual joinings, but tonight was going to be a hot one.

Without him, she would've sat all night until someone returned to that locker. Would she have checked the ceiling of the locker? Maybe. If there had been time and she wasn't worried about being discovered… Maybe. Maybe not.

Danny broke the kiss. "We're good."

"Mm hmm," she said, clutching the back of his neck in both hands to pull him down for a deeper kiss.

His mouth needed more attention. Deserved more. She wasn't done. Talk about a white knight. Everything he'd done overwhelmed her. He couldn't know how close she'd come to admitting defeat. At the last second, he'd snatched it back for her.

Wearing a smile as he withdrew, he had to hold her head to ease her mouth away from his. Though she managed to steal another couple of shorter kisses before he laughed.

"Grateful, Little Red?"

"There's a bed in the parking lot," she said, still trying to capture his mouth. "I know a guy."

"Sure you do," he said, straightening up, which immediately ended her hope of stealing more kisses. "I've got a better idea."

"Better than sex? Are you coming down with something? What have you done with my Danny?" she asked, but was intrigued. "What idea?"

His little finger twined with hers. "Know how to roller-skate?"

SIXTEEN

"THIS IS A BAD IDEA," Tess said as Danny took her hands to guide her onto the roller rink.

Her skates rolled on the slick surface, sending her into a panic. She braced to go down, but Danny yanked her to him, adjusting his own stance to catch their balance. Somehow, he kept them upright.

Peeking up at him, she gripped him tight, unwilling to let go.

"I can't believe you never learned to skate," he said. "It's like ice-skating, you ever do that?"

Shaking her head, she clung on as he used his strength to pry her nails from his tee-shirt. "Don't let me go!"

"I'm not going anywhere," he said. Relinquishing the fabric, her hands leaped to his biceps. "Open your legs." When her eyes pounced to his, a laugh quickly followed his order. "Okay, yeah, I usually do that for you, but we don't need them that wide."

"Please don't flirt with me," she said, gripping tighter as he moved backwards, his hands on her ribs under her arms. "I come all this way to get a letter and then I die before I get a chance to read it."

"Nobody died from roller-skating," he said, scooping

her aside when a gang of teenagers sprinted by. "Even the kids can do it."

"Yeah, okay, we've established I'm lacking," she said, scowling at him. "I told you, I have no rhythm."

"That's what you say, I still don't believe it," he said. "Look, it's easy. Balance, remember? We did that on the carpet."

"Yeah, on carpet it's easy."

Danny stopped them. They were out of the way of the rink entrance, but further away from the side than she'd like.

"Okay…" he said, bending his knees to take hold of her hips. "Heels together, remember? You won't go anywhere."

"Easy for you to say," she muttered, holding his arms as she adjusted her stance.

"Now all you've gotta do is shift your weight from one side to the other." Obviously, her expression didn't inspire confidence because he flashed his dimples on a laugh. "Okay." When he moved like he intended to let her go, she fired a bunch of short, desperate sounds his way. "It's okay, baby. I'm just going around the back." Her hands relaxed, though Tess didn't actually break contact as he rolled around to stand behind her. "Just like in bed when I flip you over."

"You warn me before you do that," she said, clutching his forearms, trying to pull them around her.

"Not with words," he said, squeezing her hips. "You can tell by the way I look at you."

"Yeah."

Prying her hands from his arms, he guided her into position. "Because we've been doing the dirty a while, you get to know who you're playing with."

"Uh huh," she said, noting how he angled one of her palms down and then the other. "Danny."

"I'm here," he said, still holding her hips. "Bend your knees, get low for me."

Unlocking her knees, Tess did as asked, still using his body as a support behind hers. "Usually, when you're coming at me from behind, I'm doing everything I can to get my hips higher."

The warmth of his easy snicker worked some knots from her muscles. "Yeah, well, I won't be holding you up this time… I can play with your clit if you—"

"Do not even think about putting your hand up my skirt, Danny Winger."

Another laugh. "Okay, babe. Let's do this. Left and then right, okay? Don't lean back. Keep your chin up and your shoulders back, lead with your tits."

"Great line," she murmured, glad he could be amused while she was so nervous. "What if I fall?"

All of a sudden, he disappeared from behind her. In one flourish of movement, he was in front of her, finger under her chin, gaze burning into hers. "You fall? You hurt yourself. That's all that happens. We dust you down and we start again."

Tess swallowed. "Nothing's too broken to fix."

"That's right," he said, dipping down to kiss her quick before disappearing behind her again. "Chin up. Shoulders square… feet apart, just a little. Skates straight. Left then right."

"Left then right," she said, fixated on the rink ahead. "Promise you'll stay with me."

"You go, I go. I've got your back, Little Red."

The music was happy and the roller rink full of people having a great time. Her anxiety was high, but Danny was there, and he was right: so what if she fell down? Taking a deep breath, Tess let her feet move. Danny's guidance urged her weight left, prompting her to lean more that way. He did the same the other way, and she actually moved forward without falling on her ass.

"It doesn't help that you're so amazing at everything," she said, her hands grabbing for his when they slid up her body. Tess wobbled. Danny hooked a strong arm around her ribs, yanking her up, almost taking her skates from the floor. "See."

"That's 'cause you're trying to talk and worrying too much about what I'm doing. Let me worry about the crowd." He boosted her higher. Her body still rested on his when he lost his mouth in her hair. "You concentrate on moving for me."

The rhythm of his voice gave it maximum impact. Diverting all her thoughts away from her skates and where they were, her eyes closed like they were back in the trailer. Danny must have felt her relax, because he set her back on her feet.

Opening her palms, she clamped her heels together and worked to catch her balance. "Okay, we can do this."

"You can do this," he said. "Chin up." As Tess raised her focus, the music changed to a track that made her smile. Danny gave her a squeeze. "This one's made for you, baby."

His stereo in the trailer linked to a catalog of tracks. Because Tess didn't know how to use the system, he'd set up a playlist for her. Every one of her favorites was on there. It hadn't eluded him she requested more than one Prince tune.

"Left then right," she said to herself.

On a slow exhale, Tess leaned to the left, pushing herself forward, then shifting the other way. Letting her lips move to the words of the song she knew better than her own name, she set her focus and took her time going one way, then the other.

Danny's hands loosened. Instead of panicking, she trusted him to stay close and kept on mouthing the words. They got all the way round once. Tess's eyes flicked to the opening in the side, but didn't allow herself to be distracted. After they'd passed it, Danny's hands slid away. Despite her hammering heart and the track ending, she kept on going.

Looking straight ahead, her chin stayed up, her hips low. Everything he'd said repeated in her mind. Danny had believed in her. He'd urged her on, encouraged her. She never would've done it if he hadn't tempted her into it.

Once again, he gave so much, and she had no way to repay his kindness. By the time their trip was over with, Tess would owe him a hell of a debt.

***

THEY SPENT HOURS ON the roller rink. Danny even showed her a few tricks. Tess's confidence soared. No doubt that was a lot to do with the cotton candy and ice-cream they'd shared. Thank God Luz let them park overnight; they'd never have been able to find anywhere nearby so late.

Approaching the trailer, Tess hummed Danny's seduction tune. He didn't miss her hint. Glancing her way, he was already smiling. He dug the key from his pocket—turned out the trailer did lock after all.

As he slid it into the lock, Tess sidled up behind him and wrapped her arms around him to begin unbuckling his belt. Danny didn't bother with formalities like underwear, so she expected to open his buttons and get him to attention before they even got inside.

She didn't get close. He caught her hands and turned around, keeping hold of her to put a little space between them.

He'd never stopped her touching him, not when the prospect of sex was on the table.

"What's wrong?"

He let her go to retrieve something from his back pocket. The letter. Seeing it chilled her.

"You've been putting it off," he said. "You came all this way. You should read it."

She should. Since liberating it, the paper had lived in Danny's back pocket. Once in a while she thought about it, but she hadn't brought herself to actually read it.

"What if it says something I don't want to read?" she asked, taking the envelope from him. "What if he threatens her life or warns her something's coming for her?"

H could've tried to warn her mother. Most of the time, Tess went on believing the car wreck was an accident. Any time her mental barriers fell, allowing the idea of sabotage or other deliberate action in, she quickly erected them again.

Accepting her mother's death wasn't easy. It wouldn't be made easier to learn a trip to the Rotunda might have prevented it.

"You'll never know unless you read it," he said.

"She valued her letters. Valued every one of them." The paper itself wasn't heavy, yet its significance weighted her palm. "The first day I touch them, I lose them."

"Chin up, skater girl," he said, snagging her loose

pinkie with his. "They're only words."

"Words that could change everything. Change everything I know. Everything I believe. Words have the power to alter every aspect of a person's very existence."

There was something sad about knowing H had left the letter for her mother and that she'd never read it. The poor guy may never know that she was gone.

"Not reading them would do that too," he said. "You wanted to know. We came here because you needed this closure."

Not like Danny to be so deep, but he was right. Tess nodded and reached for the trailer handle. She paused when he retreated.

"Where are you going?"

"We need beer… and rubbers," he said, continuing backwards. "You need privacy."

Appreciating what he was doing, she blew him a kiss and turned the handle to go inside. Living in a single room had its advantages. Tess never felt like they were living on top of each other, or even that Danny was in her way. Though that could be because they occupied the same intimate space so regularly.

Kicking off her shoes, she went to get a knife from the kitchen and slit open the top of the sealed, blank envelope. After putting the knife back, Tess withdrew to the bedroom. Sitting right in the middle of the bed with her legs crossed, she took a deep breath and slid the folded paper out of the envelope.

Unfolding the letter gave her a shock she hadn't anticipated. Never in a million years… "Oh my God," she whispered, reading the words written on the thick paper.

Before she was even through with the first page, a heavy tear fell from her lashes onto the sheet, blurring the words. Since losing her mother, Tess hadn't let herself cry. She hadn't wanted to open those floodgates.

But as she read the words, absorbed their meaning and tried to interpret them, her mind and heart were too overloaded to resist surrendering to emotion. The tears kept on coming and she kept on reading. Over and over again. The letter meant so much while being completely meaningless. How could it matter?

By the time she slammed the paper down on the bed and launched herself onto her feet, Tess had lost track of any meaning. In the words, in life, in everything she'd ever known. Striding down the trailer and back up, tension radiated from her. She was mad, so mad, and so lost.

Something had to change. She had to do something but didn't have the first clue what that something was.

She was passing the fridge on the way to the bedroom when the trailer door opened. It could be a crazy masked gunman. If only. Her head was in exactly the right place to take on a maniac like that. Instead, when she spun around to stomp back the other way, Danny was the one pinned under her fury.

Instantly, his smile vanished.

Shoving the grocery bag onto the counter, he came up the trailer to meet her. "What?" he asked, holding her face in both hands. "What did it say? What did he write?"

"Nothing," she said, her whole body shaking with adrenaline. "He didn't write the letter... It was from my mother."

"Your mother? I don't understand."

"It was her handwriting; I'd know it anywhere. She is C, she signed it C," Tess said, searching him with wet eyes. "I think it was him... I think H killed her."

SEVENTEEN

"WHOA, OKAY, SLOW DOWN," Danny said, pulling her to the recliners to sit them both down. "H? You think he killed her?"

"Maybe not killed her," Tess said, her determination heating. "But it's his fault that she's dead."

He swiped the tears away from her wet cheeks. "Start at the beginning. Spell it out for me, baby. I'm just a dumb grease monkey."

"Oh, Danny," she said, sniffing. "She was so in love with him. She just... She lived for him."

"And that... killed her?"

What was sense? There was none. All her life, she'd believed her mom to be a stalwart; a strong woman with no desire to lean on a man. But she had been leaning, or she'd tried to, and H wasn't there to hold her up.

"I didn't hear her," Tess said, accepting her own role in her mother's demise. Reading her words, the last words of her mother that she would ever read, really brought the truth home. "She's gone... Danny..."

Meeting his eye, she sought his understanding, hoping he had answers.

But no one did. There was no truth. Laying her hands

on his chest, Tess leaned closer, desperate for him to take the pain away.

"Babe—"

"I'll never see her again. Never speak to her," she said, facing the truth she'd avoided for weeks. "The only family I ever had. My only friend. The only link to who I am." Fresh tears tumbled from her lashes. "What do I do now, Danny? I'm alone… I'll always be alone."

As she surrendered to the tears, grief wrung a sob from the depths of her blackened heart. Falling against him, the dam restraining her anguish cracked. The pressure of her agony was so overwhelming that she couldn't seal it back up. She had to. Put everything back. She didn't want to feel sorrow anymore.

Grabbing for his shirt, Tess clawed her way up his body, her nails scraping in his stubble as she tried to draw his jaw down, seeking his mouth.

Danny gave her oblivion. That was what she needed. Under him, she'd forget. She could forget. Tess didn't want to face the truth of what lay ahead. Her life was nothing anymore. There was nothing she could do to put things back the way they'd been. She hadn't appreciated her mom. Hadn't appreciated what they had. It was gone. Forever.

Instead of giving her what she wanted, Danny resisted her kiss. "Shh, baby," he said, raising his chin to keep their mouths apart. "Don't hold it in."

Fighting to contain her grief, fearing it, fearing that it would finish her, she wanted it to stop. Weakened, tired, alone, what did the future hold? Her mother had guided her for so long, making the tough choices, keeping her safe.

Without Anne's guidance, what would she become? Her mother's strength got them through. Tess didn't have that strength. She couldn't match her mother's determination. If Anne couldn't survive the peril, Tess didn't stand a chance.

Giving up the fight, she sagged against Danny. Sobs burned from her chest to her throat. She'd been so desperate for freedom. Now that her grief saw the chance, it wanted to escape all at once.

"Little Red," Danny whispered into her hair, kissing

the top of her head before scooping her up.

Lifting her head required too much effort. It didn't matter how much despair she expelled from her heart, more stood ready to take its place.

With her face still buried against him, she saw nothing but darkness. Even the scent of his hard body or the cradle of their bed wasn't enough to calm her. Danny laid them down together and held her close, stroking her, whispering words of comfort.

She heard him but couldn't push beyond the truth that her mother was gone. She was alone. Completely alone.

***

HER HEAD ACHED WHEN she opened her eyes. The shades were down around the bed, concealing the hour of the day. Pushing her hair from her face, she sat up and took a second to orient herself. In bed. Danny's bed. Alone.

The sound of whistling betrayed she wasn't completely by herself in the trailer. Scooching down the bed, she was still sitting on the end when she leaned across to open the privacy curtain.

At the stove, Danny tipped his attention her way. "You were really out," he said, doing something with a pan that she couldn't see.

The sweet smell in the air gave her some idea what he was up to. "What time is it?"

He shrugged. "Lunchtime... I think."

Clearing her throat, she thought about a shower, realizing she was still wearing last night's clothes. "We didn't have sex."

"We fell asleep," he said, scooping something out of the pan. "Don't know when. You stopped crying. I kept holding you and... I don't know. We fell asleep."

"I'm sorry," Tess said, rising to her feet, her legs heavy and shaky beneath her.

"For not giving it up?" he asked, picking up a plate to spin and put it on the dinette table. "Could've taken it if I wanted to... I figure you've worked up some credit."

"We've never spent the night together without having sex."

The observation didn't bother her. Apparently, Danny didn't care either. He opened his hand to the table.

"Come eat."

Her head was still spinning, and her body ached all over. That was what a night of crying and screaming at nothing did. With a hand on the shower, then the closet, she steadied herself and made her way down the trailer.

The table was set. A big stack of pancakes stood in the middle by an assortment of condiments. Near the window the flame of a stubby little tea light flickered.

"Candlelight?" she asked.

He shrugged. "Best I could do."

Resting a hand on his torso, she pushed to her tiptoes; he lowered to accept her kiss. "I love it."

They both sat down. Danny grabbed her plate to put a pancake on it. As he picked up the syrup, his concentration put a smile on her face. He was determined to beat that damn syrup spiral into submission.

"Sorry for losing it," she said. "That's what I was apologizing for. I didn't mean to get... emotional."

"Overdue," he said, sliding the plate across to her. "No worries. You're not a robot."

Apologizing seemed like the polite thing to do. Tess hadn't really expected he'd have a problem. Danny didn't know the meaning of the word.

Using her fork to cut her pancake, she speared it and took it to her lips, watching him work on another spiral. "Good thing is, you're free now," she said after swallowing the pancake.

"I'm free? Cool," he said, tilting his head to watch the syrup run into itself. "Didn't know I was chargin'."

She smiled. "From me. You're free."

Done with spiral practice, his focus was on shoveling the pancake into his mouth. "What does that mean?"

Opening her mouth, she inhaled. "There's nowhere I need to be. I don't know what I'll do now. The letter didn't give me any clues about what I should do next. Short of staking out the Rotunda and hoping H announces himself if he ever shows, I don't have any idea how to find him."

"Or if you'd want to," he said, pointing his fork at her. "You said he killed her."

Nodding, Tess conceded the point, though she wasn't as vehement about it in the light of day. "That was harsh. The letter doesn't imply he threatened her, not with violence."

"What does it imply?"

Looking left, then right, worry struck her. "I left it on the bed, where is—"

"In the nightstand," he said. "I put it away."

Of course he'd taken care of it. "Did you read it?"

He shook his head, his mouth full of pancake. "It's your private thing."

She smiled and hooked a hand on the edge of the table to boost herself up enough to lean closer. "Didn't we establish you already saw me naked? You've seen me exposed and vulnerable." Admitting that wasn't easy, especially after losing it the previous night. "I don't think you reading my mother's letter will make much of a difference to my allure… that's long gone."

"So we don't have any secrets now?"

The way his lips twitched to a smile brought a laugh from hers. Such joy from a simple thing. Even if he was teasing her, she appreciated him brightening her mood.

Tess cut another chunk from her pancake. "I guess not."

"Good, then I gotta ask…" Waiting for the question, her brows rose in anticipation. "How many bikinis you packin'? We're in beach weather now and the next place we're going is right on the coast. Like right there on the beach."

"The next place?"

Didn't he hear her granting him his freedom? He'd asked what that meant. Didn't he get he wasn't shackled to her any longer?

"Yeah, it's only a few miles south. Got everything we need."

That widened her smile. "As long as there's beer in

the fridge and condoms in the nightstand, you always have everything you need."

He winked. "Bikini weather, baby."

Sometimes he was so silly. His relaxed outlook put so much into perspective. She'd fallen down and yeah, it had hurt. But just like Danny said on the roller rink, he'd been there to dust her down.

"I appreciate the offer, but I'm saying you don't have to worry about me anymore."

"I never *had* to do anything," he said. "I don't worry… about anything. You're hot and you suck my cock."

Folding her arms, she sank back against the dinette seat. That was all Danny needed to complete his world.

"You're sweet," Tess said, narrowing an eye. "In your own way."

"Come, don't come," he said, waving his fork over his plate before stabbing the last piece of his pancake to sop up the syrup. "Your call. But if you don't have any other place to be…" Then what was the point of saying no? "What about the numbers?"

She groaned and dropped an elbow to the table while scooping her hair up off her face. "Don't remind me."

The damn numbers. Still, they meant nothing to her. What the fuck? As a teen, she'd wanted to embrace tech like all the other kids in the various high schools she'd attended. Her mom was fervent in her opposition. And, of course, Anne won the battle. Since then, she hadn't thought about it more than a handful of times. For the first time, plugging the numbers into the screen was tempting. It would be so quick. So easy… So stupid.

"If I ever figure them out, I'll do something about them," she said. "All I'm doing is staring at them. I don't know what they mean."

"Put 'em in online."

"Yeah, because at least something coming for me would be progress."

Danny selected another pancake. "So… Do it."

Finding a library would be easy. Figuring out the computer might be more difficult. Danny would help figure it out.

"I don't know," Tess said, mesmerized by the flame of the candle. "Maybe it doesn't matter. My mom loved me, that's all I need to know. Why should I open the can of worms? Once it's open, there's no guarantee I'll be able to close it again."

"The easy life. Sounds good to me."

"Easy."

It would be easy to sink into life on the road with Danny. Maybe one day the Big Bad would catch up with her. Maybe it wouldn't. If whatever it was only wanted her mother, it had won.

If it wanted her and she was with Danny when it came for her…

Tess didn't want him to be hurt, but she was exhausted. After their trip and finding the letter, she'd expended so much mental and emotional energy that she was just spent.

Maybe a couple of weeks on the beach with Danny was exactly what she needed.

EIGHTEEN

STARTLED BY THE SQUIRT of cold lotion on her back, her torso rose a few inches from the flat lounge chair. The hands that pushed her down to massage the lotion into her skin belonged to the man who'd touched her everywhere. Those hands had been on her body so often they were becoming an extension of her.

Relaxing again, she smiled and settled into her happy half-slumber again.

"Sun's dangerous, Little Red," Danny said, taking his time about rubbing the lotion over her shoulders and down her ribs, his fingers meeting the side of her breasts more than once.

"So you keep telling me."

Lying face down on the flat lounge chair, she'd untied the strings of her bikini so she wouldn't have a line across her back. The Beast was just a few feet away. Home was in this perfect spot.

Her roommate was supposed to be out getting groceries. Though she had been sleeping there a while. Maybe he'd completed the errand and returned already. He'd sure got more lotion from somewhere.

The RV park really was right on the beach. A couple of dozen other trailers and RVs were lined up with them, flanking the central road. The facilities weren't anything fancy, but it had everything they needed. Just like Danny promised.

More than a week had gone by since the Rotunda mess. She'd never been happier with any decision. Danny and the beach were quite the combination and the perfect medicines for her ails.

"Beach suits you, babe," he said, sliding down the chair to work on her lower back, which seemed to include the top of her ass. "How you feel about South America?"

Tess adjusted the position of her cheek on her folded hands. "South America?"

"Sure, we can tour the coast. Just keep on driving. Stop when we like, start whenever we want."

"I don't have a passport, and what about your dad?" she asked, having brought up the second part of their mission several times that week. "When are we going to see him?"

"There's a cool seafood restaurant not far away. We could walk… get drunk, screw on the beach… again. Wanna go out to eat?"

Raising her upper body, Tess reached around to tie her bikini and righted it over her chest as she turned over. "Danny—"

"Want me to do the front now?"

His glow of optimism was just another diversion. She sat up to stall his hands before he could pour lotion into them.

"I'd give anything to have my mom around to argue with. How bad can it be? I promise I won't let him hurt you."

His lips quirked. "Oh, I'd love to see that, Little Red."

"Then let's go," she said, gripping his wrist.

He leaned closer. "I don't trust him."

"Okay," she said, using her hold on him to pull herself closer. "Least we know what the problem is. You're the one who always says nothing's too broken to fix."

"I don't want to fix it," he said. Angling her head, Tess wasn't so sure, and tipped her chin closer. "Don't do the doe eyes. I'm not gonna change my mind just 'cause you do the doe eyes."

She licked her lips. "How about if I promise blowjobs every day for a month?"

His eyes moved as his brows rose, suggesting that offer was attractive enough to consider. But he quickly groaned and took his wrist from her grip.

"I wouldn't be able to enjoy it anywhere near that asshole." He lunged forward to steal a kiss, then stood up. "Come inside when you're ready to eat. The restaurant takes walk-ins. I checked."

He disappeared around the end of the trailer, heading for the door on the other side, she guessed.

No matter what Tess said, he wouldn't be moved on the issue of going to see his father. It wasn't her place to push. Not that Danny would ever get mad at her. Maybe that was why she kept prodding at him. If he showed a real emotional aversion to visiting his father, she might understand and back off. But he never did. As easy about the rift as he was about everything, his indifference was puzzling.

The guy was his father.

Yeah, maybe it should be the patriarch's responsibility to make the first move. But with Danny traveling all the time, it would be easy to lose touch. If his dad wanted to patch things up, he'd have to first locate his son. Not an easy task.

The sea was so beautiful, she could look out at the great chasm of blue nothingness for hours. Except she'd been out in the heat for too long.

Bending forward, she retrieved her empty glass and notepad from under the chair. Sitting up, she laid the pad on her thighs and looked out at the ocean again. If only life could be as simple. The ocean was a good metaphor for life. No matter how simple things appeared on the surface, there was a whole cutthroat world lingering just beneath.

"Do you mind?"

The male voice drew her attention. An older gentleman, who she recognized from the trailer next to theirs, stood just behind her.

"Excuse me?"

He nodded toward her lap while waving a black handheld device.

"My grandson got this thing for me and I've never

used the converter."

At a loss, she shook her head. "I'm sorry, I don't understand."

He gestured at her lap with the device. "The numbers."

Tess looked at the pad in her lap. The cards were still pinned to the cover. "The numbers…" It took her a second, but she gasped and spun toward him, dropping her feet to the ground. "You know what these are?"

"The bottom ones," he said. "It's longitude and latitude, right?"

Her mouth opened at the same slow pace she used to rise to her feet. "Coordinates."

"Yeah," he said, doing something on his device. "Let me see." Tess turned the notebook toward him and he typed the numbers in one at a time. "This is supposed to change them into degrees, minutes, and seconds, give you an exact… There we go."

He turned it around to show her the screen, but it took a few breaths before she gathered the courage to look at it.

There, laid out, so simple, was an electronic map, a little pin graphic in the center. Above it were other numbers with letters and degree symbols.

Unclipping her pen from the notepad, she wrote them down. They seemed to lead to nowhere, but still she copied the vague address printed above.

A smile spread on her face. Grabbing the older guy, she pulled him down and smacked a kiss to his cheek. "Thank you. Oh my God, you have no idea… Thank you!"

Leaving him speechless, Tess spun on the spot and dashed around the end of the trailer to burst through the door, startling the damp, shirtless Danny.

"Babe—"

"I have to go to Oregon," Tess said, turning the pad to show him what she'd written. "Want to come with me?"

His gaze flicked from her to the notepad. As he read her notes, his brow came down, but it was quick to relax when he made eye contact with her. "It's not South America."

Shaking her head, Tess lowered the pad while creeping toward him. "No, but there's sex in it for you and I promise to buy the beer."

His dimple gave her his answer before his lips did. "Sold."

NINETEEN

MUCH OF THEIR ROAD trip was the same as the one they'd already traveled, just in reverse. Danny didn't complain about her dragging his ass one way, only to turn around and bring them back. As with everything else, he took the development in his stride.

Something beeped and snapped her from her sleep. Confused, she raised her head and turned her chin.

"What happened?" she asked, her voice rough from sleep. Clearing her throat, she pushed up just a little more to look around at the darkness outside. "I thought we were going to park."

"Take your time," Danny said from the driver's seat.

It was night, and they were still moving. The truck felt different too, though it wasn't until she slid her butt back and looked from the front to the back that she realized why the ride was lighter.

"Where's the Beast?"

"Parked at one of those middle of nowhere spots I told you about."

Clearing her throat again, Tess retrieved her bottle of water from the door while sitting up. "I slept through all that?"

"Only takes a minute to unhitch it."

Yeah, but Tess hadn't known she was that tired. The digital clock on the dash clued her in to how long she'd been out.

"It's almost three a.m."

"We came all this way," Danny said. "You don't want to know where we're going?"

Her curiosity brought them to wherever they were. As she looked around, trying to figure out where they were going, uneasiness tickled her neck. It was creepy. Trees. Grass. Nature. No sign of civilization.

"There's nothing here," she said. "Not a light. Not even a real road." The dirt track was smooth enough, but they weren't driving on asphalt. "I don't know if I like this."

"It's an adventure. We came, we have to say we saw, right?"

Worrying she could've brought them all that way for no reason, Tess drank some water, then ran her hands through her hair. "What if it's somebody's house? H could be the new Unabomber. He could blow us up on sight."

Danny snickered. "Maybe. Better to go at night, then people have a chance of seeing the fire."

Dropping into the cradle of her seat, Tess rolled her head his way. "What if he's angry? He doesn't want to see us? You read my mom's last letter. It sounds like he sent her a Dear John, right? Maybe that's why he never went back to pick up the other letter."

"Maybe."

She frowned. "Why is it so far away? The pickup point? If he lives out here, why do the drop-off and pick-ups in the most southern state?"

"Hawaii is the most southern state," Danny said, glancing her way just long enough to check her flat affect. "Which doesn't really matter right now."

"We can't wake the guy up at this time of day. If he's…" When the trees thinned and the path ahead widened, she trailed off and sat up straight, unable to comprehend what lay ahead. "Oh my God."

"Guess our gadget was right after all."

About a quarter mile ahead, a structure stood out in

the landscape. With ridges and peaks behind it, the darkened building only stood out because the moonlight shone above it. There were no lights on to welcome visitors or to suggest anyone stayed there. The ominous building appeared to be concrete. Sort of featureless with just the occasional steel-framed window. Only maybe three floors high with a smaller tiered floor on the top. It could be a factory or have some other industrial use. Antenna stuck out from the roof, thick and reaching, with other smaller, more difficult to make out shapes there too.

As they got closer, she noticed the wall around the whole thing. At least fifteen, if not twenty feet high, topped with razor wire, quite the first impression.

"Let's get out of here."

"What?" Danny asked. "We came all this way."

"Yeah, and now I want to leave, okay?" she said, tearing her trepidation from the structure to land misdirected anger on him.

His brow descended. "It's a building, it's not gonna hurt you."

"You don't know that," she said, shaking her head. "It could be a government facility. They could shoot us for being here."

"I didn't pass any keep out signs or anything warning us of danger."

"No, of course you didn't, because they don't want anyone to know it's here."

He exhaled a laugh. "Okay, Truther."

"Danny, please, we shouldn't be here."

Except he was still driving, and they were approaching the only suggestion of a break in the wall where two huge metal gates stood blocking the way.

"If there's nobody here, there's nothing to worry about," he said. "And if there is someone here, we'll just say we got lost."

"Got lost and stumbled on their secret government project," she said as the truck came to a halt next to what appeared to be a covered keypad. Tess leaned forward to look out Danny's side window. "What is that?"

"Guess we need a code to get in."

"Okay, well, we don't have one, so let's just leave."

"Hmm," Danny said, his fingers drumming on the wheel. "We could guess."

"And if we get it wrong, a sniper pops up to execute us."

He laughed. "Baby, we should use that imagination for role play. Didn't know you were so wild. Where's the card?"

"What card?"

"With the coordinates."

In her bag in the backseat. She twisted around to grab it and handed the card over. "What are you doing?" He put his window down and followed the other number with his thumb as he pressed numbers on the keypad. Until that moment, the other sequence had meant nothing. If his guess was wrong, they could get into real trouble. "Please don't do that. Be careful, Danny. It could hurt you."

"Zap me with a proton charge?" he jeered just as the pad flashed green.

The gate began to open. Stunned again, Tess wasn't sure she wanted to see what was on the other side. Danny tucked the card in the visor and drove forward, keeping their speed low. He killed their headlights too. The moment became more ill-omened the farther they progressed.

Sitting up poker straight, Tess fumbled for Danny, laying a hand on his arm, hoping for comfort or to convey some if he needed it. The concrete ground held no vehicles. No signs of anyone. No obvious clues. The place wigged her out.

"We shouldn't be here," she whispered like someone might hear her. "I shouldn't have brought you here."

Before arriving, she'd wanted to know what was at the end of the trail. The letters confirmed that the danger was real, but she couldn't have imagined it would look like this.

"It's completely dead," Danny said, slowing the truck to a stop halfway between the gate and the building. With both hands on the wheel, he leaned forward, craning to see the height of the building through the top of the windshield. "This is sorta cool, baby."

The wonder and excitement in his tone confounded her. All her life, Tess had been running from something unknown. If someone or something with means like these was after them, her mother was right to run, right to hide.

"Why would my mom send me here?" she murmured to herself. "Why would she want me to come here? Alone?"

Anne couldn't have known that Tess would meet Danny. If by some divine intervention she'd ever figured out the numbers, she could've found herself there. Alone. If it wasn't for Danny, she would never have got so far. His support held her up, got her through the weak moments. The gate with the keypad was enough to put her off visiting the structure. Hell, just the sight of the place had done that.

Danny put the truck in park and grabbed the card as he opened his door to leap out. "Let's find out."

"No," Tess called, unfastening her seatbelt to exit and follow him. "Danny, stop."

He was on his way to a door, another solid piece of metal, with a keypad right there beside it. Despite her calling out, he didn't slow down, and it was a struggle to catch up to him. When she did, he was just a few feet from the door.

Tess leaped in front of him, putting herself between him and the keypad. "I want to leave."

"We will," Danny said, trying to ease her aside. "Soon as we see what this place is."

Shaking her head, she grabbed for his arm when he swerved around her. "Please, it's dangerous," she said. "Danny, I don't like it."

His fingers were almost on the numbers. Tess used her body to push them aside and blocked the keypad.

He exhaled. "Let's see what happens."

"This isn't an adventure, okay? It's my life. My mom spent her whole life trying to protect me from this. Whatever it is, we should leave it alone. Let's do South America instead. I promise I won't mention your dad. Not once."

"Babe," he said, propping an arm on the wall over her head. "Your mom left you these messages because she wanted you to come here. It's only scary looking because it's night and it's quiet."

Now that he'd pointed it out… No hint of a wind moved even a single branch. There were no sounds of wildlife, no birds. She couldn't even hear Danny breathing.

He tried to push her aside, but Tess fought to stay in place. "Okay, well, if you're right, if that's what it is, how about we come back tomorrow? When it's light?"

"Tomorrow?"

Tess smiled, doing her best to appear calm and relaxed. "Yes. Think about it, if there are people inside, they'll be sleeping. Waking them up's just going to piss them off. If they're angry, they'll scare me. Let's let them sleep…" She laid her hands on his torso to get in close. "We'll go back to the Beast and I'll show you how grateful I am that you humored me."

Though she could tell he was softening to her will, he wasn't all the way there and held up the card. "I wanna know if the number works."

"We can find out tomorrow… or maybe we can just knock."

That didn't convince him. He blinked slowly, showing he didn't buy it. "We're here and the keypad is right there. It's been a month, Little Red. You don't wanna know?"

Fear was stopping her. Anne wanted her to be there. Her mom provided the numbers on the card. There were so many uncertainties about what might come next. One thing Tess knew for sure: her mother wouldn't endanger her.

She sighed. "Okay. Put in the number, we'll see if it works." She pointed a finger at him when he grinned. "But we're not going inside. We just want to know if it works. We'll come back tomorrow, in the daylight, if we decide we want to visit again." Nodding, he held the card toward her. "Me?"

"Your mom left it for you," he said, letting go of the card when her fingers took it.

Curving his hands around her hips, he pulled her forward and turned her around to face the darkened pad. Shadow made it difficult to see details, but each of the keys was surrounded by a thin glowing line, highlighting them in the darkness.

Danny was right. Anne left the card to instruct her daughter where to go. They were there. They'd arrived.

Inhaling, Tess glanced at the card. Not that she needed to; the numbers were imprinted on her brain. After the letters were stolen, memorizing them seemed smart. It was only a month ago, but so much had happened that in some ways it felt like a lifetime had passed.

Danny kissed the top of her head, reminding her he was there. He squeezed her shoulders, relaxing her and probably trying to encourage her too.

Her lips were dry and her throat narrow. Ignoring her hesitation, she took a deep breath and typed the number in. Her thumb moved for the last digit. Danny's hand suddenly covered hers, stalling her.

"Two, not a three."

Had she…? Yeah, her hand blocked the light, she'd almost pressed the wrong number. "Right."

Tiredness and anxiety had a lot to answer for. What might have happened if she'd pressed the wrong one? Maybe she should've done it on purpose. With no way in, they wouldn't have needed to come back.

She pressed the last number. The wait between inputting the last digit and the light around the keypad flashing green twice was excruciating.

A rush of heated breath cascaded through her hair as Danny's head landed on hers. "It worked. We did it."

"Yeah," Tess said, pushing her body back against his. "Now can we get out of here?"

His hands slid down her arms. He threaded his fingers between hers to lead her away from the door. Tess glanced back. They could've walked in. They could be in there exploring… or the angry occupants may have confronted them.

Whatever the building's purpose, it was something important. Its significance came in more than its size and strange location. Her fear hadn't gone, though it had lessened. They'd overcome one hurdle, yet somehow she knew it was just the first of many.

TWENTY

THE MIDDLE OF NOWHERE spot Danny picked for the Beast was beautiful. Angled to face the view of the vast lake, trees and grass and nature made up the picturesque sight. The peace was a complete contrast to what they'd found at the coordinate site night before last.

After returning to their base, they'd slept through most of the previous day. Tess guessed that was why Danny didn't bring up going back. Either that or he was enjoying ticking things off his wish list. Once he'd grilled the last of their meat, they'd laid on the grass counting stars until Danny decided he'd rather they get naked and have sex.

It didn't occur to her to be conscious of being naked outside. In that spot, they felt like the only two people on the planet. Despite her objections, he'd swept her up off the ground and carried her into the water. After she got over the freezing temperature, she forgave him with a kiss that would've become sex again if she hadn't chosen to swim instead. Danny thought just being in the water without clothes counted as skinny-dipping. Tess insisted if they didn't swim, it didn't count. Though she was really just playing.

After another night in the trailer, Danny went to get groceries. He couldn't source his weed anywhere, but there were plenty of condoms and enough beer to satisfy an army.

Her lover was at the grill again, cooking whatever he'd bought for them to eat. Sitting on her lounge chair, Tess toyed with the Hades card. Hades? H? They still didn't have answers.

They could stay there in the middle of nowhere for a while, maybe forever. Danny hadn't brought up going back to the compound. It was on his mind. He was curious. Just that fact should be enough to take them back. Danny wasn't usually concerned enough about anything to be curious. Yet he'd wanted to know what was beyond that door.

Still wary, she couldn't deny it had been on her mind too. Putting the card on the chair, she hopped to her feet and went inside the trailer. In the back of the closet, she'd stowed one of her backpacks. There were various things in it, but only one she really needed.

Retrieving the weapon her mother had left in the Figgs box, Tess tested the weight in her hand. They'd been to a gun range years before. If shooting became necessary, she could probably figure it out.

Her mom didn't like to carry weapons. With them traveling around all the time, keeping up with licenses and laws would've been impossible. They were always traveling under fake names too. Getting caught with a weapon could lead to issues. As she'd told Danny, her mom didn't like to get mixed up with official agencies. If the building they'd visited was connected to the government, that gave some clarity of her mother's reluctance. A mugshot, a fingerprint, maybe even a name or alias could bring the danger straight to them.

Except the building couldn't be dangerous. Maybe there was someone there who could help her. Someone who could put her on the right path to eliminating the danger. Taking on the threat would not be easy or straightforward. An ally would be useful.

The only thing Tess had to lose was her life. Her mom must have trusted that she was capable of doing whatever was necessary. Her only chance of ever being free came with facing her fear and going into that building. It could lead to her demise or it could liberate her. It was time. Tess needed to know.

Checking the clip, she looked at the weapon one more time before snatching the truck keys from the counter and heading out of the trailer.

"I'll be back later," she called out, without waiting for Danny to turn from the grill.

Going around the front of the trailer, adrenaline rose in her bloodstream. Danny appeared from the rear, moving quickly to intercept her.

"Okay, Annie, hold your horses," he said.

"Annie?"

"Get Your Gun, you've gotta have seen—"

"Danny."

"Look," he said, glancing at the weapon in her hand. "I don't know where you think you're going with that, but you're not going by yourself in my truck."

"Fine," she said, slapping the keys to his chest. "I'll hitch a ride."

She tried to go around him, but he put himself in her way again. "Okay, it's more than a mile to anything even close to a real road and a car probably goes by once every two or three weeks." That exaggeration didn't impress her. "*We* can take the truck." He hooked an arm around behind her neck to rest on her shoulders. "After we eat something."

"I'm amped now," she said. "And I don't want you to come."

"Mm hmm," he said, bending down to sweep her legs out from under her.

"Danny!"

If he thought about taking her to the water while she was holding their only defense, Tess wouldn't forgive him so fast. He carried her back to the lounge chair and dropped her onto it.

Crouching quickly at her side, he laid an arm across her hips to clamp her in place. "Sometimes you're a drag, sometimes you're the most luminous woman I've ever known," he said. The sentiment was enough to silence her objections. Clamping her mouth closed, Tess blinked at him. "You definitely take life way too seriously. But there is no way, in any universe, that I let you walk into that compound without me at your six. You go, I go. That's the rule, Little Red."

They didn't do mushy. Nothing even close to mushy. Especially not while it was light outside. Laying a hand on his cheek, she could read his certainty. Without blinking, he just kept looking at her, showing he wouldn't budge.

"Danny Winger," she said, her thumb moving in a slow caress. "You better be careful. If you don't find a weed source soon, you could find yourself caring about more than sex and beer."

"Tell me about it," he said, bouncing up to catch a quick kiss. "Trust me, I'm working on it."

When he took the gun from her hand, Tess sank against the lounge chair, watching him cross back to the grill.

"For a guy who was desperate to go inside, you're gun-shy now."

"Not gun-shy," he said, tucking the weapon into the back of his jeans. "We'll go after we eat… Maybe have sex and then we'll go."

Shaking her head, Tess didn't hide her smile. "Yeah," she said, tipping her head to the side to admire the view of him at the grill. "Just the essentials."

His fitness was obvious. On top of that, he was carrying a gun. Whoever was inside the mysterious building had plenty of their own to worry about. She and Danny might not be specific, but they weren't nothing either.

***

FOOD AND SEX, TWO STAPLES. Both had their boxes checked before they piled into the truck to return to the coordinates.

Tension filled the air. Not the good kind either. She'd dragged Danny into the situation. If only she could find the right words to apologize. Contrition wasn't enough. Nothing would make up for what might be about to happen.

The trees cleared, giving them a view of the building again.

"I think you should stay outside," she said.

In the light, it wasn't as foreboding, although she still didn't like the look of it.

"Outside where? The door?"

"The whole place," she said. "Just park here and I'll walk over—"

"You get to have all the fun?"

"Danny," she said, frustrated that he still thought it was some big joke. "I don't know who's in there or what they want."

"Which is why you should have backup."

"We can have a signal. How about if I don't come outside in an hour, you call the cops?"

He glanced at her but said nothing. He drove to the keypad, slipped the card from the visor and input the code to open the gates.

Tess wasn't afraid for her. She didn't have the emotional capacity to fear for her own safety when Danny was there and at risk.

"Please," she said as he drove through. "Please just leave. I promise I'll—"

"I'm not going anywhere," he said, tossing a glare her way.

It wasn't like him to glare. His frowns usually meant confusion or that he was teasing.

Tess just wanted him to be safe.

He turned the truck around to face the exit and parked parallel to the building, nearer to the door than they'd stopped before. Thank God he watched crime shows. It wouldn't have occurred to her a quick departure might be necessary.

"Danny," she whispered when he killed the engine. "I don't want you to get hurt because of me."

"Tess," he said, retrieving the gun from the door well. "We're gonna go in there together and whatever happens, it won't be your fault."

He got out without so much as looking her way. Which gave her no option except to follow. They were going in and he was going to ride the wave with her, no matter what she said.

Danny waited by the door, gun in his hand. Having been the one to suggest returning, backing out wasn't an option. With a heavy heart and stressing about Danny's safety, she input the code. The line around the keypad flashed green.

When her fingertips were an inch away from the door handle, Danny spoke. "Tess," he said, attracting her attention. His eyes were darker than usual, his expression somehow more intense. "You don't deserve this."

She didn't understand. "This?"

"This life you've led… You shouldn't have gone through what you did."

Why was he saying that? The sentiment was appreciated, but it didn't feel like the time to get into it.

He opened the door and peeked inside. Raising the gun, he went in first. This was it. They were going in. Tess held her breath as she stepped up to go in after him. The cavernous entryway held four staircases. One left and right of the door and another two facing them at either side of the space. A massive roll-up garage type door took up most of the back wall, though the ceiling was lower back there. Two of the staircases led up to the floor that ate into that space.

Danny went to the left, toward the staircase. "Come on," he said, reaching back for her.

Distracting him while he held a weapon could be dangerous. Staying silent, she hurried to curl her pinkie around his, and let him lead her up the stairs.

On the top landing, there was one central door. Going through was the only course. There was a keypad next to it. Maybe it was locked. Danny paused and tried the handle. It opened without them putting in a code.

A whisper of a sound came from his lips. What was he thinking? Ha, she couldn't figure out her own thoughts. Why would she be able to decipher Danny's?

The building was cold, in temperature and color palette. The dark gray room they left became a long gray and blue corridor. Various identical doors led off each side.

How were they supposed to find what they were looking for when she didn't know what it was? Danny took a left and kept going. The building could be a warren of corridors and rooms. Even someone who knew the plans could get lost there if everything looked the same.

Coming with a partner was proving smart. If Danny hadn't been with her, she wouldn't have known where to begin. By herself, adrenaline and determination would've waned by the time she discovered anything useful.

Danny took them through another door, and then they were ascending stairs. Confidence really did sell anything. He couldn't possibly know anything about the compound or its layout. Though she wouldn't be surprised if he knew something about search patterns or how best to get unlost. Many useless, fathomless facts lived in his lackadaisical brain. That moment was evidence it wasn't useless all the time.

He took her through a door and along a corridor, swung a left and kept on going until the middle of the passage. The way he stopped almost sent her rushing into his back. Catching herself on her tiptoes, Tess inhaled.

Their physical link dropped when he laid a palm on the nearest door. The gun in his other hand pointed up at the ceiling.

She saw his lips move, but was more intrigued by the pulse point in his neck. His heart was pounding hard. He stepped to the side and grabbed for her, putting her between him and the door. The shelter of his body, the heat of his chest against her shoulder blades, reassured her they were going to be okay.

He reached around her to turn the handle slowly. Once it was at full rotation, he paused to inhale at the crown of her head. His lips touched her hair for the briefest moment. Without letting another second pass, he threw open the door and propelled her forward.

Off-balance, she didn't go more than half a step. An arm shot around the doorframe to grab her, hauling her over the threshold. No time to think, she tried to call for Danny, but a hand clamped over her mouth, yanking her back against another hard body.

What the hell was happening? Terror coursed through her. Danny came in, gun aimed at whoever was holding her. The sight of his weapon snapped her focus to what was against her temple. A gun. The assailant was carrying a weapon of his own.

Dragged away from the door, both men were facing off, with her caught in the crossfire. She didn't get it. Couldn't get it. Danny wasn't even looking at her. His focus on the person at her back was laser precise, more honed than she'd ever seen it.

"Son," the male behind her said, his voice so deep it vibrated against her spine. "Just like old times."

TWENTY-ONE

HIS DAD! THE MAN WITH a gun to her head was Danny's father?

"This is no drill, old man," Danny said.

Except… the voice wasn't one she recognized. That deep growl, the anger, the determined intensity. Facing his father brought out a new side of him. His father… What the hell? If his father was there… She didn't understand. If Danny knew the place, why didn't he tell her about it?

If he hadn't expected his father…

He *had* known where he was going. Arriving in that specific room was no mistake. He'd put her in front of him… Danny had set it up. Set *her* up… The harsh blow of betrayal was impossible to fathom. She didn't understand what the hell was going on.

"Should've known he'd send you. It's poetic," Danny's father said, moving to the side as Danny swayed closer. "Where is he?"

"I'm alone, old man."

"Right," Danny's father said on an exhale of disbelief. Tightening his hold on her, he pulled her higher, stifling her capacity to breathe. "Where's your brother?"

Danny raised his gun higher, setting his narrow focus

right down the sight. "You tell me."

Yanked back again, the gun was pushed hard against her temple. "You want me to put a bullet in your bitch? She's fodder, right? That's what you want me to do. That's why you brought her."

"You wanna make my day? Do it," Danny said, tightening a barb of pain around her heart. She tried to object, to fight, but the guy at her back shook her to shut her up. "Do it… Now. Go! Don't hesitate, old man. Hesitation gets you killed."

"You're just standing there waving your dick around," her captor said. "You wanna do it? Do it!"

"There ain't no way I'm pissin' this moment away." Neither flinched. A dozen seconds went by, though it seemed like hours. "I thought about this, 'bout whether I'd tell you before or after… Decided on after. Cruel's what we do in this family."

Backing away, Danny's concentration didn't waver for even a flicker of a second. Not until he stopped moving near the control desk. The room seemed to be some kind of tech hub. Massive screens angled around a desk that separated into three sections. Danny looked down at the central section and flicked a cover open.

The guy behind her laughed. "That what you came for, Ares? Boy, I taught you better than that."

"Where is it?" Danny asked, strengthening his grip on the gun.

The laughter behind her trailed off. The captor repeated his statement with a chilling, sinister hue. "I taught you better than that."

"Oh yeah?" Danny asked, coming closer again. "Taught me to know my enemy too."

His gun swung an inch to the left. He fired a shot, then snapped his aim back on them.

Tess yelped as the guy behind her swore. "Sonofa—"

"That's no way to talk about my momma, is it? Wanna tell me again how much you respected her while you're holding that gun?" Danny stopped closer than he'd been before. "You know we don't walk outta this room, old man. You know this is the only way it ends."

"If that's how you wanted to end it, why'd you bring her?"

Danny didn't answer. With wild, wide eyes, Tess begged him to look at her, begged him to see the terror, but he didn't. Whoever that man was, the one pointing the gun her way, it wasn't Danny, not her Danny.

"You knew I wouldn't put a bullet in you," the stranger said. "And you couldn't put one in me unless I gave you reason. I kill her, makes it easier for you to kill me."

"No," Danny exhaled on a slight shake of his head. "Killing her is killing yourself. Do it, I'll tell you why, then you'll end us both."

The gun dug deeper into her head. She grabbed for the hand covering her mouth, but couldn't budge it.

"You think I won't?"

"I think you trained me well… I think there's only one person left on this earth you'd sacrifice anything for, everything for…" Danny said. "That's what you did. You sold us down the river so you could have her." Danny's chin bobbed her way, though he didn't take his attention from the stranger behind her. "You betrayed your own for the mistake you made twenty-seven years ago."

The hand on her mouth loosened just a fraction. "I don't believe it," the man behind her said, his tone deep, volume low. "You wouldn't."

Danny smiled, though it wasn't a joyful, happy sight. The sick twist of his lips was beyond any rage, something embedded it in the hatred that changed his whole demeanor.

"If there was anyone…" Danny said in a rumbling growl. "Anyone who could do it… Anyone who could track them down… Precious Pandora…"

The hand fell from her mouth to grab on and plant her back on the wall. In the spin, her hair twined around her head, catching on her wet eyes and trembling lips. Nothing made sense. What the hell was going on?

"Daire…" the stranger whispered, peering into her.

"It's in the eyes more than anywhere else and believe

me, old man, I looked everywhere."

The guy, whoever he was, kept his hand on her shoulder, holding her still as he scrutinized her features. Drawing in a shaking breath, Tess didn't know what he was looking for or why he was so awestruck.

"One…" the guy muttered and suddenly turned to Danny. "Carrie?"

Becoming somber, Danny lowered his gun. He blinked and swallowed before shaking his head once. Her attacker gasped in a brief sound of shocked pain. Shoving away, he stormed toward his son, fury in his gait.

Danny raised his gun again. "It wasn't me," he asserted, fixated on the man stalking his way. "It wasn't me!"

The other guy stopped. "Set?"

Danny shook his head. "I don't know who, but it was no accident… The vehicle was sabotaged, she wouldn't have stood a chance in that shit-heap anyway…" The stranger's hand scraped across his stubble. "She asked for you." What did he just say? Her attention rose. That couldn't—he couldn't mean… "At the end, she asked for you."

The guy's hand fell from his face. "What did she…?"

The gun went down in time with his chin until Danny was fixating on some spot on the doorframe, looking at no one. "She said your name… I told her who I was… She remembered me." He gritted his teeth, rolling them over each other like he loathed the words. "It doesn't matter—"

"Like fuck it doesn't matter," the stranger said, striding over, swiping the gun aside to grab Danny's shoulder.

"It doesn't fucking matter," Danny said, smacking the guy's arm away and backing off. "What matters is you lied to her, just like you lied to me."

"I didn't fucking lie. My word is steel!"

In a flash, those words struck her deep. Her lips parted, not that it mattered, she stopped breathing. "Oh my God," she whispered. The guy whipped around to look at her. "You're Hades… It's you. You're H."

"Yeah." Danny's voice came from somewhere behind the bewildered stranger. "I hope you're both very happy together."

He appeared around H, the door in his sights, still refusing to look at her. With one step, Tess slid along the wall to block the door handle just as he reached for it. His gaze collided with hers.

"You lied to me," she said, her lips dry. "All this time. You lied to me."

"Yeah," he said, his brow moving just a fraction when his chin rose.

Looking at her had been unintentional. He was avoiding her; he'd never done that. Discovering exactly what he was capable of was a hard lesson that was going to take time to process.

"All this time, you knew," she said, trying to figure it out by saying the words aloud. "All this time you knew who H was, you knew C."

"Carrie," Danny said, still evading her gaze. "Your mother's real name is Carrie-Anne… Carrie-Anne Tulay, but it doesn't matter."

Because she was dead. Every part of her chilled so fast, her fingers went numb. "Sabotaged… You meant my mother. You were with her… at the end."

His attention drifted down to hers. What did that look in his eye mean? She'd cried in his arms. Laid herself bare for him. Given him her grief and all the time he…

"You asshole," she whispered. A surge of anger smacked her hard. "You fucking asshole!" Slapping both hands to his chest, she shoved hard, wishing she could hurt him, but he didn't move. "Why? Why would you—"

"I'll move you if you don't get out the way," Danny said, an indifferent shutter closing over him.

"You won't put a fucking hand on her."

Danny's expression changed at the sound of H's voice. Seemed the whole situation was just an inconvenience. "Oh, and what are you gonna do about it, old man?" he asked, turning to address his father.

"I'll do what I have to. I'm her father."

Tess heard the word. Before she could comprehend all the implications of it, disgust hit her. "You're *my* father?" she said. Danny sank back a quarter turn. "And he's your father?"

For the first time, she saw something approaching amusement glimmer in the eyes of the guy she'd been sleeping with for a month. "Not my biological father. He raised me." She breathed out in relief. "He's your biological father." Danny swung himself around to speak to H again. "We've got DNA evidence to prove it, don't we?"

"In the vault," H said, backing up to prop himself against one of the desks.

"Which we can't get into," Danny said. "Because you're an asshole."

"That why you came here? To trade insults? You wanted me to come, son."

Danny stepped his way, raising the gun to wave it behind himself in her general direction. "Because you were supposed to come and put a bullet in your little princess. After she was gone, you'd know what it was to lose everything… Like I did."

"Oh," H said, folding his arms and crossing his ankles. "Boohoo for the little orphan boy. This where the violins fade up and the Kleenex come out?"

Not dissuaded, Danny got even closer to the man he called his father. "Yeah," he growled. "You'll need something to clean up the blood."

H stood up and slapped the gun onto the desk, which prompted Danny to do the same with his weapon.

"Please don't fight!" Tess said, recalling what Danny had told her about his father.

In the same moment she pushed off the wall, Tess faltered. Danny wasn't Danny. She didn't know him. Not the real him. All of it. Everything they'd been through was fake. And she'd fallen for it. Turning her back on them, Tess didn't know what to do, couldn't block them out, but she couldn't trust them either.

"Where's your SP?" H's authoritative voice asked.

"None of your fucking business," Danny answered.

Except he wasn't Danny. Tess closed her eyes tight.

"Give me the clock," H said. "You brought her here, which means you don't want Z to have her."

"He didn't make me an offer… Could be on his way too."

"What?" H asked, confused. "You're working for him and you don't know where he is?"

"Since when am I working for Z?"

"That's what he said."

"Never in twenty years have you trusted a word from that man's mouth," Danny said.

"Twenty-five years," H said, firm in his conviction.

"Probably longer than that," Danny said. "Twenty-five years ago is just when Pandora came into play."

H's mood hadn't lightened. "She was never in play."

TWENTY-TWO

"PANDORA," TESS SAID. The word from the card. She turned to them again. "Who is Pandora?"

"You are Pandora, Tess," Danny said.

"Me?"

H was frowning at her. Unable to believe her presence or unconvinced of her identity? Tess could identify with either possibility.

"She who will destroy the world," Danny muttered. "Temptress."

Oh, God, he'd told her. He'd used that word when they were... She was Pandora.

"Carrie's really gone?" H asked.

Grief might take time to catch up with him. The last letter from her mother was still in one of the trailer's nightstands. At least, she thought it was, Danny could have put it anywhere. Handing the letter to H, given what it said, might be cruel.

"It's your fault," Danny said to H, his candor harsh and cold. "They killed her because of you. Same reason Pandora has been running her whole life. They're in this because of you."

"I know," H said, accepting the criticism.

"What Carrie got was a relief. I don't have a damn clue how you'll keep Pandora safe now. Z blames you for everything, I can only guess he does."

"Because you haven't talked to him," H said like he didn't believe that for a second.

"Hey, I got the alert like every other operative. Only I didn't have a damn clue what the fuck was going on. You should've trusted me! I'm trained to take a bullet for you, old man. Fear doesn't exist. Fuck, you should've trusted me. Trusted your training."

"I didn't want to do that to you," H muttered, folding his arms again.

"Don't give me that shit. I would've been there."

H shook his head. "This was your life. Your home. Everything you knew. You'd do anything to protect it. I always accepted Olympus came first for you."

"If that was true, why didn't I walk with Z?"

"Didn't walk with me either, son."

"Now everything we ever knew, everything you built, is scattered to the wind," Danny said and turned to kick one of the desk supports in a show of rage. "And we can't put it together again—"

"Because I'm an asshole, yeah," H said. "You did that part."

"Can you fucking blame me?" Danny asked, driving his hand through his hair. "You don't give a damn, do you? Or what? You've put it back together and left me in the cold?"

Offense hit H so hard that it became fury before he took a breath. "I've been out there in the cold! I left them to you, every single one. What's your primary mission?"

"I don't—"

"Ares!"

Danny silenced and squeezed his lips together, holding his emotion behind the dam of his strong jaw. "Return to base."

"That's right. Fail or succeed, whatever happens, you return to base."

"I'm here," Danny said, backing up to open his arms. "I'm fucking here, and what? What the fuck am I supposed to do?" He held up four fingers. "Four people know the code to unlock Olympus, only four. Z was never gonna come back here, there's nothing here for him to kill. Fuck knows where P is, or if Styx is alive, and *you* did this."

"You knew I would come back for you. I did come back for you. Z had already killed Minotaur. We were on a clock. He told me you were his; I had no reason to doubt that. I came back. I came to get you."

Danny was shaking his head. "You lied to me. Every fuck else knew. I was the only one with my thumb up my ass when the shit came down. I would've told you straight, you never would've pulled it off."

"It wasn't my idea."

"I don't give a damn whose idea it was. Let me guess, it was the Six? Which one? Huh? Even now you still won't tell me."

"To protect you," H said, his own frustration lingering in those words.

"Fuck protection! Look at me, asshole," Danny said and lunged forward to hit H's shoulder, forcing him to look. "You created me for this."

Starting at Danny's feet, H scanned all the way to the top of his head. "You look like shit."

"Yeah," Danny said. It surprised her he took the criticism from the man he'd just been arguing with. "Haven't been training much this month."

"You doing Z's job for him? We'll need to go back to basics."

Danny exhaled his disagreement. "I'm not going anywhere with you, old man," he said, retrieving his gun and tucking it into the waistband of his pants.

"Where you gonna go?" H asked as Danny began to turn away. "What's waiting for you out there?"

Danny's focus stuck to the floor. "We don't know 'cause Minotaur is dead and you won't do a damn thing about it."

"I want to know just as much as you do, but we do that, and it starts all over again."

"I'm okay with that."

"No," H said, propping himself on the desk again. "There's nothing here to rebuild, son. It's over."

"I spent my whole life following every order. Twenty-four seven, training, fighting, working, doing everything you ever told me," Danny said to H. "And now it's just over…" He took a quick breath. "*I won't let you erase two decades of sacrifice.*" Something about that sentence was familiar. The flicker of recognition on H's face suggested he knew it too. "What you really meant was your sacrifice. You were happy for everyone else to sacrifice everything, so long as you got to play the hero for Helen."

H shook his head. "It wasn't like that."

Danny swaggered a step closer to him. "*PK is the only one I trust and he's already proved he'd pick them over me… This is the only life PK's ever known. He doesn't understand that this isn't living… I don't want to put PK in the middle either, he's so damn sharp. If he figures it out…*"

"How did you—"

"*I always look to PK and know my predicament is nothing compared to his… PK can't love. Nothing about him isn't manufactured. Controlled. Owned. I should never have let that happen either.*"

"Daire—"

"What do you think would've happened?" Danny asked. Except H called him Daire. Was that his real name? "If they found out you were communicating with her? It was against the accord, right?"

"If you read the letters, you know the truth of that," H said. "Damn, Carrie should've known better than to retain evidence."

The letters. That's why she recognized the quotes. Tess hadn't written them out with such detail on her notepad.

"They'd have killed you," Danny… or rather Daire, said. "Not before they killed Helen and Pandora… Except they weren't here, were they? Who were you closest to here? Remind me."

"I would never have let them hurt you."

"Maybe," Daire said. "You were gonna be dead anyway. What did it matter if they took me down before or after? I don't care about combat, you trained me for that. I do care that you didn't give me a fighting chance. Intel is the key to survival. You could've let me know what the fuck was coming down."

"I didn't want you in the middle."

"Because you thought there was even the slightest chance I'd choose them over you?"

"Your loyalty is to Olympus. It always has been."

"I was six years old."

"I wasn't talking about that."

"You're always talking about that," Daire muttered and moved away from H again.

H wasn't going to let Daire's accusation stand. "*Sometimes I forget. When I'm with PK, I believe that there's purpose…*" H recited. "*They sent PK overseas. I couldn't leave him. It's no excuse, I know you won't understand… I wanted so much for us, for PK, and I couldn't deliver on any of it… If I thought PK would come, I'd drag him along and we'd all be together.* You read that too?"

"I read every word, and I got it. All you went through, all of you, you blamed it on me."

H sprang to his feet. "Not a second of it."

"But you weren't missing much," Daire said, gesturing back at her without turning. "Just ask the temptress, her life wasn't one of love and luxury."

"I want both of you to be happy."

"Well then, you were right, you let everybody down."

Tess didn't want to hear more arguing. Though part of her wanted to know every detail of what the men were discussing, another part was aware of where they were and how far it was from safety… if there was such a thing.

She stepped forward. "Do you have a truck? A vehicle?"

H glanced from her to Daire and back again. "No. I hitched in and cut through the Glade."

Where was that? Was it a shortcut to a main road?

"Harry doesn't leave tracks," Daire said. "Not in the Olympusphere." Being clueless was becoming familiar. Daire put a hand in his pocket and tossed something her way. "Take the Beast."

She caught the keys. "I don't—"

"She's never hauled a trailer," he said to H. "Don't let her tell you she can do it. She'll kill both of you trying."

Daire started in her direction. The way he walked was different. His stance was straighter, more formidable, and his shoulders were broader somehow. It was insane, but the transformation was jarring. Even his eyes and hair seemed darker. How was that possible? The mean air around him was the opposite of the warm, easy glow her Danny exuded.

Standing there, in his path, Tess expected to be pushed aside.

"Daire, you can't play rogue, you suck at it." Harry stopped Daire before he reached her. "You don't do lone wolf either. You need to fight for something, son. Always have."

"Harry," Daire said, warning heavy in the word.

"I let you go because I respected what I thought was your choice. Hierarchy stands. If Z doesn't have your loyalty, you still answer to me."

"Could be bullshitting you," Daire said. "Maybe I am working for him."

"If you were, you had all you needed to draw me out when you located my Light. I'd be dead by now if Z held your leash."

"What do you want?"

"It's been almost a year. Z is still out there."

"He's taking down our guys."

"How do you know that?" H asked, though Tess wasn't sure he didn't already have his own suspicions.

"It's the only way to assure loyalty. That's what happened with your original trainers. Those were Z's orders too. He's not sentimental and won't let it go. He won't rest until he's crossed all of us off the list."

"He needs power," H said. "I figure he's going out on his own."

"Been watching the Six?"

"Two and five are already dead."

Turning in a slow arc, Daire didn't seem to expect that. "Two of them means at least eight of ours."

"Sounds right."

"Tell me you've heard from him."

"Your brother will be fine," H said. "You prepared each other well."

Exhaling a short breath from his nose, Daire's head fell. "You want us to take them on."

"It's us or them."

"You were the one who ruined everything," Daire said. "You destroyed this."

"For Olympus."

"No, not for Olympus. For your pride," Daire said, starch in his spine. "Admit it. You did what you did because you wanted to win. You wanted to take him down."

"We can argue this from now 'til forever, but we can't do it here. We've waited too long. If anyone else got your marker…"

"Z won't come back unless he's desperate. If he's desperate, he's ripe to take down."

"So you wanna wait? See if you're right?"

"I didn't say that."

"No, because you could never resist a mission," H said, grabbing his gun and striding on past Daire.

Tess scrambled out of the way so H could open the door. He checked up and down the corridor before exiting. Daire wasn't slow to follow. She couldn't think, couldn't focus, couldn't figure out what to do. Neither of the men could be trusted. The danger could be closer than ever.

Daire paused by the door. They stood there next to each other, facing opposite ways. "Where would you go?" he asked like he could read her mind. "You can hate me and resent your father, but, truth is, we're the only option you've got."

H stuck his head back in. "What's the fucking hold up?"

"Nothing," Daire said. "She's coming." He looked at her. "Right?"

Tess wasn't sure who she hated or resented. Getting away from that place seemed like a damn good idea. Given both men had guns, they could've killed her already if that was their aim.

Her head was full of questions, but she wasn't ready

to let them loose.

Nodding once, she exited to follow H on the route Daire had brought her. Daire. He wasn't the man who'd accompanied her into the building. Her Danny, the man she'd been infatuated with, was gone. She'd lost her mother. To lose someone else so soon was painful; too much for her heavy heart.

Still, what was she going to do? Lay down and die? No. Carrying on was the only option. Alone would mean drawing a line under the Danny chapter and never thinking about it again. Except he was right. She had nowhere else to go.

These two men, whoever they truly were, had answers. Answers that she needed. Her mom hadn't told her the whole truth, and this was her chance to find out. Her only chance. She'd vowed that she would tackle the danger head on, to rid herself of its specter. Before Tess could do that, she needed to learn absolutely everything about it.

TWENTY-THREE

WHEN THE TRUCK STOPPED, getting out was automatic. Anything was preferable to the oppressive atmosphere in the vehicle. No music. No conversation. Daire was nothing like Danny. That much was becoming painfully obvious. Even his posture in the driving seat was different. Rigid, both hands tight around the wheel, it was… professional.

Being in the backseat was new too. H, Hades, Harry, whoever he was, sat in her place in the front, as starched as the man in the seat next to him.

The other two truck doors closed around the same time as hers. In her haste to get away from the vehicle, she didn't think about what lay ahead. The trailer. She stopped. H and Daire continued past her, striding on with purpose and determination.

The Beast had been her home for a month. Except everything was a lie. Damn, she was an idiot. Hoodwinking her had been so easy that she deserved to be duped. He'd convinced her he was safe without her ever once questioning his nature. Why would she? Maybe 'cause her mother taught her better than that? Goddamnit.

Recalling the things she'd said, the things they'd

done… Internalizing her embarrassment didn't contain her cringe. Her seduction. She'd knocked on his door and showed him a condom. Really? Had she done that? She went to him. He didn't pursue her. That was how he'd got in under the radar.

People insinuating themselves into her life, her mother told her to be wary of that. But Tess put herself in Danny's life, assuming he was benign. She'd suspected Patrick and gone home to Danny! Though anything was possible. The two of them may have been working together. Maybe her whole life had been a con.

"Problem?"

The two men were standing at the front of the trailer, waiting for her. Waiting. She didn't want to go with them into her and Danny's claustrophobic space. They'd shared everything in there… including their naked bodies. She'd called out for him, praised him, climaxed under him over and over. All the time, he'd never existed.

Giving her humiliation voice would intensify the mortification. What was her alternative to following them? Running into the woods at sunset? It would be dark soon. They'd left later than she'd hoped. They'd delayed to have dinner… to have sex… Her eyes closed. He'd known what they'd find in that building, who they'd find, that his betrayal would be revealed. No wonder he'd postponed their departure to have sex with her. One last hurrah…

The man with the gun. The one who'd set her up as a human shield… she'd had sex with him. That same guy wasn't giving her the time of day anymore. Just a couple of hours ago, he'd been inside her. Now he was a stranger.

Had she been so desperate not to be alone? So desperate that she'd clung to the first sign of affection? It was maybe only the physical kind, but something was better than nothing. Apparently. Danny was everything she'd needed. Somehow, he'd known exactly how to play her. She couldn't deny falling for the ploy, hook, line, and sinker.

"Tess!" The abrupt bark of H's voice shook her. Impulse moved her feet. Both men were admiring the trailer as she approached. "It rigged?"

Neither acknowledged her.

"C4," Daire replied. "Remote trigger."

H's head bobbed in understanding. "Seams or floor?"

"Both."

H slapped Daire's shoulder and led the way forward. "Good boy."

Daire opened the trailer door but didn't go in. He stepped back, holding the door for H. In turn, the older man gestured for her to go inside first. Motivated by the knowledge there was alcohol inside, she didn't hesitate to go in. It was only beer; beggars couldn't be choosers.

H spoke to Daire as she stepped up. "Stand alert."

"Sir," Daire said.

What was that about? Whatever. With the fridge in her sights, she went to retrieve a bottle. H came in and closed the door. No Daire. Twisting off the cap, Tess tipped the bottle to gulp down the cool liquid.

"You should get some sleep," H said.

Bed wasn't on her radar yet. It couldn't be much after nine p.m.

She put her beer on the dinette table. "Would you like something to eat?" Tess asked, crossing to the foil covered plates on the counter. "We have leftovers, I can put them in the microwave." Stepping back, she gestured to the fridge. "Or we can cook something fresh if you don't mind waiting for the grill to heat up."

"Sleep," he said. "You should sleep."

Shaking her head, Tess was too tense to even take a deep breath. "I wouldn't sleep now."

"You don't have to worry," H said, scanning the space. "Daire will stay outside all night. He won't let anything disturb us."

Restraining her anger and embarrassment wasn't easy. "I really don't care about what he's doing."

"He didn't tell you about his connection to me," H said, inspecting her. The discerning descent of his brow prickled her irritation. "Your mother didn't tell you much about me either."

"No, she didn't."

"That's for the best," he said.

Such a breezy, unapologetic response from the man who provided half her DNA. "Excuse me?"

"It's best that you don't understand. You heard many things tonight that won't make a lot of sense to you. It's best if you don't think too much about any of it."

Oh, he was trundling down a dangerous path… Her frown was slow to form. "Are you threatening me?"

"No," he said in quick reply. "Tess, I'm your father. I will do everything in my power to keep you safe. Your mother took on that responsibility when you were young. She did her job well. Now that she's not able to do it, it's only right that I take over."

Not able to do it. Plain. Simple. Direct. What the hell? Beyond anything she'd heard that night, the attitude, the lack of sentiment, it was incredible. "Is this some kind of joke?"

For the first time, his certainty wavered. "No, why would you think—"

"You realize I'm not a child," she said, taking a step toward him. "You may be part of some fantastic global conspiracy that I don't understand, but I am capable of making decisions for myself."

"Capable, maybe, but they don't seem to be the most intelligent decisions. I will find somewhere to keep you safe, somewhere for you to stay. You won't have to worry about anything. I'll ensure you have supplies and—"

"I don't know anything about Olympus or your crazy code names or what the hell Daire planned to do with me, but I have been running for twenty-seven years. Yeah, okay, I stuck my head above the parapet and maybe that was stupid. I lost my mother; my whole world was upside down. I can admit I wasn't in the best frame of mind. I thought I could actually take you on, take on whatever we'd been running from."

"You can't do that."

"Maybe. I don't know because I don't have a damn clue what the hell mess you've made. Daire might be a fucking asshole, I won't fight you on that, but he was right. We are in this because of you."

By "*we,*" she meant her and her mother. Except she'd learned that Anne wasn't honest about a lot of things. Sure, the full story was never forthcoming. That was obvious. Always had been. But learning she didn't even know her mother's real name shook her to the core.

His affect flattened to match the deepening of his stern tone. "Your mother and I made choices. A long time ago, Tess. We did what we thought was best."

"Yeah," she said and nodded, walking up close. "And look where that got her."

His height was around the same as Daire's, so at least in a physical sense, Tess was used to asserting herself to someone of his stature. His dark gray hair had flecks of white around his temples and ears. He might be older, but he definitely wasn't inept or feeble. Whatever H was, if he'd raised Daire, he'd taught him to be a formidable foe.

"Blame me for your mother's death," he said. "You should. It was my fault. She was in danger because of me."

"Daire hasn't seen you for a year," she said. Danny had told her that. "Your precious Olympus, which I guess is where we just were, is abandoned. Whatever you did there, it's over, by your own admission." She took his lack of a reply as confirmation. "So where have you been? Daire found us." Tess exaggerated his name because although she said it, she didn't know the man. Not really. "You could've found us if you wanted to… My mom didn't go to the Rotunda every year. I know because we traveled together. If you want me to put money on it, I say you left your letters where we lived. You delivered her letters to wherever we were, didn't you? Most of them anyway. That means you found us before. She had to put hers in the locker because she didn't have the skill or the resources to track you, which was probably exactly how you wanted it."

"How did you—"

"I'm not quick," she said. "I procrastinate. It's a bad habit. Anything negative, if I can put it off, I will. That said, I'm not afraid of hard work. I do what needs to be done. I never, ever turned my back on her."

"No?" he said, grabbing her arm to pull her back

when she tried to turn away. "You put her through hell. What was running from her supposed to achieve? Every single fucking time—"

"Don't swear at me," she said, yanking her arm from his grip. "I don't give a damn who you are. You do not speak to me that way!"

"You are my child! You will respect—"

"I respect people who earn my respect," she argued. "You wanna put your hands on me in anger, do it! If you're too bull-headed and ignorant to use your words, fists will do the job for you! That's how you raised Daire, right?"

"I never—"

"My mother taught me to respect myself. Taught me to value my own contribution. Taught me strength. No matter what happens, no matter what blows we have to take, we carry on. We fight. We survive and we don't ever bow to bullies! Not ever! Easy doesn't mean right, sir." The sneer of the last word came as she stepped back. "This is a test of my strength. I don't know if I'll pass or fail, but I am in control of me. Me and no one else. I won't be led, not by you, not by anyone." Passing him in the narrow trailer, she paused at the door. "Oh, and my momma taught me never to start a fight... but she sure encouraged me to finish them."

Shoving at the door, it hit Daire and sprang back. She shoved it again, forcing the guard to step aside.

"Out of the way," she snapped, leaping down from the trailer to stalk across the grass toward the water. Half a dozen strides later, adrenaline coursing through her, she swung around to storm back. Not to go inside, but to stop in front of the sentry. "And you're no fucking better." Daire stared over the top of her head, eyes front, expression blank. "You did a good job. Excellent. Superb. I believed it. I did. I'd be lying and you wouldn't believe me if I said anything else." She sucked in a breath. "But you did me a favor. Thank you. My first real test out in the world on my own and I failed. You were very good at your job. You won. Well done." Her voice lowered to a hiss. "But don't think for one second that you broke me. No one has that power over me. No one has that right. Your lies made me stronger. I'm not weaker because you're a sick sonofabitch out looking to get his depraved kicks any way he can. You opened my eyes. I didn't want to be alone. Because of you, now I know there's no other way to be."

Returning to her previous path, Tess breathed deep, ignoring the weight of tears on her lashes. Weakness would be the downfall of anyone who gave into it. H might be an overbearing, controlling tyrant, but he hadn't given in to feelings or let weakness rule him. Maybe she should take a leaf from her father's book and focus only on what was best for her.

It didn't matter that she didn't like him. It didn't even matter that Daire was his shadow. She could learn something from their cutthroat, detached, do-anything-for-the-job attitudes. Danny had once told her she wasn't a robot. If what she'd seen of Daire was any indication, he could be exactly that. If that was what it took to survive, Tess would have to learn to be the same way.

TWENTY-FOUR

AFTER PACING ON THE lake's shore for a while, Tess sat on the bank tossing stones into the black abyss. It got cold and she got tired. For a brief moment, she considered going to sleep right there. But that might lead the men to believe they'd beaten her.

Even though it had been a mistake to trust this Daire, he was the one who'd done wrong. If anyone should be ashamed to face anyone, it should be him. H was no saint either. Not that she'd claim to be, though she'd never gone around issuing orders to strangers and talking down to them, demanding respect.

So she'd left the water and returned to the trailer, ignoring Daire, as he ignored her, to go inside. As much as she didn't want to sleep in her and Danny's sheets, doing anything else could imply defeat. And she was not defeated.

That was how she ended up in the bed, fast asleep behind the privacy curtain. It offered little protection; a little was better than none. H had declared Daire would be outside all night. Good for him. It gave her a reprieve from seeing him.

Something startled her awake.

What had…? Sitting up, she pushed her hair from her

face. Something… A noise? A feeling? Whatever it was, something unsettled her. Scooching to the end of the bed, she grabbed a hoodie from the hook by the privacy curtain and ventured out of the bedroom. The trailer was dark. Instead of finding someone in the dinette bed or recliners, nothing was out of place.

"Thirty!" came a shout from outside.

Still half-asleep and confused, she pushed open the door to find H standing twenty feet away from the trailer, looking up at something.

"What are you doing?" she asked, her voice croaky.

H glanced at her. "Go back to bed, Tess."

Just the fact that he said that like he was talking to a three-year-old prompted her outside. The grass was cool under her bare feet. The sun hadn't woken up, yet she was outside.

Going over to H, pulling the hoodie tighter around her, Tess noted him holding a small black thing and turned to see what he was looking at. In a heartbeat, the spectacle erased the remaining webs of sleep from her consciousness.

There, on the roof of the trailer, was Daire… on his hands. Upside down on his hands… As if that wasn't crazy enough, he was wearing a blindfold too.

"What the hell?" she said, doing a double take at H, who was concentrating on his little black device. "Why is he doing a handstand on the roof?" No answer. She gaped at the sight. "When the hell will he ever need to do that for anything?" She glanced around, seeking clarity. "What the hell time is it?"

"Ares!"

"Oh, four, twenty-three," Daire called, holding his position.

"And?"

"Eighteen seconds."

"Twenty-three," H corrected him. "Gimme ten."

At that, Daire's elbows bent and, still upside down and vertical, he lowered at a slow, controlled pace only to push himself back up straight again.

She couldn't believe her eyes. "What the hell is—"

"It's an endurance exercise," H said, stooping her way, keeping his focus on his ward. "He's been up there a half hour. Cramp alone could be enough to make a grown man cry." Yet H wasn't fazed or pulling back. "It requires concentration."

"And the blindfold?"

"Sensory deprivation discombobulates balance."

"I don't even know what that means," she said, swinging around to check out Daire going up and down. Eventually, he got to his ten and froze again.

"Do you want to shoot him?" H asked.

As if the moment wasn't ludicrous enough.

Her brows went up. "Do I want to what?"

H nodded toward a long black trunk on the grass by the trailer. One that hadn't been there before. "They're rubber bullets."

"No, thank you. I do not want to shoot anyone," she said, putting up the hood of her sweater, hoping it would keep some of the heat in. "Won't he freeze up there?"

"Not up there," he murmured, then raised his volume. "Attention!"

Walking on his hands, Daire turned and flipped onto his feet in one slick move. He didn't remove the blindfold, just walked to the end of the trailer and dropped onto a hip to slide from the roof to the grass.

Only when he was on his feet again did he pull the black blindfold from his head and scrub a hand over his hair. Drawing her eyes away, she didn't care about the way he stretched his shoulders in that tight black tee-shirt. She didn't.

"That is my daughter."

The menace of H's tone brought her attention back around just in time to see Daire's gaze ascend. Glancing down, Tess wondered what the hell he'd been looking at. All she saw between the hoodie and the grass were her legs. When she looked up, his stare was fixed straight ahead, and he stood to attention as ordered.

Unimpressed, H scowled. Still at a loss, she peeked down again. Either she was missing something or Daire had been looking at her legs and H didn't like it. They'd been having sex for a month; Danny wouldn't be that interested in her legs… why should Daire be?

That thought was quickly eclipsed by another. Did H know they'd been having sex for a month? Did he know they'd been intimate at all? If he didn't, what would he do if he found out? Telling him could cause violence between the men… But why should she keep secrets to protect anyone?

"Get the F-Flare."

"Sir," Daire said, turning in a quick, militaristic snap to march over to the trunk.

He opened it and brought whatever he retrieved back to H. A flare gun. Despite anticipating the sound, she jumped when he shot it. Except… what? It didn't fire any regular flare. There was a light, a small one, so small that as the projectile shot across the lake, it disappeared.

Tess was still trying to fathom the pinprick of light in the vast dark arena of the lake's surface when Daire dashed past her, shirtless and shoeless, heading for the water. Dumbstruck, she watched him vault up the rocky outcrop and dive headfirst into the water.

Her mouth open, she landed her shock on H. Not that he noticed; he was too preoccupied with the black device.

"What is this one for?" she squawked.

"This is how he earns my respect," H muttered.

"He'll freeze!"

"He'll survive," H said, making eye contact. "You think it's cruel. You're not used to our life. He is and knows what I know."

Her anger smoldered again. "And what do you know?"

"That to succeed, he must bear the burden." Gearing up to shoot him down, her chance was taken when he spoke again. "If you and I want to survive what lies ahead, Daire will be our primary instrument of success." That silenced her objections. "I'd give my life for you, Tess. I'm faster and stronger than most every other man my age. Age aside, I was recruited into this from basic training at eighteen. Daire has been training since before he could walk. From the moment he could make eye contact, Olympus has been coaching him… If we want quick and sure, Daire is the only one I'd entrust your life to. He has orders and will give his life for yours."

Drawn to look out at the water again, she couldn't see him. Couldn't see anyone. If he got in trouble or needed help, they'd have no way to know it.

"You hurt him when you did whatever you did," she murmured, still not understanding any of it. "He said you raised him. Is that true?"

"From the moment he was born," H said, still interested in his little device. "His mother was bleeding out, we were taking heavy fire… He was born in a gunfight, literally… The building was coming down around us, there's nothing left of Olympus A. Nothing except the lessons it taught us."

"His mother died?" He nodded. "Who was she?"

"First female Olympus agent."

Folding her arms, Tess gave him her attention. "And what is Olympus? What was it? Does it still exist?"

"It never did," he said. "Not to anyone except those in it."

"And my mom." H tensed. "She wasn't an agent, was she?"

"No," he said, somber. "Carrie was a variable no one saw coming. Me included."

"And there's some weird Olympus rule that you're not allowed to have sex, is that it?" From the flash of surprise on his face, he clearly hadn't expected her to be so direct. "I'm not an idiot, I know how babies are made."

"There are rules. Strict rules… Rules with consequences that were put into effect after what happened between Carrie and me."

"And what was that? What happened between you that was so awful they spent decades trying to hurt us?"

"I won't talk about that," he said, probably assuming his word would be the last.

He hadn't figured out that his authority meant squat to her. "That's not good enough," she said, startling him again. "You can't put up a wall and say no. Not to me. I'm not one of your agents."

"No, you're my daughter. A daughter who was never supposed to exist. You benefited from Daire's experience. By then, I knew what he was… What they were grooming him to become." Silencing himself, he sealed his lips and blinked to the heavens once before looking at her again. "What *I* was grooming him to become. He is a product of a lifetime of training. He'll tell you Olympus is his purpose… Until this day, he will say it. And, yes, my actions took that from him. I took away the only home he's ever known, and I didn't warn him the end was coming."

Seeing beyond the hard exterior gave her a glimpse of his burden. "Eighteen is young," she said. "You've been doing this ever since?"

"My whole adult life."

"Then I'd say maybe Daire isn't the only one who lost his home."

She didn't expect H to smile, but he did. The warmth of it took her aback. Yet the simple sorrow lingering behind touched some deep corner of her.

"I lost my home when you were two years old." What did that mean? She couldn't remember being so young. With careful fingers, he touched her jaw to tip her head up an inch. "He's right. You have your mother's eyes."

From one extreme emotion to another. The last few days had been a rollercoaster, to say nothing of what she'd been through since the car wrecked.

"I was afraid you would never know," she said as his hand fell away. "That she was gone."

His smile faded. "I should've been there. I'm sorry that I wasn't."

"I wasn't there either. She knew something was wrong. She knew it was time to go."

"She told you that?"

"We'd moved so many times that there were things we said without words. She told me we had to go soon, but I knew from the look in her eyes that something was going on, something… scared her." Tess shook her head. "Maybe if I'd paid more attention… If I'd insisted we left that minute—"

"We can't foresee the future," he said, touching her jaw again. "I know, I've met men who've dedicated their lives to trying to do just that. Maybe if you'd insisted, she would still be with us... or maybe we'd have lost you both."

"You'd never have known. Her and I would be gone, and no one would know it."

The chilling truth brought her arms around her body. Anne was her life, her only companion. Sure, it had been necessity, but they'd leaned on each other. She hadn't appreciated their bond until it was lost.

"I would've known," he said. "Daire would've known."

She sighed. "Daire didn't have a clue who I was until a month ago."

H exhaled a laugh. "You and Daire spent a year together, more than a year, when you were an infant." Shock took her breath. "You lived at Olympus... He's six years older, but you fascinated him. He had never seen another child at the beta site, let alone a female one, an untrained female one... He was protective of you, fiercely protective."

But how did that...? Being on the run with her mother was the only existence she'd ever had... at least, that's what she'd believed.

"I don't remember that," she murmured, peering into him. "How could I—"

"It's not a time we like to talk about. Your mother wouldn't have known how to tell you."

"There's a lot she didn't tell me."

"You can't blame her," he said. "If you have to blame anyone, blame me."

"I understand why she needed to protect me when I was a child. I wouldn't have understood. She should've told me after I was grown."

"And where do you begin with a conversation like that? *'Your father is principal agent of a covert organization with a shady remit and severe trust issues'?*"

The agency had the shady remit and trust issues or H did? Probably a mixture of both.

"Saying something would've been better than

nothing," Tess said. "She could've tried."

From nowhere a hand rose next to H's little device. Startled, she recoiled and was shocked to see Daire there behind H, presenting the little red tube he must've fetched from the water. With no ambient noise and just them there, she couldn't believe he'd approached without making a sound.

"Good," H said, pressing something on his device.

She hadn't noticed the tee-shirt draped on H's shoulder until he tossed it to Daire, who used it to dry his face, then pulled it over his head. For a split second, she was obsessed with trying to recall what it had been like to press her mouth to that chest. Had she ever done that? Why hadn't she done it more often?

Daire went around them and crouched to pull on the boots he must have removed before getting into the water. His clothes were wet, so it made little sense to put the boots back on.

He stood to attention for H again. "Ten point three miles around the lake. Be in your bunk in less than an hour."

"Sir," Daire said and sprinted off.

Watching him go, Tess couldn't equate what she was seeing with the Danny she knew. Danny wasn't so motivated, wasn't so physical, wasn't so bothered. He'd become a whole new person to dupe her. Witnessing just how disciplined he could be, she began to comprehend that his training was more than physical. Danny didn't exist, and Daire was a complete mystery.

TWENTY-FIVE

"IN HIS BUNK" meant sleep. No way she'd let Daire slumber wrapped in memories of them. Stripping the bed, Tess made it with fresh sheets. Maybe he'd take it as altruism. Their intimacy could be the last thing on his mind; Daire could be gay for all she knew. Danny wasn't his true self. Somehow being sex obsessed didn't seem like the disciplined Daire's style. No way.

Whatever. It made her feel better to erase as much of "them" as possible. Scrubbing both of their memories would be the ideal, but she had to make do.

While she tidied up and collected the laundry, H stayed outside. With another mouth to feed, they'd have to go into town for groceries. Fine by her. She wanted an excuse to get away from the Beast anyway. Coming to terms with the turnaround of her life wasn't easy while surrounded by reminders of so many untruths.

Daire was back from his run in under an hour, as instructed. The sun was up by the time she opened the trailer door and kicked the laundry sack to the threshold. That was when she saw Daire approaching H, a few feet from the door.

"Get some sleep," H said to Daire. "There are errands to do in town, I'll pick up my kit from the motel. We'll eat and strategize at nine."

Daire nodded once.

"You want me to wash what you're wearing?" Tess asked.

Oh… crap. The words just came out of her mouth before her brain could pull them back. Danny's clothes she didn't mind washing. Daire's… it seemed sort of rude to ask… and she still considered him an asshole. She didn't know the guy. Who knew how deep his shittiness went? On top of that, he was still wearing the clothes. The last thing she wanted was for him to strip right there.

Why couldn't she wrap her head around it? Danny naked was no big deal, so normal it was practically pedestrian. But Daire…

"He has enough to be going on with," H said. "We'll bring food back, make sure you're ready."

When H started to go, Tess bent down to wrap the top of the laundry bag around her wrist a couple of times before hauling it up to toss it on her shoulder.

"What's on your mind, agent?" H asked, attracting her attention, except he wasn't looking at her. He was looking at Daire, who seemed to be fixated on something somewhere around her abdomen. "We'll bring the truck back, if you're worried about being stranded—"

"I don't give a damn about stranded," Daire said. Obviously, training was over. Apparently that meant he was free to say whatever he liked… What was the signal of the transition? She couldn't begin to guess. "Arm yourself when you're alone with Pandora."

Oh, the… He wasn't actually suggesting… "What the—I'm not going to hurt anyone," Tess said, offended that he'd have the audacity to accuse her of being violent when she was the pursued not the pursuer. "I'm not a secret assassin." Like some people.

Neither man paid her any heed.

"Why?" H asked, closing in on Daire. "What have you seen?"

"It's like you said," Daire answered. "The marker is out there."

"You were so sure Z wouldn't come unless there was someone to kill."

"Maybe he thinks there is."

H's chin rose. "If you're in contact with him—"

"If I wanted to hand him Pandora, I could've done it fifty times," Daire said without hesitating to square up to H. "You wanna walk with her, you arm yourself. It's that or you don't walk."

She rolled her tongue in her mouth. How long would it take them to pedal down? Daire being pissed off was understandable. H had been treating him like a monkey for hours… for his whole life really. The only chance he had to grab for his own self-respect was to pick his battles.

"I just want to do laundry," Tess said, jumping down from the trailer to the grass. "You two can stand here and have your little pissing match… I don't know what you think it will accomplish…"

Wandering away, she went around the front of the trailer, hoping someone would follow with the truck keys. The bag was heavy, and she hadn't got enough sleep. Everything was a drag.

Only a few seconds later, H came storming after her. Going on straight past, he unlocked the truck and got into the driver's side. After she dumped the laundry bag in the back, she got into her usual seat, usual before H. It was then she saw him take the gun from his pants to tuck it into the door well. Daire had won the battle.

That was interesting. Why? What was the point of the battle? No idea.

H got them moving, and she relaxed into her seat. They got out onto the road. Still, he hadn't said a word.

"Who is Z?"

Tess didn't need to talk; she'd be just as happy to sit in silence. Except the only way to get answers was to push for them. Being ensconced alone in the vehicle was an opportunity not to be wasted.

"The man who was in charge of Olympus."

She frowned. "I thought you were the principal agent."

"There were three of us at the top. Me, Zeus—"

"And Poseidon," she interjected, shrugging when he tossed a scowl at her. "I read a lot about Greek myths while trying to figure this out."

"Zeus was in charge of strategy, ultimately at the top. Poseidon was resources, hardware. Personnel was my area, recruitment and training."

"And discipline?" she asked, unsure why her mind went straight there. "So how did—"

"Why do you ask so many questions? You don't need to know the details. All you need to know is that I'll keep you safe."

"No," she said, sliding down in her seat to get more comfortable. "All you want me to know is what you want to share. I don't want to spend the rest of my life running from the Big Bad Wolf."

"The only way to guarantee your safety is to eliminate Zeus."

"Because he hates me."

"He hates me," H said. "By extension…"

"But he doesn't hate Daire," she said. The name still felt odd on her tongue and to her ears. H glanced at her. "You said that you thought Daire was working with him because Z told you that. You respected that choice. That's what you said. That means you believed Daire made the choice on his own. I don't know Daire at all, but I'm going to guess he wouldn't work under a man he despised."

"He works under me."

She straightened the seatbelt between her breasts. "That's fathers and sons."

Danny's words. At the time, she hadn't accepted them. Now she wondered how much of it, if any, was true at all.

"Our relationship is complicated," H said, reminding her of her own relationship with her mother.

Some of what they'd been through had tested them. And some of her past behavior was shameful, especially in certain teen years. Could anyone say they'd been a saint their whole life? As they both got older, they developed an understanding, a way of communicating that gave each of them what they needed.

"I was a teenager," she said, recalling something H had said the previous night. He glanced her way again. "You asked about the running away. I'm not proud of it. I was a nightmare sometimes, but life was no picnic. Some unseen boogeyman dictated my entire existence. I was tired. I wanted normality."

"You can't have normality."

"I know. I know that now. But I didn't understand what my mom was afraid of. It seemed unreal to me. I wanted to be free. To get away, I thought I could change things if I just wanted to bad enough."

"Broke her heart. Her fear for herself was nothing compared to her fear for you."

"How did you know?" she asked. "The letters? I didn't know that mom was writing to you back then, but she was, wasn't she?"

"Sometimes. We didn't keep in touch as regularly as I'd have liked. I had missions, and we were overseas. Our communications were secret from Olympus, it complicated things."

"Everything's complicated," Tess murmured. "When I found the letters, I knew nothing about any of it. I couldn't even begin to figure them out." She'd rambled on to Danny about them, unaware that he knew every detail the whole time. Humiliation tried to warm her cheeks again; she blocked it out. "Can you imagine not knowing your own history? You said they recruited you at eighteen. This has been your life, been Daire's life. You take knowledge for granted. I'm the only one who doesn't know a damn about it."

"We wanted to protect you."

"Except that excuse doesn't fly," she said. "Not anymore. My mom wanted to protect me and now she's dead. It happened in a blink. We were fine, going about life, and then, she was gone. No warning. Nothing. What happens if this Z is the one responsible for taking her out? What if Z does that to you? Just like with mom, I'll be swinging in the wind. Vulnerable. I won't know who to trust and the only people alive will be your enemies. I'll learn their version of the truth. I'm going to bet their version won't paint you and mom in the best light. That's if they let me live long enough to hear anything. You'll be dead and I'll be easy pickings."

"Daire will protect you."

A snort of disbelief shook her. "For the rest of time? I don't think so. One day he'll be the same age as you and I don't know how to train him."

"By then, Z will be long gone. I promise you that."

"So it's him or me?"

"The organization is in flux… It doesn't exist as it did anymore."

"As of a year ago?"

"Right," he said. "There was a plan that didn't go down as it should have… Everyone scattered. I taught my men well, but Zeus is resourceful."

"You think he's starting up on his own…? Olympus two point oh."

"If he is, the first mission will be to eliminate everyone from the previous Olympus."

"Why?"

"Because he doesn't leave loose ends. Anyone out there who could be loyal to me is a threat. Just like you watch your tail, he watches his. Olympus has enemies. Professional enemies can become allies, if you play the situation right. But nothing will make him trust men who came up under me. None but Daire."

Confused, she frowned. "You're the closest thing he has to a father."

"Yeah, and the pendulum on that relationship has swung back and forth more than once. Olympus was Daire's life. The only home he's ever known. Losing it, in the way he did… I don't know what he's been doing for the past year, but if he ended up hunting you and Carrie, it's a safe bet to assume I'm not on his Christmas card list."

Town was just a few miles ahead. She wasn't really sure where they'd go once they got there. H, on the other hand, knew exactly where he was going. Danny was good at everything. Now she knew why. No doubt H had the same confidence. Talk about being the odd one out. She didn't even know what day of the week they were on.

"I think he's forgiven you," she said. "You were training together. He calls you sir."

"When training or receiving orders, yes. I don't know if he understands just how much he needs authority. Structure gives him security. Orders and missions give him purpose. I didn't mean for it to be that way. He took to the work. Along the way, it became what he lived for."

"He became manufactured." That was the word used to describe him in the letters. "He is PK, right?"

A rough but warm laugh lit the air. "He sure is. He knows how to comply with every training request. But when it gets informal… he's sharp… a punk kid, which is what we called him."

"You care about him. Did you ever think to tell him that? Maybe he wouldn't have been…"

In her peripheral vision, she noted H's head move in her direction. What was she doing? It wasn't her place to say anything on Daire's behalf. Some corner of her psyche was apparently having trouble accepting that Danny didn't exist. Maybe that was why she'd been so quick to speak in his defense. Either that or dealing with someone else's issues was easier than dealing with her own.

H was her father. Tied up in some complicated scheme that had taken over all of their lives. She'd never had a dad and didn't know how she felt about having one now.

"You said you've been out in the cold for a year," Tess said. "What have you been doing?"

"Moving around, keeping myself low. I should've checked in with Daire myself… except I taught him too well. If he didn't want me to find him, I wouldn't have."

She needed some of that expertise. Except she didn't have a lifetime to learn. She and her mother did well at keeping themselves hidden. Anne knew when to pack up, she had a sense for it. Tess would have to learn that too. Maybe if she hadn't relied so much on her mother's intuition, she'd have developed some of her own. Maybe if she'd done that, Daire wouldn't have duped her so easily.

TWENTY-SIX

H RAN HIS ERRANDS WHILE she did the laundry. By the time he returned, the truck was loaded up, and they still had grocery shopping to do. For some unfathomable reason, H seemed to be in a rush. Unlike her. Tess took her time at the produce section, picking everything at a pondering pace.

Her laissez-faire approach seemed to fuel H's determination to be contrary. He packed up the truck in record time, then swore under his breath at her request to stop at the liquor store.

By the time they pulled around the trees, bringing the trailer into view, it was two after nine, which didn't bother her at all. Daire was waiting, shoulder propped on the end of the Airstream, arms folded, looking mean. Ignoring him, she hopped out and opened up the back door.

"My daughter has no sense of time or urgency," H called out, she guessed to Daire.

She had ears and a mouth though. "And my father is easily riled."

"Really, girl," H said, opening the tailgate. "You need a speed other than dawdle."

She scooped up the laundry bag and spun around only to be stopped dead by Daire standing right there. Like right there. Stunned by his stealth and proximity, she didn't have the wherewithal to object to him taking the bag from her arms. He went to grab a huge duffel bag from H too.

Shaking off her daze, she returned to confidence. "I like dawdle," she said.

"I don't know how your mother put up with it."

"Are we in some rush?" she asked, picking up all of the dozen grocery bags. "I didn't know the President was coming to tea."

"I said nine," H said in a firm way that was probably supposed to put a stop to her arguments.

It didn't. "Without consulting anyone else," she said, closing the door with a hip at the same time H closed the tailgate. "Besides, your flunky was here. We had the truck, where was he going to go?"

Daire was already disappearing around the end of the trailer. H was quick to head the same way, Tess took her time. More to make a point than anything.

"We have to be where we say we'll be when we say we'll be there."

"Or?"

"Or," he snapped. "Someone may assume we're in trouble and take action."

"Without his truck?" Tess asked as Daire reappeared. "He wouldn't have got far."

H had other things in the bed of the truck, he'd told her it was full. But Daire didn't go back to retrieve those things. He came over and relieved her of the grocery bags without a word.

Left on the spot for a second after he retraced his steps with the new load, she opened her mouth to protest, but couldn't come up with the words. Damnit. Giving up, Tess followed H around the trailer and went inside.

With the three of them in there, the laundry bag and duffel on the recliners and the grocery bags on the counter and table, the Beast felt tiny. The trailer was a cozy living space, safe, even though it was confined. Danny hadn't taken up as much space as Daire. It sort of pissed her off that he was there, moving around, putting things away like the place belonged to him. Sure, it did, but there was still a disconnect in her brain that couldn't fathom Danny and Daire as the same person.

H didn't even try to put anything away, he retrieved something from his duffel then went to sit in the dinette. Hoping to open the space up a little, Tess got the laundry bag, intending to take it to the bedroom. Except she only got three steps before Daire closed the pantry and with one long stride, stopped her dead. He took the laundry bag and disappeared up the trailer with it.

Once again, he'd usurped her purpose. Pushing out her chin, she fought to contain her irritation. Shouting at him would only prove he was succeeding in annoying her, which was probably exactly what he wanted.

Retrieving a frying pan from the drawer under the microwave, she put it on the stove just as Daire started back down the trailer.

When Tess saw his hand coming toward her pan, she grabbed it up. "No," she said, holding it to her chest.

Just like the previous day, he averted his attention, avoiding her eyes. "I'll do it," he said.

"No."

"I'll make pancakes."

Shaking her head, she pointed the pan at him. "I don't want pancakes."

Backing up a few steps, Daire opened the fridge and pantry, scanning both. "Bacon, waffles, oatmeal… fruit salad? Whatever you want."

Breakfast. They'd been up for hours, yet they were only just getting their first meal of the day. "I can cook."

Daire closed the pantry and the fridge. "No, you can't."

She gestured with the pan. "I can! I'm not some super, secret agent spy, whatever, but I can put breakfast together."

Slowly, he came closer and surprised her by making eye contact. The link disabled some part of her; he got close enough to curl his fingers around the base of the pan handle, relieving her of it.

"No… you can't."

The sort of wince in his gaze clued her in. "I can't?" He shook his head once. "I don't believe it. You always ate my food."

"I spent six months in a Russian gulag that served better chow."

Her jaw swung loose.

H laughed. "He's a perfectionist, Tess. Don't take it personally."

Turning to growl at H's amusement, she moved to let Daire get closer to the stove. H didn't care that she was offended, he was reading the newspaper he'd picked up in town.

"Anything?" Daire asked.

She supposed he wasn't talking to her when H responded. "Not yet."

The muttering came in time with the strengthening of his brow.

"Might be too early," Daire said. When he got even closer, she leaped away. He opened a hand at the dinette. "Please sit down."

That wasn't quite an order, though it was more than a suggestion. Turned out she wasn't good for anything anyway, not in the kitchen. She slid into the dinette opposite H. What the hell was she doing there? These men knew each other. They were family. Whether they were fighting or not. They had a connection, a way of communicating. Tolerated each other, were familiar with their strengths and weaknesses.

Daire went to retrieve whatever he needed from the fridge and pantry. He had purpose. She was at a loose end without so much as a newspaper to read.

"What are you looking for?" she asked. H didn't lower the paper. Puffing out her cheeks, his preference for keeping her in the dark tested her patience. She released her breath in a single rush. "I think we should call him out."

Daire glanced over his shoulder, but she didn't look at him. She waited for H to lower his newspaper. Just as expected, his frown was fierce.

"Who?"

"You know who," she said, laying a hand on the table. "He's the problem, right? One man. We can take one man."

"I agree," Daire said, much to her surprise.

He didn't notice her incredulity, his focus was on H, his expression just as intent as the older man's.

When she relaxed, Tess remained steadfast, waiting for H's response.

"Neither of you know what you're talking about," H said. "We are not going to call him out." He pinned her under his scrutiny. "How do you suggest we call him out? You don't have a damn clue—"

"He hates you, he hates me," she said. "You pretty much told me you're going to be dead soon. That leaves me the only target."

"I told you Daire has orders, he will protect you."

"I don't want his protection," she said, disgusted by the idea. "I don't want to live life cowering anymore. You were happy for me and mom to live that way. You and Daire lost your home when everything went pear-shaped with Olympus. At least you had one to begin with. I have never known what it is to stay in one place more than a few months at a time—"

"Tess—"

"I don't expect your sympathy," she said, holding up a hand, recalling how he'd responded to Daire's assertion of what he'd been through. "I'm telling you, I'm done. I'm through."

"You do not get to dictate strategy," H said in a low growl that was probably supposed to intimidate her into submission.

Yep. That didn't work. "If anyone else has a better plan, I'm all ears," she said, never blinking. "But I am entitled to a say. If I don't get that here, I'll go."

"On your own?" H sneered.

"On my own," she said, strengthening her shoulders. "I'll die fighting if that's what it takes. Better that than living as a coward."

She jumped when the pan clattered onto the stove and Daire turned suddenly. Hovering at the end of the table, he waited for…? What? Was it his intention to defend his superior? Except she wasn't the one under his keen focus.

H exhaled and aimed his words at Daire. "Z has allies. If we act rashly, he will get the upper hand. We are the only ones capable of taking him down."

"Let me go find him," Daire said. "Just me."

H shook his head.

"If you wanted to take Z out," she said, "why didn't you do it a year ago?"

Daire returned to the stove.

"He's not talking about Z," H said.

More confusion and secrets. She needed to understand this from the beginning.

"What happened?" she asked, clinging to her composure. "Why did Olympus break down?"

Neither man said anything. Goddamnit, she wanted to scream. She should just leave them to their madness. To hell with them both.

"There was a conspiracy to assassinate Z," Daire said, breaking the silence. "Operation Zulu."

"A conspiracy," H spat.

"Yeah, a conspiracy. That's what they call it when a bunch of people get together to plot against someone else," Daire said, continuing with his cooking. "That conspiracy caused the Olympus exodus a year ago. Z got wind of Zulu and was coming back to execute anyone who knew about it. Everyone fled. The building was empty in under an hour. Harry wasn't on site. I was."

"Yeah, and I came back for you," H said. "Minotaur was gone. Z said—"

"That I was his," Daire said, retrieving a plate. "Yeah, we got that yesterday."

"A conspiracy..." she said. "Why after all these years would you go after him? If he's this big, scary evil—"

"It wasn't me," H said, folding his newspaper. "I was approached."

"A restructure," Daire said, scooping something onto a plate. With it in hand, he turned to slide the plate onto the table in front of her. "When?"

H laid the paper on the table and angled himself to

look at the man putting flatware down by her plate. "When?"

"Did they approach you?" Daire asked.

"Less than a year before the shutdown."

"Month."

Obviously confused, H took a second to answer. "August."

"May," Daire said. The angle of H's head shifted in a slow arc. "They offered it to me."

He went back to the stove.

The moment Daire's back was turned, H leaped out of the dinette. "You didn't tell me?"

"Like father like son."

"I didn't tell you to protect you," H argued. "I didn't want you to have to make a choice."

Those words reminded her of the letter in the nightstand. The one H hadn't read.

"I did make a choice," Daire said, measuring his tone. "I told them I didn't want it. That until you were cold in the ground of natural causes, I wouldn't even consider it." He tossed the spatula to the counter and spun to face H. "Were you so fucking stupid to think they'd stop at Z? There was no way they'd let you and Garrick take over. They wanted new blood. 'Cept someone taught me to think three moves ahead. If they'd get rid of Z so quick, you would be next. I wouldn't be a part of that."

He was angry, it was in his words, his tone. The tension in his shoulders tempted her to ease it, but he wasn't hers to touch. Never had been. His anger, his woes, they were his. Secret. Private.

"I knew the risks," H said. "It made sense to be on the inside, to know what they were thinking."

"But you didn't think I deserved to know," Daire said, pausing in his return to the stove to point at her plate. "Eat."

She didn't pick up her fork until he was cracking eggs. The omelet with mushroom and cheese was perfection. She wouldn't say it out loud, but it was better than anything she'd have produced.

"I should've told you," H said.

Like watching a drama unfold, she paused, eyes wide, fork halfway to her mouth, poised to see what Daire would do.

"Yeah," was all Daire said.

"I should have," H said, reducing the distance between them. His desire to heal their damaged relationship seemed genuine. Though what did she know. "I made a decision about what I thought was best for you."

"Or you didn't trust me," Daire said. "If you thought I'd go with Z a year ago, you thought it when the Six brought Zulu to you… You thought I would risk not only your life, but Styx, and all the guys. Why? So I could run to Z and get a pat on the head?"

"I was wrong," H said, piquing Daire's attention. Obviously those words didn't come out of H's mouth often. "That's all I can say. I made the wrong call and I'm sorry."

A long pause followed.

The room hung in silence until Daire opened his mouth to say, "Okay then."

TWENTY-SEVEN

H RETURNED TO HIS SEAT and Daire went back to cooking.

Tess couldn't believe it. "That's it?" she asked.

"What did you expect?" H asked. "I can't say anything other than that."

Putting down her fork, she leaned over her plate. "You and these mysterious 'Six' cooked up some scheme to off the guy in charge of Olympus. You didn't tell the boy you raised, the man who you said would be our primary instrument of success because you didn't think he'd side with you. The whole thing imploded, Olympus went to shit, and all you can say is 'I was wrong'?"

"What else should I say?"

With her hands on the table, she pushed back. "I don't know. But, geez, you want to talk strategy moving forward? How can you do that when nothing is resolved?"

"It is resolved."

Tess was gobsmacked. "With an 'I was wrong'? That's it? How do you know he's not still harboring some animosity that will blow up in your face the minute you're eyeball to eyeball with this Z? How does he know you won't keep some secret from him in future? How can you trust each other?"

H frowned again. "Daire walked into the control room yesterday fully prepared to kill or be killed. As did I when I saw it was him. We've had plenty of opportunities through the years to take each other down. We haven't."

Her mouth wouldn't close, she didn't get it. "And that's enough? That's enough for both of you to know that you won't turn on each other at the first opportunity?"

"Dying at my son's hands would be an honor," H said, moving his newspaper from the table when Daire put an omelet and flatware down. "I hope that's exactly how I go."

Tess's head moved side to side. "I don't trust any of you people. You're crazy."

H smiled as he cut into his omelet. "Tensions run high. Adrenaline kicks in. People say and do things they don't mean. We learn from our mistakes. That's the reality of battle. After an op, we break it down and replay it. Whether it was a success or failure, we extrapolate other potential eventualities and avenues that may have been used. Improves efficiency. Daire doesn't hesitate. If it was his choice to kill me, I'd be dead. If it was his choice to punish me, you'd be dead."

"Oh, well, that's just great news for me," Tess said, pushing her plate away. Suddenly, she wasn't hungry anymore. "And how does he know you're not out there deciding what's best for him without consulting him?"

"I know now what the repercussions would be." Him dead or her dead? "Intel is the key to survival."

Maybe this learning curve wasn't for her after all.

Daire propped himself against the counter and folded his arms. "If you don't want to call Z out directly, how do you want to do it?"

"Round up the men. As many of them as we can."

"That could take months. Longer, given we don't know how many of them are still alive. We could waste months chasing ghosts."

"Maybe," H said, still eating his omelet. "But they are at risk. We have power in numbers."

"Yeah," Daire said, pushing away from the counter to go to the fridge. "I'd agree if we revived Minotaur."

"You're hellbent," H said.

Daire reappeared with a glass. While still looking at H, he held it toward her. She sniffed it before drinking. Coconut milk. It was difficult to remember that Daire wasn't Danny when he did Danny things.

"Why shouldn't we do it?" Daire asked. "Beta is just sitting there."

"So reviving Minotaur is less about locating our people and more about getting the operation on its feet again? Say what you mean, son."

She swallowed a mouthful of the milk quickly and waved a hand. "Who's Minotaur?"

"The Olympus computer," Daire said without taking his focus from H. "Ideally, yes, but Z would never stand for that."

"We'd be sitting ducks," H said. "His access codes will still work."

"Then we strip it bare. Get hold of Garrick, gut the place, set up elsewhere. There are millions of dollars' worth of hardware in there that we can use."

"Or sell," H said in agreement. "Smart, except we wouldn't have much time. If we could get in without reviving Minotaur…"

"Only one access path with Minotaur offline," Daire said, sliding his own omelet onto a plate. "Echo entrance to control room, that's it."

"Garrick could get in."

"We don't know where he is, or if he's alive… or who he's allied with."

"Who's Garrick?" Tess asked, trying to keep up.

When Daire slid into the dinette next to her, trapping her in, Tess pushed herself as close to the window as possible. He didn't crowd her, but even his being on the edge of the seat with one leg in the aisle was too close for her liking.

"Poseidon," H said.

His tone of curiosity attracted her attention.

"Hardware," she said, picking up her drink. "And you think he'd be able to get into the system without reviving the system… How do you revive the system?"

"With a key," Daire said, setting a pointed look on H. "One of three that exist."

H was shaking his head. "I don't have it." Daire stopped mid-chew. "I don't. After the Six came to me with the plan, I knew there was a chance it would go off the rails. I couldn't risk any one of us having all three, so… I stashed it."

"Where?" Daire asked.

H ate some more. "Miami."

Daire dropped his fork and sank back. "Are you fucking kidding me?"

It wasn't even remotely funny, but her lips twitched. Daire, or Danny, had just driven all the way across the country and back again. If he wanted to follow H's breadcrumbs for Minotaur's sake, he'd have to turn around and go all the way back.

"What?" H asked.

"Garrick would be easier to find," Daire muttered.

"You're right, we don't know if he can be trusted."

"Same could be said about all the guys. I won't be the only one you pissed off," Daire said. "You've left us out in the cold for a year. Z could've caught up with them."

"He'd never trust men who trained under me… Except you."

"Always except me," Daire said, pushing his own plate away. "If I'm so fucking amazing, why aren't we setting up on our own?"

"Money."

"Right, but we just agreed that Olympus Beta is a cash hoard."

"Not including the actual cash hoard in the vault," H said, a smile quirking his lips. "You want to set up on your own?"

"I think if Z is doing it, we should start where he would. We talk to the people he would talk to. From their reactions, we figure out what he's up to. We're a year behind on this, old man. Before we do anything, we need intel."

"So we start with the money."

Daire sucked in a breath and stood up to take both his and her plates. "Two and five are dead. Six is the only original left."

"Six was our squealer."

"Yeah, I figured that one out all by myself," Daire murmured while scraping the food into the trash.

Seeing such a tasty dish go to waste was disappointing.

Dragging her mind from the food, she blinked at H. "Squealer?"

"The one who told Z about the plan to assassinate him," Daire answered, removing the sink cover.

"You don't have to answer her questions," H said.

"Yes," Tess said, relaxing, spreading both hands on the table. "H thinks I should be a good little female and simply cower in whatever hidey-hole he finds for me."

"Not a bad plan," Daire said, putting the plates in the sink, then turning to retrieve H's, which was now empty. "Call him Harry. Only people who don't know him call him H unless we're in the field."

Should she thank him for the advice? No. Their scales weren't tipped anywhere near gratitude.

"And women who birthed his children," she said instead. "That's how you signed your letters to mom."

"Details were risky. Contact was risky... It was ridiculous. I should've known better," Harry said. After a breath, he straightened up. "Where are they? The letters?"

Oh... ah. Closing her mouth, the next confession would not be easy. "Actually, I..."

Daire grabbed a towel to dry his hands and crouched. He flipped up the kick-plate under the kitchen unit and then stood, tossing a familiar cosmetics case onto the table. Stunned again, her stupor was instant. Some part of her suspected him as the thief when he'd quoted the letters to Harry. But for him to be so blatant about producing them...

Harry put a hand over the case and slid out of the dinette. "Excuse me."

Just like that, he left the trailer. The letters were personal to him and her mother. It was sort of comforting to know he wanted to be alone while revisiting those memories. Except after the echo of the door closing silenced, the air

settled. She and Daire were alone in the trailer.
Alone.

TWENTY-EIGHT

DAIRE WAS FINISHING up with the dishes. Tess considered going outside, but didn't want it to appear like she was following Harry. Going to the bedroom wouldn't achieve anything either.

Just like in the truck with Harry, instead of being silent for silent's sake, she'd get answers instead.

"You want to tell me how you did it?" she asked, receiving no response. "You were there when my mom died. You were with her… You didn't think that I'd be interested in that?"

"I thought you'd be dead before it ever came up."

Another thorn in her crown. "You wanted him to kill me? Why not just do it yourself? You had opportunity." She'd slept naked next to him for a month, there'd been plenty of opportunities. Except he chose not to answer again. "You can at least tell me how you ended up at Buckhorn?"

"Got myself hired," he said. "Yeah, I was there when your mom died… I was on scene, hung back, watched it all unfold and saw who towed the wreck."

"And you knew I'd come looking for it?"

"Figured you would," he said, draining the water.

Tess leaped from the dinette to grab the towel for the

dishes before he could. He didn't make eye contact, but she smiled anyway. One small battle. Yet the victory was sweet.

"And if I didn't?"

"Then it didn't matter," he said. "I'd have found another way."

"I don't understand," she said, drying the plate, then putting it away. "Why? You couldn't have known that my mom…" Before the words left her tongue, she figured it out. "Goddamnit… You put the cards there. It wasn't my mom at all." No response. She exhaled a laugh. "Man, it must have driven you nuts that I took so long to figure out the numbers." His silence tormented her irritation. "Figgs? You set that up?" A chilling thought shuddered through her. "He disappeared. Did you—"

"Paid him to go on vacation," he said, dropping into Harry's vacant dinette seat.

Instead of tucking his legs under the table, he kept both feet planted in the aisle, manspreading all over the place. Everything he did seemed designed to irritate her. Honestly, Danny never took up so much room. Maybe she just didn't notice it so much when she had no problem occupying the same space.

Letting him know that his behavior was getting to her would give him too much satisfaction.

So Tess simply picked up another plate. "Figgs was so… weird. All jumpy and sweaty."

"He didn't want to help… I persuaded him."

The slow drawl held enough warning to erase any doubt over what he meant.

"He was scared," she said, putting the plate down. "He was scared of you…" Recalling that day, she exhaled a breath of disbelief. "My God, what was breakfast about? Why follow me? What if I wanted you to come in with me?"

"He wouldn't have said a word. I'm good at my job."

In a state of disbelief, she couldn't remember what it was like not to be stunned by new revelations every twenty seconds.

Something tickled the back of her knee. A warmth. Light pressure. Someone was touching her. Oh, the… Sitting there, his elbows on his thighs, the tip of his fingers glided up an inch before she backed off.

"Are you kidding me?" she asked, grabbing for the edge of the counter at her back.

He sat up, burning the ferocity of his gaze into her. "I hated you for years."

"Hated me?"

"None of it was your fault," he said. "But I didn't get that, not when I was a kid."

"I don't understand."

"He left, after you were born. He was gone until..."

"Until what?"

When he surged to his feet, shaking his head, Tess gasped and pushed back against the counter. He'd been so much closer to her in the past. Yet the new presence that hung in the air around him gave his proximity a much more oppressive edge.

"It's not my place."

How he conveyed words in such a growl without his lips moving more than a millimeter was impressive. How could one man undergo such a transformation in such a short space of time?

"You didn't care about that a few days ago. It wasn't your place to lie your way into my bed, but you did it anyway. You lied to me for sex."

"Not for sex."

"For what? Shits and giggles? You wanted me to humiliate myself? To bare my soul to you so you could feel superior? Or is it exploiting women's weaknesses that gets you off?"

Without waiting for an answer, Tess turned, intending to leave, but he dropped a hand to the counter, blocking her way.

"I hated you for years."

"Guess I have some catching up to do. I didn't know who you were until yesterday... I still don't know who you are."

"I'm trying to tell you," he said, his volume low. "Harry was all I knew, and he left because of you and your mother. That's why I hated you."

"You did want him to kill me," she said, searching his fathomless expression. "You took me to that place because you wanted him to—"

"I put myself in your path to punish him. I was angry. He ripped my home away from me. I needed a mission to focus; you were the only way to hurt him."

"Me and my mom. Who you just happened to be with when she died."

Unapologetic, his scowl was determined. "I own what I do. If I'd killed her, I wouldn't lie. If I'd done it, I wouldn't have needed you."

"You were following her."

"Yes."

"What was the plan? Kidnap her?"

"She remembered me," he said, somehow both in awe and perplexed at the same time. "I didn't think she would."

"Even if she didn't recognize you, she knew who you were. You were in the letters." He inhaled like he intended to speak, but there was a pause and then nothing. "I already don't trust you and I don't trust your Harry. If I don't get answers, I'll walk."

"You walk and Z will find you."

"Maybe he'll be more inclined to answer questions."

When Tess tried to go the opposite way, he dropped his other hand to the countertop, blocking her in from both sides. Looming over her, he bathed her in his shadow. It didn't feel like the same shadow she'd basked in with Danny.

Daire was close. Too close.

Raising her chin, Tess met his eye. Such a deep, dark brown, filled with so many unknowns. So much meaning, yet impenetrable. What would it be to dive in and never look back?

"Z is not an option for you."

"No?" she asked, doing her best to hide the tremble in her breathing. "Then you better give me answers. I don't have the patience to keep begging for scraps."

He parted his lips to inhale. "After you were born,

Harry left Olympus to live with you and your mom. Z didn't like that. The Six didn't like that. Death is the only release from Olympus. When you were two years old, to make their point, they took you from your parents. Brought you to Olympus." Which must have been when she and Daire played together. "Eventually, negotiations led to Carrie coming to stay with you at the beta site. Harry wasn't allowed to see either of you… You were there just over a year when they struck the accord. You and Carrie were permitted to leave. Harry was to cease all contact."

"That's why we were running? Because they couldn't stop writing to each other?"

"No one knew they were writing. I didn't know it… But it was more complicated than that. After you and your mom left, things changed. Z had taken Harry's home. Threatened what he loved. From then, their hatred grew. Z kept tabs on you and your mom, was always trying to track you down."

"To use us against Harry?" He nodded slowly. His eyes were low, not on hers, on her tongue as it slid across her lips. "You need to back off."

He didn't move. "Anger drove me to you. I hated what your existence did to Harry when I was a kid… Then he took Olympus from me. Putting you in front of him, taking you from him, it seemed right."

"The perfect revenge."

"In theory."

"Yeah, because he didn't put a bullet in me. That was a nice surprise, you telling him to shoot me… Did you really have to have sex with me before we left?"

An electric charge amped up around them. Fizzing and snapping, the air grew thicker, more humid. More dangerous. Stupid. She didn't want him to know her thoughts. Spilling them was careless. She needed to be vigilant about opening her mouth.

"I knew after, if we weren't dead, you would hate me."

"Top prize to you," she said, wishing she could move without touching him.

To get him out of the way, she'd have to push his arm. Except after what she'd seen that morning, he'd be able to resist if he wanted to. Strength seemed to be his forte.

"You were never weak."

The murmured compliment narrowed her eyes. "What?"

"You had no weakness to exploit."

"Is that what you think?" Folding her arms, she breathed in, doing what she could to maintain her barriers. "That I had no weakness? I broke down in front of you, I was a mess."

"That doesn't make you weak. Emotion like that is powerful."

If that was power, he could keep it. "I was so desperate not to be alone that I clung to the first human who looked my way." Which was exactly what he'd wanted. "It was pathetic. I probably deserved a bullet just for that."

"As a kid, every day was a new lesson. A new challenge. Then I grew up and it was mission after mission. I did my mentor proud. Impressed my superiors. Did everything right. But I lost it all anyway. I didn't know what else there was, what life could be without Olympus. I'd never lived outside the confines of the Olympus rules. They were all that mattered. All I focused on. Everything in my life was about living up to expectation, surpassing expectation… until you."

Her lowered gaze rose to his at the gentle whisper of those last two words.

"Me?"

The intent of his probing eyes deepened. "I had never lived a minute without expectation hanging over me. Either what I put on myself, or from Harry and Olympus. But you wanted nothing from me."

That wasn't exactly true, but Tess wasn't about to remind him of how she'd pestered him when her mood got frisky.

"I won't trust you just because you try to make believe we were something that we weren't," she said. "Everything was a lie."

He shook his head. "No," he breathed. "The first time, yeah. Maybe the second, but somewhere the lie became real."

"No," Tess said, bending her knees to duck away when he reached for her face.

It wasn't ideal that she was by the fridge with him blocking her route to the exit, but at least he wasn't looming over her… not so close anyway.

"I know it can't happen, that it won't," he said.

"Yeah," she asserted. "Because I don't have a damn clue who you are. You…" Tess gestured up and down at him. "This guy, he's a complete stranger to me."

"You know this me better than you knew that me. This me understands what you went through. I know what your existence was. What it is to lose your guiding light."

Shaking her hair from her shoulders, she held her head high. "I already admitted I wasn't thinking straight after my mom. Maybe if you'd been a gentleman and pointed that out…"

Except why would he? Daire wanted her in his trap, and she'd skipped along into it, oblivious to reality.

"I didn't intend for it to happen like that."

"Yeah, and I'm clearly the superior physical presence in the room," she said, her words laced with sarcasm. "I didn't force myself on you."

Not exactly.

"All you wanted was me. No pressure. No expectation, just… me."

While cocking a hip, Tess folded her arms. "Just a shame you couldn't show up."

"You didn't need a guy like me then… I would've scared you."

Daire didn't scare her, not exactly. Maybe because she'd seen him training or because she didn't have the capacity for fear while her head was such a mess. What was going on? What would her life be?

Whatever happened in the future, at least in the immediate future, her path was destined to parallel his.

TWENTY-NINE

MAYBE UNDERSTANDING how he did what he did would help. As it was, she couldn't relax around him. The guy was a stranger, yet he knew things about her. Things that even she didn't know.

"How did you do it?" she asked. "Change yourself so completely."

"Training isn't only in combat. We're required to do whatever is asked of us. Sometimes that means going undercover... Harry is big on eliminating embarrassment. When we're not doing combat training, we're honing other skills. Skills that will be useful on missions or for ingratiating ourselves... Embarrassment is a cousin of fear; that's one of Harry's lines. So whether it's line dancing in a honky-tonk bar or standing up unprepared on open mike night, he teaches us to face pretty much anything. Hesitation gets you killed. He instructs us to ignore hesitation, to suppress it. If we can do it with embarrassment, we can do it with fear."

There was a weird kind of logic in there. One that made complete sense to her. Unfortunately.

Undercover... so he was used to adopting all kinds of false personas. Changing at a moment's notice, just like he'd done when switching from Danny to Daire.

"Is there anything you wouldn't do under his orders?" she asked, thinking again that Harry relished treating Daire like a performing monkey.

"No," he said without hesitating.

"Even if you knew it was wrong?"

"A lot of what we do is morally wrong." He thought for a second before correcting himself. "Did. What we did was morally wrong."

"But you want to start over."

"It's the only life I know."

"Knew," she said, correcting him like he'd corrected himself a moment ago. "It's the only life you knew. You've been living a different kind of life this past year."

"This past month," he said, taking a step toward her, forcing her to reverse. "I won't hurt you, Tess."

"I thought that before you put me in the path of my father's bullet. It will be harder for you to convince me of it again."

"I made a mistake."

Tess shook her head, raising a hand to stop him coming any closer. "I'm not my father and I'm not you. Saying you were wrong doesn't erase what you did. I'm not that forgiving. You stole from me. Those letters were everything to me. You knew that losing them upset me. How did you get them?"

"You told me you were going out. I knew you wouldn't be in the house."

"When? I was with you the whole time from…"

"Your date with Patrick. I was looking for something else. When I found the letters, proof Harry violated the accord, I couldn't pass it up."

"Is that why you asked me out? To find out when I wouldn't be home?" she asked, though the answer was obvious.

His proposition on that first day at Buckhorn was nothing more than a ruse. He sure didn't do it because he was attracted to her. She was a mission… nothing to him. A means to an end.

"I'm good at what I do," he said. "Very good at it."

Tess didn't need to be told that. Everything was a mess. Was she lost or found? Saved or damned? The world was no longer the one she'd grown up in. Leaving Daire and Harry would be the simplest course. Leaving meant no longer facing embarrassment every minute Daire was in the room.

"Where would I go," she whispered.

"You're not going anywhere," Daire replied.

She hadn't wanted an answer. The question was for her, not for anyone else. Anne had made decisions about their safety, but she tried to be as considerate of her daughter's life… as much as she could. Tess had to take control of her own path. It was past time.

"I don't want to be here," she admitted. "I don't want to be close to you. Looking at you every day."

He got a step closer. Tess didn't raise her head, but put a hand out to stall him again.

"You don't have to look at me," he said, the bassline of his voice flat. "If you want me to vacate, I will. I'll live outside, train outside, it's all I need. You only have to give the order."

No matter how much she scrutinized him, she wasn't able to recognize the man in front of her.

Incredulous, she stated, "I am not your master. I would never want to be."

"I had a mission," he said. "In my head, when there's an objective, I carry it out. I decided to put you and your mom in front of him. After your mom was gone, it was you. I had to get you to Olympus. I knew that wouldn't be tough. I knew as soon as Harry got the marker he'd come. Just the possibility it could be Z would bring him there."

"It wasn't Z, it was us. It was you," she said. "I don't even know what the marker is."

"The code," he said. "That we put in the first night. It sends a beacon to the three principals."

"You said four people knew the code."

"I knew it," he said, his shoulders dropping just an inch. "I know a lot of things about Olympus that I shouldn't… that others don't."

"Why?"

"Because it's my home. Because Harry taught me well."

"You took me there to hurt me."

His lips thinned, but it was the tick at the angle of his jaw that she noticed before he spoke. "Yeah… The mission was to get you into that room with Harry. To show him I was capable. That he couldn't take from me without consequences."

"You wanted him to kill me."

The innocent confusion of his searching eyes implied he wasn't so sure. "I knew my objectives. I hit my objectives… But I backed off…" he murmured those last words to himself. "Before I met you, I expected that once we were in that room with him, none of us would leave alive… Except I didn't threaten him. I didn't up the pressure or force his hand…" Whether or not he'd figured it out, Tess wasn't the only one talking to herself. When his gaze drifted to her, he strengthened his stance and tone. "If I'd wanted Harry to kill you, I'd have given him no other choice… I gave him a choice… I didn't want him to kill you."

"You did when you set these objectives, this mission… That was your goal."

"My goal was to get his attention."

"To impress him," she said. "Say, 'Hey, dad, look at me! Look what I can do!' was that it?"

He flattened a hand on the closet and fridge doors, blocking the hall. Not that she'd have been able to get past anyway.

"I was alone. I didn't have a damn clue what I was doing. My life has been orders and rules… Suddenly that was gone."

Some part of her identified with what it was to have everything change in a heartbeat. She'd relied on her mother's instructions. While Tess had only Anne, Daire had a whole phalanx of whomever. But it didn't matter. When the shit hit the fan, he'd been tossed out on his ass with no idea who he could trust or how to just be in the real world.

"You lied to me," she said. "And now I know how good an actor you can be. If you want me to feel sorry for you—"

"I want you to stop looking at me like I'm someone else," he snapped.

That brought a whisper of a laugh from her lips. "You *are* someone else… Whoever you were, the guy who gave me a place to crash and traveled with me across the country and back again, you killed that guy. He's gone. It wasn't bad enough that I lost my mom; I had to lose the only support I had too. So 'I was wrong' and 'I'm sorry' won't work with me. I won't trust you. I can't."

"I wasn't wrong. I was weak," he snarled. Tess didn't understand, but didn't back down. "You were… you became…" Frustration stunted and stalled his words. "Goddamnit!"

Spinning around, he stalked down toward the recliners.

"This is not my fault," Tess argued.

He flipped around, pinning her under a scowl so ferocious she could feel it in her soul. "I failed my mission because you got in. Because you became my goddamn weakness. How the fuck did you do that?"

"Me?" she asked, affronted that he could direct anger at her. "You knew from the start that it was all bullshit. Not like you didn't have plenty of chances to tell me the truth or disappear on me. You could've left any time. No one forced you to stay with me."

He marched back toward her. "Do you know how many people are out there right now looking for you? Harry had twenty agents under him, not including me and my brother. The Six, Zeus, Poseidon, there's a chance every single one of them wants to take you down. Hurting you is the best way to get to Harry. The best chance to recruit or destroy him. You're his weakness."

"Oh, so now I'm his weakness? Make up your mind."

His hand rose between them. Curling his fingers into a tight fist, he loosened and did it again, the muscle in his arm working as he squeezed the air. "You're at risk. I saw what happened to your mom. I watched her spin out… saw her hit…"

Her anger circled the drain, disappearing into oblivion. "But you went to her. If she spoke to you..."

"Yeah," he said, bowing lower. "I went to her. There was nothing I could do. She knew that, just like I did. She said his name, asked for Harry... Told her it wasn't Harry, I was just a punk kid. She smiled..." He straightened, his hand falling to his side. "Touched my face, told me I... I was a good kid... that I needed to get to you before they did..." In the next pause, Tess held her breath, anticipating more, desperate for another second. Instead, Daire grew rigid. "Your mother knew you were at risk. You need to know it too. You need to face it. Accept it. Then accept that I'm your best chance for survival."

Going from her mother's last moment to the danger of the future was a difficult switch.

"Your plan was to lead me to my death," she said. "You think it's easy for me to accept that I can suddenly trust you? All this time you knew everything about me, you knew more about me than I knew about myself. You knew how my mother died, who my father was, what I'd been running from. You knew everything and never once hinted you were anything more than the junkyard dog."

"Once I was in it, I couldn't risk you walking away. I couldn't risk that you'd walk away," he said. "I had to get you to Harry... If you tell me to walk, I'll walk. Harry will die for you. He'll do whatever he can to keep you safe... But he won't go as far as I can."

"He already told me that," she said. "He already said that you were our best shot."

"Then let me be your best shot."

Breathing out, Tess ran both hands through her hair. "I don't know who you are. You're here. Fine. I'm here. We'll just ignore each other."

"We have to make decisions."

"Harry won't listen to me... And I can't claim to know as much about any of this as either of you can."

"Do you want us to stash you somewhere and—"

"What? Come back for me when it's all over?" She shook her head. "What if neither of you ever come back? I'm done hiding. I meant what I said about living as a coward."

"Yeah, not a good idea to call Harry a coward."

She gritted her teeth. "I am not one of his agents."

"Olympus is all I ever knew. It's all Harry knew since he was a kid," he said. "It screwed with everyone's head. I'm used to taking orders. He's used to giving them."

"I'm used to being treated as a human being. Not a mindless robot."

"You're anything but a robot."

"I'm sorry I'm not all cold and controlled," she said, trying to go past him.

He got in her way. His body blocked her path, bringing hers to a halt. "You're never cold," he murmured. "Little Red."

When his finger rose to her temple, her attention ascended to his. He brushed the fingertip through her locks, tucking them back behind her ear.

"Don't," she whispered. "Don't call me that."

"You were the first and only person I ever chose for myself."

"Mission," she said, stepping back, swiping his hand aside. "I was the first mission you assigned yourself. Doesn't make me feel special. Keep your distance. I'll do the same."

Before he could respond, the trailer door opened. Daire turned; she took the chance to get past him. Harry came in, closing the door behind himself.

"Money," Harry said, talking over her, so she guessed he was addressing Daire. "Pack it up. We're hitting the road."

THIRTY

"WE HAVE TO HIT SIX FIRST."

"You want to punish him," Harry said. "Anger won't erase what's happened."

Sitting in the back of the truck, Tess had her elbow propped on the door, her hand in her hair. It had been a long time since she'd said anything. Daire and Harry were more interested in their own back and forth.

"Anger's your way of life, old man."

"It's not healthy. You shouldn't let it rule your head," Harry said. "You won't make smart choices if you make them in anger."

"You've been mad at Zeus for forty years."

"No, not that long," Harry said from the passenger seat, glancing at his ward, the driver. "The first ten years it was more aggravation than rage."

That was maybe the closest thing she'd heard to a joke since they'd started driving three hours ago.

With no music and no banter, it felt longer than both the drive across the country and the one back again combined.

"Garrick is an option," Daire said. "You want to approach him. Find out what he knows. What he's planning."

"Garrick was the best. *Is* the best. But he's no leader."

"You think he's waiting?"

"He's an observer."

"Which means he's been gathering intel for a year."

"Most likely," Harry said. "He'll be useful to us, in time. But we can't waste time looking for a passive player."

"I'm never averse to taking an active role."

Tess didn't even think about what she was doing. For some reason, her head swayed from her hand and she glanced around just in time to glimpse of Daire's eyes in the mirror, pinned on her.

As fast as they met, she drew them away. "Can we have music?" she asked. "Maybe the radio. I think you disagree with each other just for something to do."

"Debate is healthy," Harry said. "Prompts innovative problem solving and decision making."

"Except you're not making any decisions," she said, undoing her seatbelt and grabbing the shoulders of both chairs to boost herself forward.

Squeezing between the seats, she lunged over to open the glovebox and raked through the cassettes.

"What are you doing?" Harry asked. "Sit back in your seat. It's dangerous to be doing that while we're moving."

"Thought your buddy was a super-agent," she said, finding the desired tape and shoving it into the deck. "He should be able to drive in a straight line while I wave my ass in the air."

As the music started, she dropped to sit in the middle of the back seat.

"Tess—"

"Let me tell you what I've heard since we got on the road," she said. "Both of you fundamentally agree that information is key. Neither of you have a lot of love for Zeus, but both of you respect he shouldn't be underestimated. Olympus is out because, A) it's already in the rearview. B) you can't access your precious Minotaur. And C) you hang there too long and Zeus will sneak up on you. So instead of staying there, waiting, you want to speak to your Six, or what's left of them, to ask for money for a new venture."

"Asking for money gives us a read on them," Daire

said. "Doesn't matter if we get it. Their reaction is what we want to assess."

"You're explaining something she doesn't need to know," Harry said.

Daire didn't respond. But that was okay; Tess could speak for herself.

"You are used to having agents under you and, from the sounds of it, unlimited resources," she said. "You don't have that anymore. Believe me, I'm not wild about it, but for now, the three of us are it."

"You won't be taking part in anything," Harry said. "As soon as we can, we will find somewhere for you to stay in hiding."

"Think about leaving me anywhere and I guarantee I won't be there when you come back for me."

Harry twisted a little and paused before turning around to look at her. "Why do you insist on being difficult?"

"Same reason you insist on being ornery," she said. "It's in the blood, I guess."

A murmur of an almost silent laugh came from the driver's seat. "If she's with us, we can keep an eye on her."

"You say that as though I'm the problem," she said. "I won't cause trouble."

"You are trouble," Harry said. "With a capital T. We can't have a woman involved in ops."

"Why not?" she asked. "You said Daire's mom was an agent."

"An agent? Absolutely not," Harry said. "You will never act in the field."

Hooking her arms onto the shoulders of both front seats, Tess pulled herself to the edge of hers. "Daire does."

"Daire is trained."

"You can train me."

Harry laughed. "I don't have enough years left in me… or the patience."

Tess sighed. "Look, I'm not interested in being a super-agent. All I want is the freedom to live my life my way… Isn't that what you want? You're only doing this for your freedom."

"And revenge," Daire said. "Harry wants revenge too."

"And what do you want?" Tess asked. "Say you catch up with this Zeus or he catches up with you? Do you want to kill him or join him?"

The expectation of an answer came from both her and Harry.

"Sit back," Daire said. "Put your seatbelt on."

"Why? Because you might drive into something out of spite?" Tess slid her ass to the back of her seat and did as asked. "These six guys, The Six, you call them by their numbers. One, Two, Three, Four, Five, and Six. You said Six is the only original left. You also said Two and Five are dead. Were they originals?"

"No."

"And you said that they wanted to restructure. They approached both of you because they wanted things to change," she said, tipping her head back. "I don't know how long Olympus has been a thing. Daire's mom died as Olympus A crumbled and he's six years older than me, so it has to be over thirty years, forty years."

"Does she have a point?" Harry murmured.

"She's getting to it," Daire said.

Nice they were happy to talk about her like she wasn't there. Their input wasn't required anyway. "It suggests the newer members of your Six were the driving force behind the changes. Six told Zeus, so we know his loyalty is there. I'd say One, Three and Four are most likely next up in Zeus's crosshairs... unless they've struck a deal with Zeus already."

Daire's head moved like he glanced in the mirror again. "If you're looking to save people, baby, there are people more worthy."

Baby? Did he just...?

"We save them, they'd be grateful," Harry said. "Unless they've already struck a deal for financing with Zeus."

"Why would they do that if they were the ones who wanted him out?" Tess asked.

"Zeus is a dangerous guy, a persuasive guy," Daire said. "If he confronted them—"

"They'd do everything Z said to save their lives… One is most likely to be above that. He has resources of his own," Harry said, leaving that to pique her curiosity before changing the subject. "It'll be dark when we arrive. Hunting season."

"You want to get straight to it?"

"No need to waste time," Harry said. "We'll park your rig, rent a car…" He took his little black device from his pocket. "I'll make reservations."

Suggesting he was going online. Being so close to a connection to the web made her uneasy.

Her busy mind distracted her and her attention drifted to the rearview again. Daire was facing front, doing his job, watching the road. The strong line of his brow was relaxed, it wasn't taxed by thought. He seemed at ease, from what she could see in the narrow reflection of the mirror.

Thinking of Danny was an odd consolation, imagining he was still there, alive in her life… Her heart knew it wasn't true. The rest of her was humiliated by reality. Forgetting about the danger, plotting, and deceptions, her thoughts floated back in time. To the roller rink, to the cherry on his shake, the taste of his mouth…

Danny didn't exist.

But she wanted his comfort. Wanted him to curl his little finger around hers, to pull her close…

When the eyes in the mirror moved, they locked onto hers. Hers stayed put. She should tear them away, but the snare of his attention was too powerful. Losing herself in that moment, it took a second to register the track coming from the speakers. Danny's seduction tune.

Had she known that song was on the mix she selected? Maybe. Her muscles relaxed, her thoughts slowed, and everything became okay again. For just a glimmer of seconds, she wanted to stop being worried, stop being angry and scared. She wanted a piece of Danny's peace. He'd been able to calm her with his touch, with his kiss… with his hands.

Daire was still looking at her. Fixated on her in the mirror. Hating him would be easy. She could hate him for lying to her, hate him for betraying her, for making her feel something, for giving her security, then snatching it away.

But when he was looking at her like that… His quick wink should've startled her, disgusted her. Instead Tess's lips curled. Danny used to wink at her like that. To comfort her, play with her and connect them even when they couldn't touch. Not that they couldn't touch often.

Daire hadn't just slept with her to gain her confidence, he'd made her believe he wanted her every minute. Danny anyway. Talk about overkill. Wouldn't the occasional intimacy have sufficed? Instead, he'd taken it at every single opportunity. The reminder took her smile and her gaze from the mirror. Danny wasn't there. He'd never be there again.

"Done," Harry said, putting the device back in his pocket. "We should eat on the road, so we're ready to go out as soon as we arrive. I've rented tuxes too."

"Tuxes?" Tess asked, her chin rising. "You want me to wear a tux as well?"

"You'll stay in the room," Harry said. "It's the safest place. I won't leave you in the trailer when we're a distance from it. Better that you be in the building."

"While you two go and… what?"

"Count cards," Daire said.

"Ares!"

"What am I going to do?" Tess asked. "Snitch on you? When you said money, I thought you meant we were going to meet one of your Six. Your benefactors."

"Three is a third generation casino owner. His family got in on the ground floor."

"So, wait," she said, sitting up straight. "One of the people who funded Olympus is a Vegas millionaire?"

"Billionaire," Daire said. "He inherited the role from his father. The family have mob connections and associates in the intelligence community."

"You're only encouraging her," Harry muttered. "Best she doesn't know too much."

"I have a right to know," Tess said. "This is my life. It's been my life. I'm finally beginning to understand the mess of crap I was born into. God, what would've happened if I had kids of my own? What happens if I do? Am I supposed to run with them?"

"You won't be able to trust any man who proposes marriage," Harry said. "Not until we know Z is dead."

"I don't need to be married to have kids," she said. "Shouldn't have to tell you that, Harry. Were you married to my mom?" That question didn't require an answer. "I have to know what is going on so I can make decisions about my future. What if I want to get married or have kids? I don't think that's unreasonable."

"Your mother knew the danger," Harry said.

"But she had me anyway," Tess said.

"It was a different time then. You should know better than to be careless with men."

She snorted a laugh. "Yeah, you'd think, wouldn't you? Careless is the only way I can be with men, daddy," she said, using the title as an insult. "Careless is the only way I can make sure they don't get ideas they'll spend more than a night with me."

"Tess—"

"Mom was careless too. That was us, the careless duo. Grab a guy for one shot on the carousel, then it's off to the next one."

"Your mother knew how to protect herself. I'd hope you do too. Being caught out is too easy," Harry said then added under his breath, "Believe me, I know."

Glancing up, Tess found Daire's eyes on her in the mirror again. It was one time. He didn't have to think about it. Except... Tess could only know what was in his head if it was in hers too. It was no big deal. The back of her fingers slid up the inside of her arm toward the scar of her implant. They were protected... weren't they?

THIRTY-ONE

TESS WASN'T EXACTLY uneasy for the rest of the journey. Her mind just wouldn't settle. Still, they went through Harry's steps, parking the Beast, climbing into the rental car that was waiting for them, and then into the hotel.

The casino was buzzing with people, lights, movement, smells, sounds; it was a mass of organized chaos. She got little chance to enjoy it though. Harry and Daire whisked her into an elevator and up to a standard room with two queen-size beds. There were three of them, but no one commented on that.

Sitting on the bed, flicking through the television channels, Tess wasn't really watching anything. The men were moving around, getting ready for a night in The Strip's hubbub. It wasn't like she was jealous. Being in the mass of people would only send her head spinning. Still, it wasn't nice to be sidelined without consultation.

A clean-shaven Harry came from the closet, his hair slicked back. She wouldn't tell him, but he cleaned up nice.

"You are to stay in here," he said, stopping at the end of the bed. "Do not leave this room. Not for any reason."

"What if the building is on fire?" she said, looking past him at the TV screen.

"Stay here until Daire comes for you."

Blinking up at him, she stopped flicking. "You'd send him *up?* Away from the exit?"

"He's trained."

She sighed. "So you keep saying."

Returning to her flicking, Tess didn't sense Harry's frustration until he stalked over and grabbed the remote from her hand.

"Pay attention," he snapped, tossing the remote to the end of the bed. "You stay here, do not leave the room."

"You said that already."

"Daire and I will have the keycards. You won't have to open the door to anyone."

"Except room service."

"No," he said. "Do not order food."

She sagged. "You expect me to sit here and stare at the walls until you get back? It could be days for all I know."

"It shouldn't take more than a few hours. I will come up and check on you if we're going to be longer."

"I make no promises," she said. "We ate hours ago. I might want cake or something. I bet they have good cake."

"You're infuriating," he grumbled.

Tess pasted on a broad smile. "Just warning you in advance to expect the minibar to be empty when you get back. Is there an ice machine on this floor?"

Harry raised his arm to free his watch from under his shirt cuff. "I will get you ice… and food. Stay there."

He about-faced and marched out of the room, closing the door a little harder than was really necessary. Flipping over, Tess crawled to the end of the bed to get the remote. On her knees, she'd just started flicking again when Daire came out of the bathroom.

"Where'd Harry go?"

"To fetch me food," she said, turning off the TV and sinking down onto her back, driving her fingers into her hair. "Geez, I'm going out of my mind already."

Daire came over to stand between the two beds and looked down at her lying in the middle of hers. "I realized today I didn't apologize."

"You don't have to," she said, springing onto her feet,

knowing exactly what he was talking about. "The less we talk about what happened between us, the better."

The wide window offered a view of the lights and sights of the desert city. Putting her back to him didn't block him out. When he approached, she could feel him coming, could feel the pull of his gravity.

"I do have to apologize. I didn't… It shouldn't have happened."

"We said that at the time," she said. "You not being who you said you were doesn't change that."

"I should explain. I wish I could…"

The uncertainty of his words brought her around to face him. "You're an asshole for lying to me. But there were two of us there that night, I didn't think about it either."

"I didn't like seeing you with him… it's the only excuse I have."

Her brow lowered. "With who?"

"Your date… In that bar… You were smart to spill the drink."

"Oh my God," she breathed. "You were watching us."

The thought that Danny was in the same position she'd left him in that night was laughable now that she discovered he hadn't even been in the trailer.

"It was the only way to make sure you were safe," he said. "You can't trust any man's motivation."

"So Harry said," Tess said. By now, she should be used to calling herself an idiot. "No way could any man actually want me. All they care about is Olympus, right? I get it."

Side-stepping, her aim was to go around him, but he stole her arm to hold her there.

"Every man wants you," he said, his grip loosening. "Harry's warning was… he has a strange way of showing he cares."

Curiosity got the better of her. "Does he know?" she asked. "That we were… together?"

Daire shook his head. "He's no idiot, but he hasn't asked for confirmation. Don't think he will."

"What would he do? If he found out we had sex?"

"I don't know… Shore leave wasn't something we got in Olympus. The women from my past are exclusively mission related."

Olympus dictated everything, including his sex life. Tess didn't want to feel sorry for him. Yet there were times it was impossible to ignore how Olympus had screwed him. When she'd read the words in Harry's letters about PK being manufactured, the ramifications hadn't sunk in. Not until she faced the evidence.

"Harry told you who to be with."

"Mission directives usually came from Z," Daire said. "Sometimes we'd be granted field autonomy… Harry would make those calls."

His comment about her being the first he'd ever chosen for himself began to make sense. "Must feel good that you pulled off your first planned and executed solo mission. Shows you don't need them. You're capable on your own."

"Capable of screwing up. Yeah," he said. "Do you want me to get you a test?"

Pregnancy, right, Tess wasn't sure where her head was. "No," she said, trying a smile, though it wasn't close to genuine. "I have the implant, we'll be fine. Don't know how you'd explain that one to Harry."

"I'll step up if it's needed," he said. "You have no obligation to keep secrets for me."

"Harry and I aren't exactly close. He has less rights to know about my sex life than he does yours. You want to tell him, tell him."

"He knows I lied to get close to you," Daire said. "Like I said, he's no idiot."

Which meant Harry probably at least suspected something had happened between them.

"Why wouldn't he say anything?" she asked.

Maybe it was don't-ask-don't-tell. Harry was smart enough not to ask a question he didn't want the answer to. Certainly not so soon after patching things up with his errant protégé. When your kid ran away from home, you were just grateful to have them back. Blasting them for every naughty act would only lead to pushing them away again.

Daire gave a cryptic answer. "It's like he said, hierarchy stands."

It wasn't immediately clear what that meant. Then she remembered how quickly Daire had answered her question about what he wouldn't do under Harry's orders.

"So when you're out tonight…" she started, "if he tells you to sleep with someone, you'll do it?"

The answer was none of her business. Why did she even ask the question? Waiting, scrutinizing every nuance of his expression, she anticipated an answer. His eyes left hers. The aversion wasn't like before, he wasn't avoiding her, he was searching for something… Something inside himself.

"He won't. We only want Three's attention."

"But if he asks you, you'll do it," she said. If Harry suspected they had a connection, he could hope to break that link by sending his apprentice to bed with another woman. "You said it can't happen, that it won't… You meant us." She'd known that at the time. "It's nothing to do with respect for Harry or your missions, you said that because you knew he'd never order you to be with me. Nothing will ever happen between us until you're given a directive. But that directive will never come."

It shouldn't matter. But, for some reason, the pressure of anger pulsed through her. Maybe it was the lack of choice. That someone else would think to make decisions for her, for anyone. Harry didn't have that right over her. Olympus didn't either. They shouldn't have it over Daire either.

"It doesn't matter," Daire said. "You wouldn't want anything to happen between us… would you?"

The simplicity of that query vented some of her anger. He was right. She shouldn't be thinking about who made decisions like that. Even if it was allowed, if Daire was given permission, she'd never let it happen. They couldn't be intimate ever again. Wouldn't be.

"No," she said and turned away. "Of course I wouldn't."

He stopped her getting any further by catching her

little finger with his. Her chin sank slowly until she could see that point of contact. Daire was a stranger. But his touch…

"If there was a way to fix this, I… I would do it."

Some part of her wanted to comfort him. The guy might be some super trained efficient machine, but had he known love? Had he known comfort? Harry wasn't exactly the most tactile or expressive guy. He expected a lot from his charge and always pushed him to give more.

"I used to have a friend," she said, hyperaware of the vast black sky reflecting the energy of the city back down on itself. "Guy was so laid back, he thought being upright was some sort of expert yoga move. Wasn't really the kind of guy to get himself stressed about anything, but every once in a while he'd say something real, something profound…" Raising her focus to his, Tess's expression softened. "He used to say nothing's too broken to fix." The admission startled him. "Maybe things can't be put back to exactly the way they were before, but with enough hard work, anything is possible."

The room door opened. Without turning to check who was coming in, Daire's finger drifted away from hers. Harry approached with a tray and an ice bucket.

Daire couldn't help being who he was, but that didn't change his priorities. Despite the negatives of his upbringing, he liked the regime. Taking orders, carrying out missions, those were his life and the only one he'd known. The one he chose. Tess wouldn't change him, couldn't. That meant she had to be stronger in protecting herself.

"There," Harry said, dumping everything on the dresser by the TV. "Now don't leave this room and don't open the door to anyone."

With a mock salute, Tess went back to sink onto the bed again. "Yes, sir. I'll park myself right here."

Harry glanced from her to the food and back again. "You don't want to eat?"

"Not now," she said, snagging the remote to put on the TV. "I'll get to it in my own sweet time."

"Trouble," Harry muttered. It seemed he found focusing on Daire much easier. "Ready to do this?"

"Yes, sir."

At an almost march, the two men left the room without looking back. They had a mission. Good for them.

Sighing, she slouched against the pillows. Living on the road, with men who didn't trust her or believe her competent, was going to be tough. Tess wasn't dumb enough to think that she was as capable as them. Still, it would be nice, for once, to be more than just an inconvenience in someone's life.

***

TESS HADN'T MEANT TO fall asleep. The television was still on when she awoke. Sitting up, she scanned the space, trying to remember where she was and what was going on. The hotel. The mission. Harry. Daire. Three.

Inhaling, she cupped her face with both hands to scrub away the remnants of slumber. In the truck that day, she hadn't been able to sleep. When Danny was driving, she'd never thought twice about drifting off. Somehow, it wasn't the same with Daire and Harry in the front. Sleeping would've meant missing the chance to gather information. The men were open and direct when talking to each other. Not so much with her. Eavesdropping wasn't the most enlightening plan, but it was what she had.

The dim illumination of the wall lamp didn't help wake her up; the noise of the room door handle did that. Taking her face from her hands, Tess waited in silence. It moved again. If Harry or Daire were trying to get in, they sucked with keycards. There wouldn't be anything wrong in using the peephole, would there?

She got as far as the end of the narrow hall leading to the door when it opened, stopping her dead. Not Harry or Daire. A stranger. A mean, capable looking stranger. The two of them looked at each other for a couple of seconds.

"Who are you?" she asked, trying to decide if she could rush him and escape. "I'll scream if you—"

He raised a weapon. Without saying a word, he aimed and fired. Gasping in a scream of surprise, the piercing impact stung, but it wasn't agony. Maybe her brain hadn't got the message she'd been shot. But it wasn't a bullet. A small silver dart jutted from her shoulder. Not a bullet, a…

Her mind slowed, the room spun, and before she could say a thing, the black veil of night consumed her.

THIRTY-TWO

LONG BEFORE HER EYES actually opened, Tess was aware of lying on something soft, of being warm and loose. The clean scent of the pillow beneath her head complemented the freshness permeating the air. The drowsy fog didn't ascend from her senses even after her eyelids parted.

She tried to focus through the glare of bright light shining beyond the window. The hotel. Her memories faded in and out. The light, the window... she wasn't in a high-rise building anymore. There were plants outside, some kind of trees, houses, greenery... It wasn't The Strip.

Sitting up, she clutched her heavy head to prevent it from falling into the pillow again. Her mouth was dry, her senses dull. What the hell had happened? Where was she? All she could remember was Daire walking out with Harry.

Something had happened after. Something... Grabbing her shoulder, Tess pushed the thin strap of her dress aside to search for evidence of the dart. The smallest red prick confirmed it wasn't a dream. She'd been shot... with some kind of tranquilizer. That would explain her being so groggy.

Shoving the white covers away from her body, she glanced up at the wispy white fabric draped over the metal frame above the bed. Wriggling to the edge of the mattress, the platform bed was almost at floor level. After liberating her feet from the canopy, cool tile met her soles. The hard surface was a nice juxtaposition to the sumptuous bed. It was something to cling to, something solid and real.

Her head still ached. At her first attempt to rise, she failed and immediately dropped to her butt. Catching her forehead on the heel of her hand, she didn't think about the pain or the confusion. She thought about Daire. About the man who'd dedicated his life to a cause that cast him out. Whatever he was thinking, wherever he was, either he'd be basking in glory or drowning in defeat. Why was he plaguing her?

The room. The building. Wherever she was. It wasn't the hotel. Her father and Daire could've orchestrated the "kidnap" to stash her somewhere out of their way. It was that or the dreaded Z had caught up with her.

Giving herself another minute to cast off the weight of sleep, Tess took stock by figuring out what she could see. Straight ahead was a low dresser with a television on it. To the left was a door, on the same wall as the head of the bed. A window occupied the wall behind her. Avoiding the light definitely helped her head.

Opposite the end of the bed were three doors. The one closest to the windows was tinted glass, so it probably went outside. The other two were closed. Three options. One to the left. Two to the right.

Forcing herself onto her feet in a wide stance, she opened her arms to get her balance. Memories of the roller rink flashed by. She wished Danny was behind her again, there to keep her steady. Forget that. Forget him. He wasn't real.

Her predicament was very real. Unfortunately.

While so foggy, it wouldn't be the best idea to storm out to confront whoever had taken her. The alternative was taking her time lounging in bed. No way. Drawing in a long breath, she bolstered her energy, intending to charge toward the door by the nightstand when it opened.

Holding her breath, waiting, she anticipated who might join her. If it was Daire or Harry, at least she'd know their plan didn't involve respecting her wishes. Still, they were known factors, better than the unknown.

The door opened further, and a man came inside. Another stranger. Probably about Harry's age, his vivid blue eyes were keen, alive, aware.

"Pandora," he said, closing the door behind himself and gesturing to the bed. "Please make yourself at home."

Without shame or contrition, he passed the dresser to seat himself in the wingback chair in the corner.

Tess stayed on her feet, fixated on him. "Who are you?"

He brushed something from the leg of his pants, then curled his fingers around the arms of the chair. "James Garrick."

Garrick, Tess knew that name. "Poseidon."

His lips curled. "I wasn't sure how much your mother told you."

"My mother is dead."

His lips flattened. "Yes, I heard. I'm sorry."

He'd heard? Did that mean he was responsible or that news traveled fast in the Olympusphere? As long as he was giving her answers, she wouldn't make a break for it. Lowering to sit on the edge of the bed again, the delay would give her head more time to clear.

"Why am I here? Are you working for Zeus?"

"No," he said, his expression morphed from somber to serious. "The opposite."

"You're working against him? Why? And why am I here?"

"I can't trust Zeus now. Not that I'm sure any of us ever could. Even if we came to an agreement, he couldn't be trusted to stick to it. Z will always be most concerned with his own interests."

"Isn't everyone?"

One side of his mouth lifted. "You have Harry's shrewd mind."

She wasn't so sure about that, or so sure that she wanted to be compared to her father. "Why am I here?"

"Because you are Pandora," he said. "There's a lot to

explain. A lot you have to understand. In the meantime, consider this your home."

"Does Harry know I'm here?"

"Not yet. But he will," Garrick said. "I don't intend to keep you here against your will. I imagine a lot of your life has been dictated by others. That is not why I had my man retrieve you."

"Then why?"

"Would you like a tour? Something to eat? We have fantastic facilities here. There's a pool, a gym, a wine cellar… There's even a games room and a movie theatre."

"Where are we?" she asked, glancing around again. "What is this place?"

"It's the home of one of our benefactors," Garrick said. "He gifted the place to our cause… for the time being."

"Our?" she asked, her brows rising. "I know you don't mean me."

"I hope once you hear our plans that you'll be open to joining us."

"Me?" Tess asked and shook her head. "I'm no super-agent."

His smile suggested he enjoyed her description. "No, but what I need, only you have the power to give."

"What is it?" she asked, unable to imagine what she could offer.

At the hotel, Garrick's guy would've had access to her possessions. The Beast held the balance of whatever was hers. Tracking that down wouldn't be a challenge for the great Poseidon.

"Not what. Who." Standing up, he opened the two mystery doors. "My men bought some things for you to wear." Behind the first door was a long, walk-in closet. The central door led to a bathroom with a shower over the tub. "Take your time, bathe, dress, come downstairs when you're ready."

He went toward the exit.

Before he got there, she asked, "How many men do you have?"

"Five," he said. "You shouldn't fear them. They were

trained by your father. Their allegiance to him is absolute."

"Olympus men," she said, thinking about the plan suggested in the Beast to gather them up. "You brought them here.

"It's a long story, Pandora," he said, opening the door. "Like I said, take your time, then come down and join us. I'll tell you everything you want to know."

He departed and closed the door. Such a brief introduction, yet the promise of answers gave her hope. Leaping up, she wobbled and cradled her head, remembering a little late that she hadn't got over her slumber yet.

Poseidon, the man they'd thought passive, was being proactive. Tess wanted to know everything. How long he'd been there, what his plan was, and what he wanted from her. She'd have to pace herself while catching up with reality, but lingering wasn't an option. Answers were finally within reach.

THIRTY-THREE

THE HOUSE, SORRY, MANSION, was gorgeous. With tiled floors, curved and straight corridors, it was easy to be awed by the place. And get lost in it. The rounded wall opposite her bedroom concealed a circular area that overlooked an office/boardroom. Beyond, a mezzanine revealed vast living space dominated by a towering fireplace.

Even that was dwarfed by two-story high windows showcasing the huge stone and slate patio out back. Everything was big, expensive, flashy. Was that just Vegas, or did the obvious wealth say something about Poseidon's benefactor?

After a few wrong turns, she found a staircase to descend and followed another long curving corridor on the lower floor. Voices became clearer, though not enough to pick out specifics. She stopped in the fireplace room. A glass door with some kind of external water garden stood opposite the raised seating area. It looked like there was a path. Like an exit.

If she wanted to get out of there—

"Pandora!"

The shout startled her. Straight ahead, Poseidon stood at the other side of the fireplace. Garrick. Maybe it was better to think of him as a human than an invincible deity.

"Come and join us," he said, stepping aside to gesture her over.

Her answers were there. That's what Tess kept saying to herself. Answers… and if the various deep voices she'd heard were any measure, a bunch of guys too.

Past the column of the fireplace was a long dining table surrounded by aluminum-back chairs and a fish tank wall. More wealth. Of course a regular wall wouldn't do.

Garrick gestured for her to continue with him. A pool table at the far end of the house was the first thing visible in the next area. The huge retro kitchen only got a passing glance. Five men stopped or turned to look at her; it felt right to return the favor.

Like it was show and tell or she was some art exhibit, they drank her in from head to toe and back again.

"Beguiling," one of the two men standing by the pool table said.

"But will she bring misery to the human race?" the other asked.

"Yes, you're right," Garrick said, putting an arm around her to draw her deeper into the room. "We have Pandora."

Those who weren't playing pool were sitting in the various seats or at the low curved bar next to it.

"She's hot," one of the seated guys said. "Don't see Hades in her at all."

"None of you met her mother," Garrick said, ushering her around in front of him. He laid his hands on her shoulders. "She was beguiling too. Pandora, meet your father's soldiers. Boze, Lowe, Zip, Milo, Albany."

As he said each of their names, the men raised a hand to offer a wave or casual salute.

"I'd say it's nice to meet you all, but I don't want to lie straight off the bat," she said, narrowing her gaze on Albany. "You shot me."

"Guilty," he said, leaning on his pool cue. "Following orders, ma'am."

"Please take a seat," Garrick said, directing her onto a vacant couch facing the pool table.

The three men seated in the same area watched her walk around and sit.

It was unnerving. The men were gripped by her every subtlety.

Being the freak show in a room of super-agents wasn't much of a warm welcome.

"The first thing you should know and always remember is no one here will hurt you," Garrick said, striding to an armchair on the other side of the room. "You are valuable. Very valuable."

"No one ever says they won't hurt me just because I'm such a great gal," she said to little response. "What are you all doing here?"

"P brought us in."

"Each of the men here has a synthetic isotope in their blood," Garrick said. "It was an experimental procedure, something we were running when the Exodus happened."

"When we all scattered from the beta site a year ago," Milo said.

Yeah, after Zeus learned of the plot to assassinate him, Harry sent an alert telling his men to bolt. That much she knew. Now the incident had a name.

"How much do you know, Pandora?" Boze asked.

The men's scrutiny intensified.

"I know enough," Tess said, knowing better than to blink first. "Doesn't tell me what you're all doing here."

"The isotope control module is the only thing that can trace subjects. Unfortunately, it's a prototype, we didn't move past the initial stages. The control module only works in a narrow radius, less than a hundred miles and it's not precise. As these men came into its field, I, or we, worked to recruit them."

"Still doesn't tell me what you're doing here now."

"Regrouping," Garrick said. "I don't have Z's strategic skill or H's operational expertise. My role is to facilitate mission needs."

"So gathering everyone together is just your way of maintaining Olympus status quo?"

"Things can never go back to the way they were,"

Garrick said. "Z is an enemy of Olympus now. Tracking Harry would be impossible, even for me. If, somehow, I'd found him, none of us would get near him. All we could hope was that at some point, he'd approach the Six."

"Or what's left of them," Boze said.

"Two and five are dead," she said, judging the reactions on the surrounding faces.

Albany and Milo put down their cues. She hadn't heard any balls ricochet, yet, apparently, the game was over. They stood in front of the tall windows, their backs to the patio.

"Three was the easiest to monitor," Garrick said. "We waited for Hades to show up, it was all we could do."

"Third generation casino owner," she said. "If you knew it and Harry knew it, doesn't Z know it?"

"Z is in Europe," Garrick said. "I've been monitoring him."

"How do you…" Tess pushed to the edge of her seat. "If you know where he is and that he's so terrible, why didn't you finish the mission?"

"End him?" Boze said.

"Wasn't our mission," Lowe said. "Harry has the objectives, but he hasn't issued orders… at least not to any of us."

"Couldn't be Ares mission either," Zip said.

"Why not?" she asked, recognizing the code name as one Harry used for Daire.

"Because his brother is the assassin," Lowe said.

"And Ares was in the dark about Zulu," Zip added.

Operation Zulu, also known as, the plot to assassinate Zeus.

Daire's brother. Tess looked from one male to the next. She'd heard Harry and Daire talking about a brother. If these men were doing the same, he couldn't be present. Whoever he was, whatever he was, he was in the wind or dead.

"That's what you're all waiting for," Tess stated, clarity washing over her. "Orders."

"We're not complete enough to make a move."

"Harry will have more success tracing and recruiting

his people," Garrick said. "He's done it before, he can do it again."

"Why not go to him?" she asked. "You said you were waiting here for him. You must have known he was in town."

"Not until he arrived. We've been waiting, monitoring the hotel's security, hoping he'd come for Three. We didn't expect him to show up with Ares and Pandora."

"Changed things," Boze said. "Getting close to Harry was always gonna be tough."

"Getting close to them together is impossible," Milo said. "Even if we got one of them alone—"

"The other would take us out before we could explain."

"What?" Tess asked. "That you're holed up here hoping someone takes care of the problem for you?"

From the shock and confusion reverberating around the room, she guessed they hadn't expected her to be so blunt.

"We came and got you, didn't we?" Albany said.

"For what?" she asked, focusing on Garrick. "What do you want from me?"

"To bring them here."

"If this is Three's house and they want to talk to him, won't they come anyway?"

"They played at his casino last night," Garrick said. "Cheated at his casino to get his attention."

"Problem for them?" Albany said. "Three's in Panama… running from Z. Everyone's running from him."

Three being in another country was a problem. No chance of a rendezvous. And, as far as she knew, her father and Daire didn't know this splinter Olympus faction was on their feet ready to act.

"So you plan to use me," she said. "To dangle me in front of them to bring them in."

"No," Garrick said as a couple of others shook their heads. "If we're confrontational, they'll go on the offensive."

"Even with five of us," Lowe said, indicating himself and the others. "We'd never take on Hades and Ares and win… It's too big a risk."

"We can't afford to lose anyone else," Albany said.

Noticing the way they shared glances, then fixated on the floor, Tess witnessed their grief.

"How many have you lost?"

"Two confirmed," Garrick said. "Most are still unaccounted for."

"We need Hades," Lowe said. "His discipline will get us on track. He'll get us to where we have to be."

"We're scattered without his guidance," Milo said.

Her father was these men's confidence. Their bedrock. Just having him in their midst would strengthen them.

"I gotta say," Zip said, pushing back in his chair. "Seeing Ares felt like a weight off."

"Damn straight," Lowe said.

"Agreed," Albany said.

Boze nodded. "He's the backbone of the team."

"If we get him with us. We'll be unstoppable."

That was a dangerous line of thought. No one was invincible.

The faction had so much admiration, so much respect, for the two men they'd stolen her from. Their deference was intriguing and enlightening. It gave her a clearer understanding of how important Harry and Daire were in the operation. How crucial they were.

Since they'd rejected her first guess, she asked, "What's the plan?"

Garrick smiled. "You have to invite them to join us."

Oh, she didn't like that. The monolith of responsibility quickly eclipsed the weight of trepidation.

How could she be the one to summon them? It could be a trap with her as the lure. Still, these Olympus men could be their salvation. Either that or they were seducing her with talk of solutions while intending to erase both Harry and Daire.

Daire.

Her stomach clenched. There were so many questions, so many what ifs. She should have quizzed him instead of being concerned with his lies.

Anger was justified, given how he'd betrayed her. But

he was a man whose entire world was subterfuge and politicking. He needed a mission. A focus. And he'd chosen her.

"No," she said. "I won't do it."

Some corner of her psyche wanted to declare it wouldn't matter. That even if she called up their hotel and got through to Daire or Harry that they would laugh in her face before walking into potential danger. But she wasn't sure that was true. Potent hesitation held her back.

Garrick inhaled. "If you don't ask them to come, weapons down, through the front door, they could kill every man in this room to get to you."

Killing wasn't necessary. If these men were going to be loyal to their mentor and equal, she didn't want to be the reason one harmed the other.

"I can't," she said. "I won't be the one to bring them here."

"It's your job," Boze said. "You're Pandora. Tempting is what you're supposed to do."

"Your words, not mine," she said. "I'm not refusing because I don't think they'll come. I'm refusing because I don't know any of you. I don't trust any of you."

"How can we change that?" Garrick asked. "We don't have a lot of time."

"Yeah, they'll be tracking us already. If someone doesn't make contact before they locate us…"

"What?" she asked when Lowe trailed off. "If someone doesn't make contact before they locate us, what?"

"They'll come in shooting," Zip said.

"Or just blast us off the face of the Earth," Milo added.

Responsibility. Another dose shot through her. She didn't want to be responsible for these men losing their lives and didn't want to decide Harry and Daire's fate.

"Let me go to them," she said. "I'll go to the hotel and explain what I've seen here."

"Nothing to stop you taking off or not telling them," Boze said.

Rolling her tongue behind her parted lips, hypocrisy

reeked. "You want me to trust you, but you won't trust me?"

"It's dangerous out there," Garrick said. "We let you go and something happens… Hades blames us."

"Something happens like what? Like I am abducted? Those responsible for that are right here." Her focus lingered on Albany. "I need more time. I need to think about this."

"We don't have time," Garrick said, leaving his seat to go over to the bar. "It's almost sundown."

Sundown? They'd taken her at night. A whole day had passed.

"Why is it so late?" she asked. "Why was I out so long?"

Garrick picked up something from the bar and then came back her way. "We had to wait for your blood analysis to process," he said, pressing numbers into the phone in his hand.

"My blood analysis? Why the hell would…" Harry hadn't recognized her, so there was no reason for these men to know what she looked like. "You were checking who I was."

"Yes," Garrick said, raising the phone to his ear. "Good news, you're disease free too." Once he heard what he was waiting for, he held the phone to her. "Time to decide."

Expectation closed in from every angle.

"If they're gonna hit us, it will be in the dark," Lowe said. "Time's up, Pandora."

She didn't like to be rushed, but her only choice was to take the phone and listen to it ring.

"Hades," came the biting reply.

With her attention fixed on Garrick, she struggled to decide. She could hang up, but if these guys had nefarious intentions, they might kill her if they deemed her useless or insubordinate.

"Dad?"

"Damnit," he said on a long hissing exhale. "Where are you? I told you to stay put."

"I'm… with Poseidon." Silence on the line. "They want you to come here. You and Ares."

"Who are they?"

"Five of your men. Poseidon… Me."

Her father had only been in her life for a couple of days. He was curt and demanding. So far that was all personal experience had taught her. But, for some reason, hearing his voice actually kindled emotion. She did want him there. He'd know what to do. Know how to handle things. Tess needed him.

"Light-Sprite…" She'd only heard her mother use that pet name. A tingle to her tear ducts took her attention down. "You will be okay."

"I know," she said, drawing in a long, calming breath. "They say they won't hurt me. That they don't want to hurt you. I don't know if they're telling the truth. I don't know if it's a trap."

"It doesn't matter," he said. "We're coming. Where are you?"

She looked to Garrick. "I need an address."

"I'll send our location to his base unit," Garrick said, taking something from his pocket to press buttons.

"Got it," Harry said.

Either he could hear Garrick or the message had gone through.

"Tell him he and Ares are not to be armed."

"I heard him," Harry said, a deep displeasure in his low voice. "If he's harmed a hair on your head—"

"They haven't hurt me yet. But if they do—"

"We'll take every one of them down, Light," he said. "Stay there. We're on our way."

The line went dead; she held the phone up to Garrick. "If you're lying, no God will be able to save your soul."

A scoff of a laugh came from behind Garrick. "Definitely Harry's daughter."

THIRTY-FOUR

PACING IN FRONT OF the huge double-height window by the fireplace, Tess muttered, "Right thing, wrong thing."

The men, including Garrick, were around the dining table on the other side of the fireplace.

She itched and tingled, anticipating what may or may not happen. Daire had been an asshole. That didn't mean she wanted him dead. And she'd had little chance to get to know her father. They needed more time. But it was possible she'd called them to the slaughter.

Still obsessing, there was no way to reach a conclusion until what happened, happened. The glass front door burst open, stopping her dead. Daire was halfway across the room, her in his sights, zero awareness of anything else.

Relief propelled her to mirror his determination; they met just as he reached the step up to the split level. Even though she was one step higher, he still had to bend his knees to level their eyes.

"You hurt?" he asked, grabbing her waist. "Look at me."

He cupped her face to check her eyes, cheeks, and jaw, then ran his fingers up through her hair and down her neck, checking her scalp and spine.

"I'm fine," she said, laying her hands on his chest. "I'm not hurt."

"What happened?" he asked, squeezing her arms and hips, apparently still checking for tenderness or broken bones. "How did they take you?"

"It didn't hurt. I wasn't hurt… It was a tranquillizer dart… I think."

Her fingertips went to her shoulder, attracting his attention. He zeroed in on the spot, pushing her fingers aside and easing down the strap of her dress to run his thumb across the red mark left by the dart.

His jaw tightened, thinning his lips, gritting his teeth as he inhaled through his nose. For a split second, his eyes were on hers, then he was whirling around to face the others, shielding her with his body.

"Who was it?" he demanded.

Tess edged aside to see her father in the open doorway, gun in hand. Garrick and the men were crowded next to the fish tank.

"Ares, the men were acting on my orders," Garrick said.

It was only as Daire's hand came around to his back that she noticed the gun in his waistband.

When his fingers curled around the grip, she plastered both hands on his to stall him. "No," she said before he could free it. "No shooting."

His hand loosened from the gun to twist and take hold of both of hers at the small of his back.

"What's the play, Garrick?" Harry asked. Transfixed by Daire's long fingers trapping all of hers, her father's words faded through. "Using my own child against me? My own men?"

"No," Garrick said. "Not against you. For you. With you… We needed you here, but it was too risky to approach you."

"Needed me for what?"

"Come in," Garrick said. "We'll sit down and talk."

"Stratego," Boze said. "It's time to hit back."

"Hit back," Harry murmured. The front door closed.

"You want to take him down."

"If we work together, anything is possible," Garrick said. "All we want to do is talk."

Harry probably looked to Daire, maybe even took his time deciding. Yet, less than a minute later, the men turned to head back the way they'd come. She leaned further to witness Harry crossing the room after the agents, the gun no longer in his hand.

Daire started forward, but instinct closed her fingers around his, bringing his attention around. Once he was looking at her, she forgot her reason for holding him back.

"Babe?" he whispered, swiping the hair from her brow. "You wanna leave?"

"You came."

Although she'd suspected he and Harry would retrieve her, the confirmation was profound, humbling.

"Always will," he said. "Any time you need me."

Her father had been the one on the phone. She hadn't even asked Daire to come, yet there he was. Why? She couldn't figure out his reasoning.

"Following Hades orders?" she asked, pushing her fingers deeper between his.

He swept her hair from her jaw and ran the back of his fingers down her cheek. "When I walked in that room and you were gone…" She shouldn't have let her eyes close, but they did. His caress was enchanting. "Babe, I'd have killed every living soul on this earth to get to you."

The determination in that admission opened her eyes. His were filled with potent conviction. Emotions were running high, Tess understood adrenaline was responsible for overreactions. Still, even if he didn't mean it tomorrow, he meant it then.

The line between Daire and Danny blurred. It had been over a month since they'd spent so long apart. They'd been taken from each other. She'd been taken from him. It didn't matter that she wasn't hurt; the possibility had been enough to scare him. That's what Tess was looking at. Behind his anger and frustration, she could see it: he'd been scared for her.

"No expectation," she murmured. "Remember? I have no expectations of you. I am not your master. I don't give you orders and you don't owe me anything."

Daire continued to stroke her and was on the verge of saying something when his expression blanked. His hand fell and he whipped around, pulling the gun from his waistband to aim it at the guy standing in front of the fish tank.

Zip. He raised his hands. "Hades needs you."

Carefully inching around Daire, she slid a hand down his arm to lay it over the weapon, lowering it from its target. Zip was shaken. Pointing weapons at each other couldn't be normal. Or if it was, the aggressor probably didn't look as feral as Daire.

Zip backed away a few steps to disappear into the dining room.

"You need to calm down," Tess murmured.

"I need to hit something," he grumbled, his words almost lost in the pant of his breath.

She smiled. "No, you don't," she said, relieving him of the weapon with little effort. "You're amped."

His head snapped around, locking his focus onto her. Danny never looked at her like that. Still, she could read his mind. Could feel the heat. Could understand exactly how he wanted to vent his adrenaline.

For the first time, she wondered what Daire would be like in bed. Danny had always been incredible, always took care of her needs. But there was no urgency, nothing even close to what she read burning from the man beside her.

"There are seven men on the other side of that wall," she whispered.

Why had she said that? The fireplace wasn't even really a wall. There was space at either side to allow people to move through the different open-plan areas. Did she say it to remind him that if he touched her, she'd summon the men to save her? Or was she reminding herself that taking action would lead to the discovery of their intimate connection? Former connection, that's what it was. Former. They weren't connected. Not anymore.

Yet, with their eyes still locked, he wound an arm around her waist and clamped her body tight to his side. In a silent inhale, her lips parted, drawing his eye.

Damn her body for reacting. Hormones warmed her skin, sending tingles and tickles to every intimate corner. Her stomach tightened in response to the instinctual desire he provoked. The tremble of her breath was automatic. As was the straining of her nipples against the fabric of the sundress that she hadn't considered tight until that moment.

Danny's name was on her tongue. Except Danny wasn't the man looking at her. Danny had never aroused her so completely and thoroughly by wrapping a single arm around her. Thinking of her ex… if he could be classed as that, reminded her of the betrayal. Except now, it didn't feel like she'd been betrayed; it felt like she was betraying his memory.

Everything was such a crazy mess.

"You have orders," she whispered, refraining from licking her dry lips because if he kissed her… "Ares."

In a second, he changed again. Growing rigid, he picked her off the step and put her onto the same level as him. Then he opened his arm, gesturing for her to go first. She hadn't been asked to join them, but it didn't seem like Daire would go anywhere without her.

Hoping she didn't appear as undone as she felt, Tess led the way to the fish tank, presenting the dining table of men to the man following her.

Harry sat at the top of the table, Garrick at the opposite end, nearest where she stood. There were four chairs at either side of the long, narrow table. The five men dubbed Harry's soldiers were seated, three on one side, two on the other. Daire walked the length of the table to stand behind Harry, his hands linked at his back.

There was space on both sides of the table, but Daire didn't choose to sit. It could be a strategic decision. On his feet, he could move faster and see more. There was a lot of glass too. He probably wanted to guard his leader's back. They still didn't know what they'd walked into. She didn't know either.

"Tess, honey, you don't have to listen to this," Harry said.

From the expressions around the table, she'd guess the guys weren't used to Harry being anything other than his blunt, decisive self, giving orders.

"I have nothing better to do," she said, deliberately not taking his hint.

"I don't know whether to be reassured or scared that she has Ares' gun," Albany said on a snicker.

"Your brains would be decorating the floor if she hadn't saved your ass," Daire said.

The smiles dropped from the faces of all the men.

Albany laid his hands on the table. "Guess someone lost his sense of humor in the last year."

Daire took one step.

Without even looking, Harry knew it and raised a hand to stop him. "Stop dicking around, all of you. Ares, you remember the Zone Project? The synthetic isotope?"

"Yeah," Daire said, still glaring at Albany.

"That's how Garrick got these guys together."

"It was only a prototype."

"Yeah," Harry said. "So it's not far-reaching or exact, but it's something."

"Where's the Trident?" Daire asked, switching his focus to Garrick.

"Z has it."

Harry rose a couple of inches from his seat. "Are you insane? What the fuck did you—"

"It was that or my life," Garrick said. "He came back to Olympus for more than his Bolt."

Biting her lip, Tess wanted to ask what they were talking about. Except Harry didn't like her to ask questions. Doing it in front of his men wouldn't improve his openness. It turned out that there was no need to ask. Someone knew that she wanted the answer without her even opening her mouth.

"The three keys capable of reviving Minotaur," Daire said, surprising more than just her. "The Bolt, the Trident, and the Scepter."

"Zeus has the Bolt and the Trident."

"Took waking Minotaur off the table," Lowe said. "Until we got Hades back."

Harry shook his head. "I don't have it."

"Don't tell me—"

"Not Zeus, no. I figured there was a chance of things falling apart when Zulu was first discussed… I stashed it."

"Where?"

"That doesn't matter," Harry said. "We animate Minotaur and Z will be on the first plane." He tipped his head up to address Daire. "He's in Europe."

"I can't track him exactly," Garrick said. "But when he passes through a checkpoint, I get a hit."

"Good," Daire said. "I'll be on the first flight."

Boze threw up his arms. "Now we're talking!" He leaned toward Harry. "Send us to him."

"No," Harry said. "I haven't seen any of you in action for a year. All of you are out of shape." Again, his chin rose Daire's way. "All of you."

"Alright, old man, I hear you," Daire muttered.

"We get these guys in shape," Garrick said. "I'll keep running Zone, hope others stumble into our radius."

"Won't pick up Styx," Daire said on an exhale.

"Think he's still alive?" Lowe asked.

"Yes," Daire said, one side of his mouth curling though his resolute attention remained unwavering. "He hasn't killed me yet."

"You and Styx weren't in Zone."

"We're not guinea pigs," Daire said.

"No one ordered you to do it," Albany said, implying that he and the others hadn't had a choice.

"Three is in Panama," Harry said. "What do you have on One and Four?"

"Six is who we want to trace," Boze said.

Harry opened his hand on the table. "No one is touching Six."

"We can't trust him," Boze said. "Doesn't mean we can't kill him."

"One's gone dark. No surprise there. He has the

deepest connections," Garrick said. "We're monitoring Four."

"Awaiting orders," Lowe said.

All expectation turned to Harry. With the sun sinking low in the sky and the lights from the distant Strip glittering, she couldn't imagine they would take action that night.

"Orders are to get in shape," Harry said. "Everyone eat. Sleep. You're on Omega regimen."

A groan went around the table, though Garrick laughed. "You were all so desperate to have your Stratego back. This is what you get."

Harry left the table first. The others followed as they were given orders. "Lowe in the kitchen. Boze, I want a full inventory of hardware. Zip supply list. What do we need? What do we have?"

Garrick stood up. "It's good to have you here, Harry."

One man nodded at the other, then Garrick disappeared past the fireplace.

"Milo, Albany, you two go back to the hotel, bring our things here."

No one hesitated to do what they were told. After receiving orders, everyone disappeared until only she, Harry, and Daire remained. Harry pushed in his chair and turned, probably intending to talk to Daire.

Tess stepped forward. "What about the Beast?"

Harry looked at Daire. "I can send Boze for it."

"I'll do it," Daire said. "Tomorrow."

With a nod, Harry accepted that. Daire got more input than the others, which, for some reason, made her proud.

"I want a full lay of the land," Harry said, his volume low. "I want you to know every corner of this place. Every exit, every cover position. Everything. Inside and out."

"Sir," Daire said.

Just like the others, Daire went off to do as instructed. It was only then her father's attention swung around to her.

Wearing a wide smile, she didn't hide that she was kidding around. "I could go get the Beast, if you give me cab money to get there."

"Says the girl who has never hauled a trailer, let alone hitched it to a truck," he said, sauntering over. He laid his hands on her upper arms. "Were you hurt?" She shook her head. "I'm sorry my men were heavy-handed."

"It wasn't your orders," she said. "They didn't hurt me. Just a little pinch… I was freaked out though."

Tess wasn't sure she'd have admitted being scared to anyone else. They didn't know each other, but after seeing the way the men responded to him, she could tell her father was a positive force.

"You don't have to worry about any of them hurting you again."

"Garrick said they wouldn't… You're not suspicious though? They're all here, we don't know for how long… It could be lies. Zeus could be waiting to strike."

His head bobbed, though he didn't appear worried. "Anything is possible." He smiled. "But I trained these men. They've gone into harm's way under my orders for a decade, some of them for longer. And never forget what I said about Daire."

Being their primary instrument. "I understand you have history with everyone here. It's just…"

"You trusted Daire and he led you into a trap," her father finished her thought.

Damn, Harry was smart. Tess couldn't decide if his being able to read her mind was a good thing or not. He hadn't referenced any kind of intimacy and still seemed to be smiling, so she guessed all was well.

"You're right to be vigilant," he said. "You always should be. But when you got in trouble, you did the right thing."

Tess shook her head. "Garrick made me call. I considered hanging up and telling him to go to hell."

"But you didn't. When you need help, when you're in trouble, there's nothing I wouldn't do, Tess. Nothing."

She believed him, almost as much as she'd believed Daire when he said he'd come to her aid no matter what. If everything was as it appeared to be, they could be in a safe haven. If not, their time could be running out.

THIRTY-FIVE

DINNER WAS AN INTERESTING mix of Daire saying nothing and everyone else telling stories, enjoying reconnecting.

Tess didn't say much either. Not just because eavesdropping was her foremost intelligence gathering method, but because it paid to be wary. Relaxing could mean getting too close to people who could screw her over.

There was plenty to eat. Too much. At least that's how it looked at the start of the meal. By the end, every plate was clean and there wasn't much left.

They didn't linger at the table. As soon as Harry said it was time to clean up, the men got up to do just that.

"The master is yours," Garrick said to Harry. "It's upstairs and has a separate living area with kitchen facilities and the largest balcony in the house. Also plenty of closet space, two bathrooms, separate hot tub."

"Life of luxury," Harry said.

"I knew you'd want Ares close. The men have been building a barracks and training assembly in the basement. You should check it out before you retire."

"Needs work," Daire said, picking up his water glass. "Gimme a week, we'll get it up to inspection spec."

Garrick's amusement was broad. "We've missed you too, Ares. Doesn't surprise me you've done your reconnaissance. By now I'm guessing you know the house better than the rest of us."

She was coming to hate the code name. Growing up in Olympus, Daire probably heard it every day. No wonder the guy found it so easy to play another person. Did he even know who he was half the time?

"New environment is no reason to let standards slide."

Lowe wandered over to collect glasses from the table. "Never been the class clown, but you used to know how to have a good time, Ares."

"It's been a year for all of us," Harry said. "Training will loosen everyone up. Tess, stay here while the men clean up."

Harry rose from the table in sync with Garrick and Daire. They went out onto the patio and stood in a close group. That wasn't part of any tour or a friendly catch up. Those men were exchanging secrets.

They stayed there for the next half hour while the guys in the kitchen chatted and cleaned up. Bored with pretending she wasn't staring at the men outside while eavesdropping on those in the kitchen, Tess sprang out of her chair. Garrick's comment about Daire knowing the house reminded her that there was a house to get to know.

Creeping away from the table, she passed the end of the fish tank to go down the narrow corridor by the kitchen. Walls of wine from floor to ceiling tempted her into the cellar. Maybe there was still hope.

Selecting one red, she drew the bottle halfway out. Now, was there a corkscrew somewhere around that wouldn't require venturing into the kitchen full of super-agent assassins?

"Take it upstairs if you need something to help you sleep."

Startled, she turned to see Garrick in the doorway with Daire, Harry, Lowe and Boze behind him.

Daire slipped past Garrick to come over and push the

bottle back into its slot. "Not while there's a chance the tranq is still in her system."

"Everyone is going to bed," Harry said. "It will be an early start."

"I remember," she said, recalling what her father had put Daire through the morning after they met.

Tess didn't know the time. It had been a long day, even for her, and she hadn't woken up until it was almost over.

The men parted to allow her past, directing her toward the front of the house to another staircase. All she could do was ascend and head for the curved wall, knowing that her room was opposite it.

Seeing her bag on the bed was a relief. At least some of her things were there. Going through them, she half noticed Daire coming in behind her, but paid him little heed. If he wanted to double check window and door locks, that was just fine.

From inside the bag, she retrieved her toothbrush to prepare for bed. Daire didn't seem to be going anywhere, her father and Garrick were still by the door too. Why were they loitering?

Lowe appeared between the principals and tossed something to Daire.

"What's that?" Tess asked.

Harry came over to cup her face. Tipping it up, he kissed her forehead. "Get some sleep, Light."

The others filtered out when he let her go. Everyone except Daire. He was laying something on the floor.

Before Tess could ask what it was, her bedroom door closed, trapping her inside. The not exactly huge bedroom. With a bed... And Daire.

"What are you doing?" she got around to asking when he kneeled on the floor.

"This room is secure. Everyone gets ten minutes to settle in their berth before I do a final security sweep."

He sprang to his feet.

She went closer to see a bedroll laid out. "You want me to sleep on the floor? What's wrong with the bed?"

"The roll is for me," he said. "I'll be bedding down in

here."

"On the floor?" she said just as he turned to face her. "I mean in the room." Because the first comment suggested he might be welcome in the bed. "I thought you were sharing with Harry."

"Harry can protect himself, and he wasn't abducted from his last bedroom."

"Daire," she said, backing out of his path when he headed for the door. "You don't have to watch me twenty-four seven."

He turned the door lock and went to check inside the closet. Sharing a bedroom with Daire. Being in a confined space all night… with Daire…

"Why do you have so many clothes here?" he called from the closet.

"Garrick said his men bought things."

Daire appeared in the doorway. A completely transparent babydoll nightgown dangled by its skinny strap on his broad forefinger.

She smiled. "I guess they have particular tastes."

The canopy curtains that had been loose earlier in the day were now tied to the thin metal frame over the platform bed.

Slipping the sandals from her feet, she kicked them aside and slid the straps of her sundress down her arms to wriggle out of it. Being freed from her clothes felt good. Dropping onto her back on the bed, Tess spread her arms wide.

"Some days are more surreal than others," she said, arching to hook a heel on the edge of the bed to boost closer to the middle. "Though I guess every day is just another day at the office for you."

"Not every day."

The direction of his voice opened her eyes. He was standing at the side of the bed, directly over her. If he was Danny, he'd be eating her or riding her already. But he wasn't. The vision of the man he was, tall and dominating, casting his formidable shadow over her, was alluring.

She could point her toes, raise her leg, slide her foot

up his inner thigh, tease him until she tempted him to be hers again.

She didn't want him. Shouldn't want him. Shouldn't be thinking about how the weight of his body on hers would be pure security. How it would promise her a safety even Danny couldn't have offered.

"What would you do if someone walked in right now?"

He didn't pause to think about his answer, it came immediately. "Tear out his eyes and his tongue."

Tess laughed. "What? Could be an ally, one of your buddies, you don't know."

"Any man who lays eyes on you like this will lose them," he said, riveted by every detail of her body. "I'll cut out his tongue so he can't tell his tale."

Her underwear wasn't that revealing. He'd seen her in less. Her bikinis exposed more skin. The intense spotlight of his eyes rolled through her. Waves of warmth cascaded over her, rising in force until every inch of her was seared by the ownership he exuded.

Danny never wanted to own her. He'd never asked to. Never even hinted at it. But that was all she felt under Daire's scrutiny as it slithered over her, coating her in his protection, in his strength.

His next inhale was slow. He held it for a few seconds, then released it at the same speed. In a twist, he crouched to swipe up her dress and shoes, then vanished into the closet.

Tess rose to support her weight on her elbows. "You like things tidy," she said, figuring out something else about him. "You're a neat freak."

"Less of the freak," he said, coming out of the closet to retrieve her bag from the end of the bed before returning to the walk-in.

"Then why are you unpacking for me?" she asked, climbing off the bed to stumble into the closet to confirm her suspicion. Yep, he was putting things away. "I guess we're staying."

He paused, bag in hand. "You don't feel safe?"

"I don't know anyone," she said. "No, I don't feel safe. But would I be safe anywhere? Even if I run, if I leave here, walk away from you and Harry… I don't know what way is up anymore. I wouldn't be safe in a hotel, in a trailer, drifting across the world. Until I know the truth, until I understand Olympus and what it is you do, I don't know what I'm running from. Hell, I could get in a car, drive a thousand miles, live happily for a year and still never know Zeus if he walked right up to me and shot me in the head." Tess smiled and folded her hands on the doorframe to lean against it. "Well, I'd probably know it for the fraction of a second before I died."

Daire dropped the bag and started toward her. "Babe…" he said, hesitating the moment the word came out.

"It's okay," she said, knowing he was second guessing the slip up. "What? What were you going to say?"

He took his time about replying. "No one will ever hurt you…" He came a step closer. "I know I hurt you. I know my tactics were… cruel and underhanded. I'll dedicate my life to protecting yours, to erase the hurt that I caused you. You didn't deserve it."

"You said that the night I met Harry. The night I lost my Danny."

"Pandora—"

"No," she said, pushing away from the doorframe to narrow the last of the space between them. "No code names."

"They detach us," he said. "It's important to keep that distance."

If he wanted them detached, Tess would respect that wish. He'd lied about being Danny, which could mean he'd lied about being attracted to her. Except, if she'd been a simple job, he wouldn't have said half the things he'd said to her since the night the truth was revealed.

The man in the bedroom had been attracted to her. But it didn't matter. Regardless of whether he wanted her, he'd made it clear that his life belonged to Harry.

"Okay," she said because it wouldn't be fair to pressure him.

No expectation. Everyone expected something from him, so she never would.

Going around him, Tess got the bag he'd dropped and started to put her things away.

"I don't want to—"

"It's okay," she said, showing him a quick smile. "You don't owe me an explanation." Not for being dedicated to the life he loved. "I'll finish here. Your ten minutes are up. You said you had a job."

He nodded once and left the room. As soon as Tess heard the door lock, her hand dropped.

Daire in her bedroom. It better be just for that night. Restraint hadn't been in Danny's repertoire. In contrast, Daire was proving himself capable of a huge number of things. Maybe he could handle it… Was she so confident in her own ability?

***

AFTER QUICKLY PUTTING her things away, she grabbed her toothbrush and got ready for bed super quick. By the time Daire came back, she was under the covers, eyes closed. She heard the snap of the lock and then nothing. Not a sound.

She wasn't asleep, not really, but her eyes stayed shut. The bathroom door opened. There was no light or sound of it closing. In there she heard movement. He brushed his teeth, flushed the toilet. The door closed and then nothing.

In the darkness, concentrating on her breathing, every breath made her more self-conscious. Daire was silent, but each of her exhales echoed in her ears. She sure wasn't any kind of secret super-agent.

Giving up, her eyes opened. "What is an Omega regimen?"

"No excess. No indulgence. Strict diet. Rigorous exercise. Ample sleep."

No question or comment about her faking sleep, he simply answered her.

Picking up her covers, she crawled down the bed under them until her head came to rest in the bottom corner.

Ambient light from outside reflected off the canopy above her. "Why do you answer me? Harry doesn't like it."

"He's never ordered me not to."

"If he did, would you stop?" No answer. "I'm sorry. I know you follow orders. But you can tell me why you do it."

"You deserve to know. You're in this as much as the rest of us…" True. She was glad someone finally acknowledged that. Though from what he said next, it had to only be half the truth. "I tell you because after lying to you, hurting you, I vowed I'd only ever give you the truth… to the best of my ability." Another pause. Tess was glad of it. She needed time to process. "You will always have the best of my ability… I know sometimes it won't be good enough. I failed you last night."

Rolling onto her stomach, she peeked at him over the edge of the bed. "How did you fail me?"

"They took you."

"I'm not your responsibility."

In the shadows, it was difficult to see him. His shape was familiar, the lines of his body, the texture of his skin. They used to talk in the night sometimes. Most of those times their words were dirty or arousing, or they were requests for intimacy, not that Danny often asked. He was more action than discussion.

"I miss him," she admitted, rolling onto her back again. "It's stupid, right? He was never real. But sometimes… I still expect him to be there next to me… or to feel his hands on me."

It had been a few days. Still, it was taking time to get to grips with the truth that Danny wasn't real.

"I'm sorry. I am."

"I didn't say that to guilt you," she said. "You were doing your job. I just figure if you're giving me honesty, I should do the same… Though, I guess you could be lying. Maybe you're only being nice to me to gain my confidence again."

"Why? I had it. If I still needed it, I wouldn't have revealed myself."

"Maybe," she said, shrugging at no one. "But you taught me anything is possible."

"If only that were true," he muttered.

It was on the tip of her tongue to ask what he meant. Considering the answer might not be easy to hear while they were lying there alone in the dark, Tess sat up to grab two pillows from the head of the bed instead.

She stuffed one behind her head and tossed the other over the end of the bed at him.

"We should get some sleep. You'll have a long day tomorrow."

Silence. They weren't together. Weren't touching. It made little sense, but lying the wrong way on the bed, as close as she could get without joining him on the floor, made her feel better. He'd hurt her. Humiliated her. Yet she still needed him.

Daire. Ares. Danny. Whoever he was, he was as lost as her.

"I miss him too," Daire said, surprising her by saying more. "I miss the way you trusted him. Miss letting myself loose."

"It was an easier time, for both of us."

"We could still be there, in that RV park, nowhere to be, nothing to do."

A forlorn sort of smile tugged at her lips. "Or in South America… on the coast. Weed, beer… rubbers, we wouldn't need anything else."

"Nothing but each other." It was a nice dream. Shame it could never happen. "I miss you, Little Red… I miss your body against mine. Miss holding you while you sleep… It was a gift. The time with you… Time I should never have had with anyone."

Tess shifted her head on the pillow. "You deserve love as much as anyone else. Deserve to care and be cared for… You're not a robot either, even if that's what they trained you to believe."

"They trained me to believe I'm better at my job when I'm disciplined, when I don't give in to weakness. I can't say it's not true."

"Maybe it is. I don't know much about being a secret super spy," she said, rolling onto her chest to peek over the end of the bed again. "But I know you're a human being with a heart and a soul. I know everyone is better when they have something to fight for. Your mom gave her life for Olympus. I'm willing to bet she wouldn't want her boy to do the same. Not for nothing."

Olympus didn't exist. That's what she'd been told. If Daire was only what Olympus gave him, he didn't exist either. Ares might be okay with that. She wasn't.

THIRTY-SIX

THE NEXT DAY, TESS was in the closet trying to figure out if there were any new clothes that she'd actually wear. The bedroom door opened. Huh. It was later in the afternoon and shouldn't be time for dinner. Who would come to find her?

The closet door opened to reveal Daire. "Come on, we're going out."

He didn't wait for a reply and disappeared back the way he'd come.

Ducking down to grab footwear, she dashed after him. "We are?" she asked, hopping into her shoes. "Where are we going?"

"There's a cab waiting outside," he said, descending the stairs faster than she could.

A cab? Hotfooting it after him, she got her first glimpse of the external water garden when Daire held the front door open. She didn't have much time to admire it. He planted a hand on her lower back, and urged her quickly down the path, then opened the cab door.

"Where are we going?" Tess asked after he got in with her and the cab started moving.

The driver knew where they were headed, she was still in the dark.

"Gotta pick up the Beast."

Yeah, he'd said that was on his agenda. Why was she going along? Not that it was a problem. With nothing to do, the day had dragged. The guys were training. She'd heard them out back and at lunch in the kitchen.

Daire kept his focus out front, maybe monitoring that the driver was taking them the right way. The life of a super-agent involved a lot of paranoia.

"Does Harry know I'm here?"

She had thought nothing of following Daire and was an adult who didn't need her father's permission to go anywhere. Daire did though. The hierarchy dictated his life.

"Only way I can guarantee your safety is to be with you…" he said, then seemed to rethink his wording. "Is to keep you in my eyeline."

Put a lot of things into perspective for her. "That why he let you sleep on my floor last night?"

"Why he'll keep letting me do that," Daire said, glancing at her. "Your safety is my primary mission."

"I thought your primary mission was to find your way home."

He didn't respond, but didn't take his gaze from hers either. Edging her hand closer to his, she kept staring into him as her pinkie slipped beneath his on the middle seat. He didn't pull away his hand or his focus.

Whatever line they were treading was easier for her than him. She didn't owe her father anything. Daire didn't feel the same.

"Home doesn't have to be a location," he said, noticing her tongue darting out to moisten her lips. "Damnit."

His eyes closed before he turned his head. The finger shielding hers moved away too. No expectation. She had no expectations of him. Everyone in his life wanted something from him. Amidst her embarrassment over his double-cross, it was easy to keep her distance. It didn't seem to matter how disparate their lives were supposed to be, how different they were, they were together, connected. Even when neither of them should want it.

The rest of the journey went by in silence. The cab

driver took them right up to the Beast's plot. As Daire paid the guy, Tess got out of the vehicle.

The silver trailer had been the closest thing to a home she'd had in a long time. Not just because they'd lived there, dragging it from one side of the country to the other, but because she'd been happy there.

The truck was parked right next to the trailer. Daire would have to attach one to the other and then pull it back to Three's house. Except Tess wasn't so sure that she wanted to go back there. Not while her happiness was in front of her, so close.

The cab drove off and Daire passed by, retrieving keys from his pocket. He'd unlocked the door and freed the stairs before she noticed his frown. Yeah, she couldn't stand there on the road indefinitely.

Jumping to it, she started to move, so he went inside. Tess wasn't far behind and was careful to close the door without letting it bang.

They'd parked the Beast and gone straight to the hotel. So they didn't have to worry about any kind of hook ups or draining anything. Still, Daire was moving around in a much more methodical way than Danny, ensuring everything was secure and nothing was loose.

"Grab anything you need," he said. "It's easier to get it now than going up and down the stairs once we're parked in the garage at the house."

Yes. Okay. Made sense. Why was she all over the place? His prompt was appreciated; someone needed to kick her.

They'd only packed essentials for the hotel. Most of her things were stowed in the Beast. She opened the closet to grab one of the paper grocery bags. The only other option was her suitcase, and that was in the bed of the truck. That's where it was the last time she saw it anyway. Her sewing machine was there too. They'd be taking the truck back to the house. If Tess could get some fabric, she might be able to start making money again. Work would keep her occupied.

Tossing a couple of things from the closet into the bag, she continued to the bedroom. Upon opening the nightstand drawer, other than the abundance of condoms, the first thing her eye fell to was the envelope standing against the side. Sinking down to sit on the bed, the bag fell from her hand, then her fingers were on that envelope, retrieving it from where it had been since Danny put it there.

With it in both hands, she stared at the white rectangle, almost afraid to slip the paper from its cocoon.

"You okay?"

Daire's voice pulled her out of her thoughts.

She looked over her shoulder at him standing in the mouth of the hallway, on the threshold of the bedroom.

"Yeah," she said, her attention returning to the envelope. "We should show this to Harry."

"Sure."

Had she wanted him to agree with her so readily? In some ways, Harry was unshakeable. If she hadn't read his letters to her mother, she might believe that he didn't have any feelings at all. Seemed that was the way he wanted his men to think anyway.

She was still trying to convince herself that it was a good idea when Daire spoke again. "I got something for you."

He wasn't on the threshold anymore; he was sitting on his side of the bed with his back to her. Tess laid the envelope on the nightstand and slipped off her shoes to curl her legs as she twisted around to look at him.

"You got something for me?"

"When we were in Florida," he said. "Before you figured out the numbers." His drawer closed and then he was turning. A long ball-chain hung on four of his fingers while he cradled something in his other palm. "I didn't know when to give it to you or if I should."

"What is it?" she asked, scooching closer to see what was in his palm. It looked like a bullet, black, maybe a couple of inches long. The chain was threaded through a metal loop at the top.

He coughed. "It's a… Your mom's ashes are in it. You can twist the top off. It's no big deal. I just thought you'd prefer her with you. Near to you."

Speechless, Tess couldn't believe he'd done

something so thoughtful. That he'd done something so personal. Danny wouldn't do something like that. Danny wouldn't think of it. But Daire, he knew the value of traveling light, of how quickly she had to move sometimes. And he knew how she missed her mother, how she cherished that relationship.

He cleared his throat. "If you don't want it—"

"I want it," she said, bouncing to the middle of the bed. "I do."

Without meeting her eye, he raised it up, and she ducked forward to let him loop the long chain around her neck. It fell to her chest, and she curled her fingers around it, holding the bullet in her fist.

"Thank you," Tess said, her eyes warming. "I don't even know how to… Thank you."

He bobbed his head. Was he uncomfortable with her gratitude? That was what she thought… until his eyes snagged on hers. Gratitude wasn't on his mind. He'd realized it first. They were alone… in what had been their bedroom… on their bed.

"I shouldn't have—"

"Yes, you should," she said, crossing the last few inches of bed between them to take his face in her hands. "You absolutely should."

Pulling him closer, she couldn't help herself, couldn't stop her need from joining their mouths. She tasted his hunger, his craving for her, the potent heat of sweet desire racing for its climax. He was more than she wanted. More than she needed. Her fingers slid from his face and her arms wound around his neck as he held her waist to guide her onto her back. Coming down on top of her, he fulfilled her wish with his promise.

Opening her legs to accept his body between them, Tess grabbed for his face again when his mouth left hers. It didn't go far. His hands drove up her outer thighs, pushing her dress from her hips until it was over her head and gone.

"Daire," she begged in a gasp before he kissed her again.

Dominating her with his desire, his fingertips

skimmed down her body. With more than basic entitlement, he scooped her from the bed to erase the barrier of her bra. Tess couldn't feel everything all at once. It was too much. The heat of his kiss pressed to her mouth for a moment, then those lips were on her neck, branding her skin with the scorching demand of his possession.

This man. This lover. He wanted to own her. Wanted title to her body and everything that came with it. Her anger, her fear, her love. His kiss proved his rough claim to her soul. It conveyed his intention to put her before anything and anyone else. To keep her safe, to hold and occupy her existence with his own.

"Please," she begged as his entitled mouth ravished her breasts. Doing more than just kiss her, he bit and sucked, bruising her, marking her in a way neither of them could ignore. "Oh God, Daire, please."

With her fingers in his hair, her body rising and writhing, undulating with the rhythm of his need, Tess handed her life to him. More than any physical danger that could ever harm her with its violence, she gave him her future, her present, her identity.

He tore his kiss away from its mission to yank off his tee-shirt. Before her hands could even find his skin, his mouth was in her cleavage. Opening it to drag his teeth across the sensitive flesh, his urgency couldn't match hers. No matter how frenzied his devouring need became, it was nothing to the pulse of her pounding heart that fought to get nearer to his.

"I need you inside me," she pleaded, her knees sliding higher on his body, testing and claiming whatever they touched. "Daire."

He squeezed her breast, preparing it for the heat of his mouth. Just that quick caress wrung another whimper from her soul. Joy tightened her stimulated gut when the buckle of his belt rattled. Until that moment, she feared he'd come to his senses, that something might tear them from their desire.

His mouth left her skin and he reared up. In one slick move, his body slid up hers, their eyes met, and he pushed into her. A ripple of instant pleasure spilled through her.

"Yes," Tess said, her mouth never closing, her eyes never leaving his.

He pulled back and pushed into her again. Taking what he needed with such deliberate intention, there wasn't an ounce of equivocation. Daire didn't only want her body, didn't only want to occupy her, she was necessary to his existence, essential. Tess couldn't explain it, didn't know how she knew it. Moving in time, their haste heightened the closer they got to their end. As much as she never wanted their joining to be over, its completion was vital to the next beat of her heart, the next breath he took.

"Daire," she whispered, the pressure of her pleasure building.

His hips sped up, pushing her deeper into the guarantee of what only he could give. The tension snapped and a loud yelp of climax burst from her lungs as she tightened around him. He didn't stop; she wasn't sure he'd be able to if his life depended on it. Her pleasure pressurized again until the burden collapsed once more and her body was thrust into a harsh ache of pleasure so acute it was almost painful.

As the blur cleared from her vision, she saw him grit his teeth and propel himself into her, delivering himself to his own promise. Panting, unable to think, Tess tried to smile as he descended from his peak, but she didn't have the ability. With a weak arm, she touched her fingertips to her lips and lifted them to his, giving him the closest thing to a kiss she could muster.

He stayed there above her, scrutinizing her, though it seemed more for himself than for her. Whatever he was trying to work out, Tess wasn't sure he got to any conclusion before moving away. They were almost exactly in the middle of the bed. Or she was, Daire didn't move her or even lie down, he shifted to sit on the edge of the bed, where he'd been when she kissed him.

THIRTY-SEVEN

STRAIGHTENING HER ARM, her fingertips touched his spine. He didn't move away, but he didn't say anything either. Tess didn't know what to say that might reassure him. Sex before had been part of his mission. Getting close to her, giving her whatever she needed to keep her close, he'd been with her for a purpose.

Whatever they'd just done wasn't for any mission, not that she knew about, and it wasn't sanctioned by Olympus either.

When he didn't react to her fingers, she took them to her cleavage where the bullet he'd given her was nestled. Somehow, the chain had stayed in place.

"I have to tell Harry," he said and couldn't sound less happy about it.

"You said he wasn't an idiot," Tess said. "He probably knows we were together before. You didn't want to talk to him about that."

"This is different," he said, bending over to grab his tee-shirt from the floor. He pulled it on, his jerky movements angry. "He needs to know."

Tess sat up. "I think before you tell him, you should tell me." His head jolted toward his shoulder, though he didn't go so far as to turn around. "What is it you want to tell him? That we had sex? You're an adult, Daire. It was consensual. You don't have to explain yourself to anyone."

"You don't understand," he said, shaking his head. "It isn't as easy as that."

"As easy as being attracted to each other? It's not a crime," she said. "If anyone should hate themselves for what just happened, it's me. You're the con artist who duped his way into my bed. And here I am, opening my legs for you again."

Daire turned, but as soon as he noticed she was still naked, he stood up. "I didn't mean for us to…" He bent to swipe her clothes from the floor and tossed them onto the bed in front of her. "That's not why I brought you here." He breathed out, driving his fingers through his hair. "Harry gave me the go to bring you. Jesus."

"What is it I don't understand?" she asked, donning her bra. He'd only pushed her panties aside. So once her bra was on, all she had to do was put her dress on over her head. "You follow Harry's orders, I get that. But he didn't order you not to have sex with me, did he?"

"He wouldn't think he had to," he muttered. "Some orders are implied."

"No," Tess said, pouncing to her knees to shuffle down the bed and grab his tee-shirt in both fists. "There are no implied orders. Not when it comes to your feelings. He can't order you not to be attracted to me." Leaning back, she tried to make him look at her. "Are you going to tell me you're not attracted to me?"

"Tess…"

"That's better," she said, relaxing to rest her forearms on his torso. His height and the low bed meant her fists were just below his ribs. "Thank you for remembering my name."

"I didn't forget your name."

"No, but you said code names detach us… Do you want us to be detached?"

The way he searched her brought both anger and sympathy to the fore. Tess wanted to help and to understand. She understood that some things weren't about words. But if he didn't let her in, if he didn't lean on her, she wouldn't be able to make anything better.

"What I want doesn't matter."

"It matters to me," she said. "Right now, it's all that matters to me." The groove between his brows deepened, betraying that statement didn't help him at all. "Was this a con? A lie? Did you have sex with me for a reason?"

His fingers curled against her cheek. "Because I couldn't help myself," he said, letting himself feel her for a moment before exhaling. "I'm supposed to be stronger than this."

It wasn't fun witnessing Daire beating himself up. "We don't have to go back," she said, slipping her hands under his tee-shirt and watching the fabric move as she stroked and scratched him beneath it. "We have everything we need right here. We could hit the road, you, me, and South America."

His silence built the tension until it was so thick Tess could feel it pressing into her from all angles. Forcing herself to peek up at him once and again, she wanted to read his thoughts, to know what he was thinking and whether she'd just offended him. His expression wasn't one of offense; it wasn't of joy either.

"If I could, there wouldn't be anyone else I'd give it up for."

At least his rejection was clear.

Sinking down to sit on her feet, Tess's hands slid free of his shirt to fall onto her lap. "You're choosing him. Harry."

"Baby, it isn't—"

"It is," she said. "Olympus is your life. It doesn't matter that it doesn't exist. What we have in Three's house is the closest you've had to it for a year. You want it."

"It's…"

He sucked in a breath and sealed his lips. Not because he didn't want to tell her something but because he couldn't. As his hand went through his hair again and she caught on to just how bewildered he was, Tess suddenly got it.

"You've never talked about your feelings before… You've never even been allowed to have them."

She'd known that his obligation to Olympus was rooted in his upbringing. Every moment of his life, every second, was dictated by his training and what was best for their agency. Harry was his mentor and his father. But it wasn't like a regular parental relationship. Daire didn't rebel, not like other kids might. Like he'd said, Olympus was life or death. He couldn't disagree with his commanding officer. It could mean either his life or someone else's was put in jeopardy.

"I don't know what the hell is going on," he said, sinking onto the end of the bed near where she kneeled.

Some things weren't so different. Tess had been allowed to have feelings and had been allowed to show them. But just like Daire, she couldn't love or have relationships. Her mother would tear her away from one life to drag her to the next before anything close to a serious relationship could develop. Another difference was, she'd been allowed to be mad about it. Allowed to argue with her mother and voice her displeasure. All Daire could do was say "yes, sir" and do as told.

"I don't know what Olympus does," she said, wondering how significant their missions were. "You talk about missions and orders… I don't know what their aim is… I'd never heard of Olympus before this. Is it governmental?"

He shook his head. "The original Six had ties to governmental agencies, business, or crime factions. It started with Two, the original Two… It was his idea to have a private agency, one that acted in the best interests of the country. Without oversight to slow them down… We don't have to worry about a governmental budget or public opinion, it's completely secret. Only those in it and the Six know it exists… for sure anyway. There are others who suspect… allies of those on the inside."

"The best interests of the country," she murmured.

"Yeah, and humanity. Missions can be anything. Everything from infiltrating and monitoring a domestic fringe group to toppling an international regime."

Surprised, she blinked at his profile. "You've done that?"

"Sure helped," he said. "That's why it's important for

us to be at our peak. For us to be ready any minute for anything… These internal arguments, the politicking, it slows us down. While we're not at efficiency, things are being missed. Sometimes we're just collecting dirt on some politician with dangerous ties, but it could be we're responsible for averting a terrorist attack. When we don't do our job people suffer, people die."

Her muscles relaxed. "And here I am, telling you it's okay to walk away from it."

"Little Red…" he said, twisting to lay a hand over hers. "There's no one else I'd consider doing it for. But Harry…" He breathed out a laugh. "Last week I was so angry I couldn't wait to punish him for agreeing to Zulu…"

"You were angry, but you understand why he's important… Why you're important."

Petty animus aside, they were a unit. The men of Olympus, for whatever reason, hadn't believed Zeus was being faithful to their organization's aim. Understanding the scale of their project helped Tess to understand why they were so quick to put their personal feelings aside. Each of the men in Three's house had worked with or under Harry for a long time. They'd been in the field together, in battle together. Of course there would've been bumps and the latest one with Zeus was a big one. But none of them would've signed their life over to Olympus if they didn't believe in its purpose. Being that the group was a secret, these men couldn't have family or friends snooping into their intentions. All they had to rely on was each other.

As her chin drifted to the side, he put a hand on her face to bring her focus to him. "You're important. My primary mission will always be to keep you safe."

She shook her head. "Olympus is your primary mission. I understand now. What you do, what all of you do, it's selfless. You give yourselves over to the cause completely. You can't afford distractions, can't afford to put anything ahead of your objectives. You need to help Harry, to train your men, to get back to your purpose."

Tess didn't know what she felt for Daire. She hadn't known the truth of him for long enough to trust her emotions.

Whatever they were.

With Danny, things had been so easy that there was no urgency or need to put names to whatever they were. Daire was the kind of man who liked specifics. He liked labels because they were clear. Good guy. Bad guy. Kill or be killed. Stand up or take cover. Advance or retreat.

His life meant something. People talked about wanting their life to be important, to make a change or have a significant impact before they shuffled off their mortal coil. No one would ever know Daire's name. He wouldn't have medals or commendations, but she didn't doubt him for a second when he told her the truth of what he did. He saved people, their lives and from suffering. He gave himself to humanity. Put the greater good ahead of individual desires.

She touched his jaw. "Can I ask you one more thing?" He nodded. "What's your last name? Your real last name."

He frowned. "Canon," he said. "Two ns, not three. Why?"

"I want to remember your name," she murmured, mesmerized by how his stubble felt beneath her fingertips. "You won't ever be Ares to me. I don't want you to be Danny or anyone else with me. Just be Daire, just be you, whatever the honest you is in the moment."

He leaned in a little closer to mumble, "The honest me would have you on your back a lot more than the restrained me does."

First a smile and then a whisper of a laugh. "Yeah, I've got to admit, I'm sort of sorry I won't find out where Daire's sex drive falls on the scale." Still wearing her smile, Tess put a hand to his shoulder and swayed forward to rest her forehead on it. "Though I guess I know how you always had the energy for it now."

Being a super-agent required him to be in tip-top condition. By any regular person's standard, Daire was way beyond fit. By Harry's standard, Olympus standard, they were all out of shape.

His mouth disappeared into her hair. "Assume where you're concerned, it would be infinite. I can't imagine not wanting you. For even a single second."

Raising her head from his shoulder, she didn't move away. "You're better in bed than Danny."

The sight of his smile released a flood of delight inside her. When he laughed, Tess thought she might burst. Her smile stretched to a grin that made her cheeks ache.

"I don't even know how to take that, babe," he said, catching a quick kiss.

"It's a compliment," she said, sitting back on her feet when he stood up to go to the closet. "Danny was incredible in bed, always satisfied me, more than satisfied me… Daire gave me more than something physical."

He closed the closet door to look back at her. "And you can keep it, because I won't give it to anyone else." Turning around, he opened the fridge to grab a bottle, which he offered to her. "Want a beer?"

The question harked back to the first time they'd been intimate. "Is it cold?"

He came over and touched the side to her cheek. "Yep."

Tess curled her fingers around the bottle. "Share it with me," she asked as he twisted off the cap.

"Can't," he said, handing it over. "I'm on Omega."

As Tess took her first mouthful, his head tilted on a frown. "What?"

"Don't know the rules of sex on Omega… I thought I knew all the rules."

"Rigorous exercise," she said, curling her fingers into his jeans pocket. "You didn't break a sweat, but I'm sure I got your blood pumping."

"If only you knew, babe," he said, drawing a fingertip from her temple to her jaw.

Sex was usually controlled by Harry, the same way everything was. That was why they'd never be able to do it again.

"You don't have to tell Harry you sullied his little girl," Tess said, letting go of his pocket to take his hand off her face. "I support your decision." Rising from the bed to stand up, she felt the warmth of his body and wished she could sink herself into it, into him, but that wouldn't be fair.

"Olympus wins. I won't try to compete with it. I won't put you in the position of choosing between me and your integrity."

With her beer in hand, she turned to walk away.

Daire's fingers tangled in her hair when he caught her cheek to draw her back. "Everyone is better when they have something to fight for," he said, looking her in the eye. "You are my something... Little Red. You'll always be my something."

"So much for being easy," she said on a sigh. "Kiss me, Agent." Laying her arm on his chest, Tess pushed onto her tiptoes. "It'll be our last, so make it a good one."

Admitting the end wasn't easy. Pain actually bedded itself deep in her gut as his mouth touched hers. She wanted his kiss. One would never be enough. But it was all they had left.

THIRTY-EIGHT

A WEEK WENT BY WITH Daire on her floor at night and training all day. They didn't talk in the night anymore. Tess could almost feel him inside her when she closed her eyes and breathed in his proximity. Several times she'd thought about slithering onto the floor and pressing herself against him. Her hands could wander, her lips might seek his, and then… It wasn't fair to think like that. Her promise not to put him in that position was honest. She couldn't compromise him. Wouldn't.

Except living in the same room meant sharing the same space again, just like in the Beast. Sure, there was more of it between the bedroom, closet, and bathroom, but that didn't stop their scents mingling in their joint territory. It felt like theirs… like they were something together.

Daire felt it too. He didn't say it, but that awareness kept him from going to bed at the same time as her. She'd go up to bed while the men were jeering each other in the kitchen after dinner. Even if she wasn't tired, Tess would go to the room and soak in the tub or read. No matter what, she'd be in bed with the lights off before he came in and locked the door behind him.

Harry didn't want her to go out of the house on her

own. With the guys training and them being in the one place, he granted her the right to have things delivered. He gave her a credit card with an alias that she was to use when placing orders over the phone or requesting samples.

Daire was the only one allowed to check the mailbox or receive deliveries. The guy had plenty to do without worrying about checking her numerous packages for anything suspicious as well, but he never complained.

Designing and sewing clothes gave her a distraction. She might never get a chance to sell any of the outfits if she couldn't go to stores who might sell them for her. Still, Tess kept on doing what she knew.

Sitting at the dining table, Tess finished up with her latest creation. A cocktail dress of the sexy, slinky variety.

Standing, she held the dress up, admiring the shimmer of the fabric. Garrick came striding past the fireplace. When he spotted her, he came to a swaying halt.

"Pandora," he said.

She was getting tired of the guys always using her code name. "Mr. Garrick, we don't usually see you out of your office before dinner."

No one was in the kitchen cooking, so she didn't think they were approaching meal time.

"I was looking for your father."

"He's out with the guys. They're doing one of their runs," she said, draping the dress over her arm to retrieve the small metallic cylinder from next to her sewing machine. "I know because he gave me this panic button."

Garrick smiled. "He's protective of you. He always has been." Strolling closer, his expression became something more serious. "Forgive me for noticing, but I haven't seen the two of you talking much."

"Harry and me?" Tess shrugged. "He's busy."

"Yes," Garrick said, the smile he offered was placating at best. "I just always assumed if he got the chance to… Losing Carrie must have been difficult for him, for both of you."

Not her favorite topic of conversation, especially with someone she hardly knew. "Yes."

"She was his weakness. Always was. Sherwood knew it too."

Tess frowned. "Sherwood?"

"Zeus," he said. "Ulysses Sherwood… We use code names because it—"

"Detaches you," she said, stroking the fabric of the dress. "I know."

"There was a time we were friends, all of us. Olympus was a huge undertaking. All three of us walked away from everything we were before, we gave ourselves to the cause." Something she knew all too well. "When your father met your mother… He saved her life. We were unaware he continued to see her… They met in secret… I found out later that Harry didn't know your mother was pregnant until she was almost at term. When you were about six months old, Harry left the Olympus Beta compound… he completed his mission and returned to base only to disappear an hour later… Ares was beside himself, no one could calm him… Hades was gone for eighteen months. Sherwood and I, we knew it was unlikely Harry had been victim to any terrible fate… Sherwood got to the bottom of it… He tried to control it, tried to minimize your mother's exposure."

"Which he did by kidnapping me?" she asked.

Garrick frowned. "I'm surprised you remember. He took you on your second birthday… Daire's eighth."

"Excuse me?"

He exhaled a laugh. "The two of you share a birthday. Your father didn't tell you?" She shook her head. "It was after that things really soured between your father and Zeus… Your father made it clear how much he valued Helen… which was perhaps his failing."

"Helen?" Tess asked, remembering Daire had once used that name too.

Slipping his hands in his pockets, Garrick inhaled. "Your mother's code name… Helen… of Troy."

"The face that launched a thousand ships," she whispered.

"She started a war, yes," he said. "No one denied your mother's beauty… or her allure… which I suppose is why she gave birth to the original temptress."

Tess tossed the dress and panic button to the table. "Who comes up with this stuff?"

"Code names were more Zeus's thing than mine." Which was probably how he ended up with the most powerful one. "You should talk to him about your mother… about what happened in that time."

"Zeus?"

"Harry," Garrick said, his eyes narrowing. "There's still so much you don't understand."

"I don't know that he'd be honest with me. He's busy with his men and seems to feel… to think…" His head dipped forward, prompting her on. "That I'm two years old."

Garrick laughed. "Well, he lived with you until that age… after that, after your mother took you from Olympus… he never saw you again."

The letters implied how Harry cared for her, if she was indeed the Light he referred to. Since Daire took her to her father, he hadn't shown the same dedication. It wasn't completely on him; Tess hadn't made much of an effort either. The time he spent with his men made it difficult for them to find time alone. If she'd tried to reach him, asked him to make time for her, he may have done it.

Her mother's death was still unreal. Talking about it, and about her in the past tense, could bring reality crashing in. Tess wasn't sure she was ready for that. Not with everything else that was happening.

Dragging herself from her reflection, Tess straightened up. "What did you need him for? Is it important?"

"Yes…"

She didn't think Garrick was done with his response, but the front door opened and the sound of a bunch of adrenaline-high men spilling inside silenced the rest of his words. It took a minute for them to reach Garrick, who wore a smile as he turned to greet them.

"Hydrate. Shower," Harry said, coming in at the rear of the bunch. "Then dinner duty."

"We need to talk," Garrick said to Harry.

Her father nodded once, and the two disappeared as the other men filtered away toward the back of the house. All except Daire.

Tess was smiling, watching the rowdy gang disappear, and didn't notice Daire was looking at her until they were all gone.

"You're staring," she said, picking up her dress to hold it against her body. "What do you think?"

"Beautiful," he said, wandering around the table. "Oh, you meant the dress."

She laughed. "Are you flirting with me, Agent?"

"Maybe," he said, coming up close.

"Look at that," she said, checking him out, or as much of him as she could with him standing so near. "You worked up a sweat."

"Running in the desert," he said.

She wasn't sure why his eyes were alight with mischief or why he was leaning in.

"You're in a good mood."

"Mm hmm," he said, his body coming into contact with hers.

Tess laughed again. "You know someone could walk in here." He just nodded and didn't back off. "Something serious is happening."

"I know."

Her next laugh was louder. Tess laid a hand on his damp tee-shirt. "With Garrick and Harry."

He brushed her hair from her brow. "What?"

"I don't know. Garrick just came in here looking for Harry. I asked if it was important, he said it was… Did you know they called my mom Helen of Troy?"

"The face that launched a thousand ships."

That Tess had said the same thing brought a smile to her lips. "I don't think she meant to start a war."

"Helen or your mom?"

Tess rolled her eyes. "My mom… I don't know the real Helen of Troy… if there ever was one."

"She didn't start the war," he said, laying a hand on the back of the nearest dining chair. "The men started the war."

"In the story?" Tess asked. "If she went willingly then yes, it was the men's fault, but if she didn't…"

"There's no better reason to start a war."

Tipping her head up, she showed him her frown. "No better reason?"

"For love… for the woman you love… I love."

"Daire," she exhaled his name, pressuring his chest, not that her pushing made an ounce of difference. "What's gotten into you?"

"I'm keeping my distance," he said. She just raised her brows and glanced down at the non-existent space between them. "This is distance… compared to how close I want to be."

Apparently, getting the blood pumping raised his mood and his libido. In having fantasies since they'd last been intimate, Tess believed herself to be the one out of line. The only one still infatuated with the idea of being intimate with him.

"I am not tempting you," she said, though it was difficult to keep a straight face. The notion that they might ever be able to play with each other was enough to kick up her pulse rate. "I am not doing anything."

"You're not backing off either," he murmured, licking his lips as he zeroed in on hers.

True. It hadn't even occurred to Tess to retreat. Although the dining table was at their side and she had a chair behind her, there was still space for her to flee if she wanted to run away.

"Are we playing chicken?" she whispered, pushing to the tips of her toes.

"You better hope not, baby. You wouldn't stand a chance."

"Okay," she said, sliding her hand higher. "Then be a gentleman and don't put me in that position."

"Don't feel like being a gentleman right now," he said, his fingers skimming up her hip to her waist. "You said be whatever the honest me is in the minute." She nodded, relaxing her jaw. "The honest me wants something."

"Is this the unrestrained you?" His dimples almost wrung a delighted laugh from the tips of her toes. "I need someone to help me take the sewing machine upstairs... and you need a shower."

"I think you might be dirty now too," he said, his lazy gaze falling to her cleavage.

He'd been leaning on her for a while, not long enough, but he was suggesting she'd need to shower him off her. The shower might be a good idea, though there was no way Tess ever wanted to cleanse him from her soul.

The whispered words of his seduction song that came from his lips put a smile on hers and strength in her hands.

"I've tried my best all week not to think about your slow hand, thank you, my Heart. You're not making it easy for me to be magnanimous about your integrity."

"My integrity is for you, Little Red," he said, pulling her close to rest his mouth on her hairline. "I have a reason. Hit me when I was out there, when I'm sick of it and ready to jack the lot in... I have something to do it all for. You're the something I want to keep safe. Now I train to be ready when you need me... You're what it's all for."

The idea that she was so important to him seemed to thrill him. Tess wasn't so ecstatic. Raising her chin to look into his eyes, her expression of doubt didn't match his of satisfaction.

"You have to do it for you," she said. "Or else you'll blame me for missing the life we could've had together... or you'll get yourself killed."

He frowned, but before he could respond to her, his brow twitched, and his eyes moved. Like he heard something she didn't. He took a step away and turned just as Harry appeared around the fireplace.

"Ares."

"Sir," Daire said, no trace of the playful, aroused man who'd just been touching her.

"You're supposed to be hydrating."

"Sir," Daire said and started to go the way the other men had.

"No," Harry said, stalling his ward. "No time for that

now. Something's happening, you're needed at the top."

Daire went after Harry when he returned in the direction he'd come. Tess had known something was going on. Garrick had said it. But it wasn't Olympus business that put a frown on her face. Tess had told Daire not to choose; she'd made the choice so he didn't have to.

They couldn't be together. No matter what. Not just because the country needed his expertise. Not because she trusted him more than anyone else on earth to keep the population safe. And not because his skill and dedication would save lives.

Tess couldn't distract him. As long as he hoped they could be together or that she'd be there for him, his head wasn't where it needed to be. They couldn't be together because Tess would never forgive herself if she was the reason he wasn't concentrating at a crucial moment.

Daire needed to keep strangers safe. Hundreds, maybe thousands of them. Tess's only concern was him. Her job was to keep him safe, and that meant ensuring his head was in the game and nowhere near her panties… or her heart.

THIRTY-NINE

DINNER WENT BY IN ALMOST silence. Garrick, Harry, and Daire were so lost in their own thoughts that their scowls became contagious. The men who'd been in such high spirits on their return from their afternoon desert run were stoic and mute.

Everyone ate and afterward, as usual, everyone went to complete their tasks as assigned on a schedule she'd never seen. Harry, Garrick, and Daire went out to sit on the patio. Instead of sitting around waiting to see if something would change or someone would explain the somber mood, Tess left the table.

She should go upstairs to her room. If she was playing by usual rules, she should retire for the evening and read something in the tub. If Tess was the dutiful team player, that was what she'd do. Except she wasn't being treated as an equal to everyone else in the building.

Daire was the first to notice her step onto the patio. Tess didn't plan to put him in the awkward position of having to silence whatever was being said and kept her distance.

"I need a minute, Harry."

He didn't even bother to turn around. "Later. We're busy."

"Not later," she asserted. "Now."

It was unlikely anyone expected her to be so forceful with the man who made so many of the rules. He twisted in his seat to look at her for just a second before standing up. Tess went back into the house to head across the dining area. Although the doorway was glass and one wall a full height fish tank, she went into the wine cellar and waited for him. After he was inside, she closed the door.

"Tess, you can't—"

"My mother chose her life," she said. "She chose to love you. Chose to have me. Chose to agree to the accord that allowed her and me to leave Olympus. She chose to write to you. Chose to keep your letters."

"How do you know—"

"I'm not a child, Harry. Yes, everyone keeps telling me I'm your daughter, but blood isn't enough." Some of his obvious anger ebbed to confusion. "You can't issue orders, tell me to sit and stay like a good little soldier, because I am not one of your soldiers." She stepped closer. "You know nothing about me. Nothing other than we share blood. That's enough for you, it's not enough for me."

"Tess," he said. On an exhale, he rubbed his forehead. "This is not the time for petulance."

"Is that what it is? I told you that if I didn't get a say, I would leave. Remember that conversation?"

"You're safe here. We're keeping you safe."

"There's more to life than safe," she said, showing some flexibility. "Don't you see that we're missing an opportunity, maybe the only one we'll ever have. I've talked more to Garrick and your men than I have to you. You don't know me, I don't know you either."

"You think this is the time to be playing catch and trading stories?"

Tess wasn't happy to be subjected to his ridicule. "I think my mother is dead. I think you're the only family I have left, but existing in the same space doesn't bond us. You think it's your job to keep me safe because you're my father or because you're an Olympus agent, I don't know. Your men mean more to you than I do. We have a chance to change that, a chance to mean something to each other… What do you think mom would want? If she was here right now, would you be ignoring her like you ignore me?"

"Your mother understood what I do," Harry said, the insistence of his firm tone growing. "She sacrificed us for what I do. We sacrificed it. It wasn't an easy decision to make. You can't possibly understand what it is to be so obsessed with another person, to be in love with the only thing that ever mattered to you… the most important thing in your world, and to walk away from that."

Didn't she? Tess didn't even have to turn around to know that Daire was looking at her. Even in that moment with the fish tank at her back, she knew he was nearby, knew he was monitoring what was going on even if he couldn't hear it.

"Then explain it to me," Tess said, going closer to pick up her father's hand. "I want to understand." And maybe if she understood more about her parents' relationship, she wouldn't be doomed to make the same mistakes they did. "I want to trust you. To believe in your conviction, to support you. I want you to be my father… You're a stranger to me. I know more about you from your letters to mom than—"

"You shouldn't have read those," he said, withdrawing his hand and turning his back on her.

Although it hurt to be shut out, Tess pushed her shoulders back and kept on going. "They were all I had left of her. I didn't even know what they were… I didn't know who you were."

"That was the way it was supposed to stay. Anything you know about me and what I do puts you in more danger. Carrie put her life on the line to birth you. I don't know why she'd… Any danger she was in before that… Choosing to have you signed her death warrant."

That implied that… The tingle of hurt in her nose came just before the heat in her eyes. "You never wanted to know me. You could care about me for what I was to mom, you knew what I meant to her, but without her… You said that being caught out was too easy… You didn't even know mom was pregnant until the very end. If you'd known sooner, if she'd told you…" As he turned to the side to meet her eye, she didn't have to ask the question, let alone hear any answer to it. Closing her mouth, Tess nodded, accepting the truth. "Okay." She managed a smile, even though her lips were shaking. "Thank you for being honest."

Going out of the wine cellar, Tess resented the tear that slipped from her eye. As she vaulted up the stairs, she swiped it away. Harry hadn't known that her mother was dead. He'd been free of Olympus for a year before her death and he hadn't tried to reach them. Given what she'd just learned, Tess wondered if that was her fault. Maybe her father would've gone to her mother if she was by herself. If he'd been with Anne, maybe she wouldn't be dead.

If Harry resented his daughter for putting the woman he loved in danger, it was possible her mother felt the same way. Tess had split the couple apart. Just by existing, she'd put a wedge between them. Without a child weighing them down, maybe Harry and her mom would've fought to stay together. It would be easier to run without worrying about the ongoing needs of an infant.

Going into her bedroom, she didn't pause even to turn on the light. Tess went straight into the closet and grabbed the bag she'd had at the hotel. Travel light. Her suitcase was still in the bed of Daire's truck. She didn't care about leaving clothes, but without her sewing machine, she wouldn't be able to make a living.

Tossing her essentials into the bag, she departed the closet to enter the bathroom. Money. She'd need money. The money her mom left at Figgs office… Except… Her mom didn't leave that money or the weapon, Daire left it to set her up.

Ironic that he'd managed to do it just by introducing her to Harry. Her father got his punishment alright. In the form of her.

"There isn't a chance in hell you'll get past me."

Glancing at Daire leaning on the bathroom doorjamb, it didn't surprise Tess that she hadn't heard him approach. His stealth mode was impressive at the best of times, and her head wasn't even close to being in the game.

"Please don't," she said, striding forward, intending

to go past him.

Daire didn't move and actually laid a hand on the opposite doorjamb to block her way. "You won't get past me."

"He sent you up here to tell me that? Goddamn man is a coward. He really does make you fight *all* his battles for him."

"Tess—"

"No," she said, ducking away from his hand when he tried to touch her face. "You don't get to use what I feel for you to fix this."

"Nothing is too broken to fix."

She almost couldn't bring herself to look him in the eye, but she did, aware of how much hurt and anger burned from within her. "Tell that to the man who wishes I'd never been born."

"He wishes I'd never been born either," he said, too casual for her liking. "Imagine how much easier his life would've been without a newborn to keep up with and a toddler kicking around the complex."

"Your mom died, she didn't choose to leave you."

"Neither did yours. So far we're equal."

"I didn't spend years hating you for splitting Harry's focus."

His ease vanished, and he stood straight. "Hey now, baby," he said, trying to touch her face again. Tess backed off further. If he touched her, she'd fall apart. He came into the small room, closing the door at his back. "I don't hate you now. I was a kid. A dumb kid. Who knew nothing about anything. Soon as I met you I knew I was wrong to blame you for something that wasn't your fault… Just took me a while to get my head out my ass when it came to admitting how I feel about you."

"Daire," Tess exhaled, the bag falling to her side when her arm loosened. "I am so tired."

"I know, baby," he said. "You've been running a long time. Lost a long time."

"I always thought I knew who I was," she said, not fighting when he took the bag from her hand to put it on the vanity. "I thought I was strong and determined and sure. I thought I could handle anything."

"You can." Her head shook as it drooped. His fingers slid onto her cheek, losing themselves in her hair as he raised her attention back up. "Tess, you are the strongest person I ever met. Without a goddamn doubt." That sounded like lip service if ever she'd heard it. "You are. Your mom died, you were alone, completely alone, and you didn't give up. I go out there into the field with backup and almost limitless resources and there are times I waver. You don't waver."

"I'm wavering," she murmured.

He smiled and adjusted his hold to run the tip of his thumb across her lip. "No, you're not. You're pissed at him and you're hurt, but just like always, you had a plan before you even reached the closet. You're not afraid to be out there on your own, without backup or resources. You do whatever you need to do. You find a way to get through it."

"I need my suitcase from your truck. My sewing machine is too heavy to carry for long."

"You are not going anywhere. My Heart, that's what you called me, right? You were mine long before we ever walked into the Olympus control room... even if neither of us realized it." When she tried to look away, he strengthened his grip. "Tess, I can't make you happy. I can't change who Harry is. He's an asshole. Yeah, you should've known that when you realized I was the same. Takes one to raise one... But, baby, he does love you. He's hurting over Carrie. He can't show it, he doesn't have the time, or the luxury... Three is on his way back into the country." That surprised her, which he saw and acknowledged with a nod. "We don't know what game he's playing... He left because he feared Zeus, because he wanted to protect his ass by being far away from it."

"Now that you and Harry are here, he's not afraid."

"Maybe," Daire said, shrugging, watching his thumb stroking her lower lip. "We won't know until he gets here. His flight is due to land in a couple of hours. It's possible he is coming back to be a part of it, to bankroll whatever mission we need to take Zeus down... or he's working with Z and we'll have to scatter fast."

"Scatter. Like the Exodus?" He nodded. Tess inhaled. "If it's this easy for you to tell me, why can't Harry do the same?"

"Harry loves you," he said. "He's not *in* love with you." Did she hear him right? His smile narrowed his eyes and lowered his volume as he bowed nearer. "You do the doe eyes and I'd find a way to switch the sun with the moon for you. I'd split the world in two if it would make you smile, Little Red."

"You can't be in love with me," she said, though her heart grew with desire to lose itself in him. "Harry resents me for forcing him to walk away from my mom."

"I will never blame you for us missing the life we could've had," he murmured. "Giving me to the mission, to Olympus, it's such a brave, honorable act. I am in awe of you, baby."

She couldn't blink, couldn't drag her gaze from his, even as a tear rolled from her lashes. "You'll be distracted, in the field, if you think of me. I couldn't take another breath if you weren't out in the world, keeping it safe… They used me, my mom, against Harry. They made him what he is, afraid to feel."

The pad of his thumb slid across her lips again. "I will never be afraid to feel… not for you, my Heart."

"We can never be together."

"I know. Harry wouldn't allow it and if anyone knew what I felt for you…"

They'd use her against him, just like they'd done with Harry and her mom. "I don't want to be your weakness."

He smiled, his lips wide and satisfied, showing his dimples and the mischief in his glittering eyes. "Too late." Taking his thumb from the corner of her mouth, he wiped away her tears with both hands. "No one will ever know it. You don't have to be afraid for me, Little Red. You don't have to be afraid for the world."

"What if I'm not strong enough? What if I change my mind and beg you to leave Olympus for me?"

"I would never have my Heart beg for anything… Whatever happens, we'll deal with it together. Even if we can't be together, we will always know the truth."

"That history is repeating itself?"

His smile vanished. "That will never happen. I'd raze the continent before I'd ever let anyone hurt you."

"Thank you for being with her. I never got a chance to say that I… It means something to me. That she didn't die alone," Tess said, stepping closer and laying a hand on his chest to confess her own secret fear. "I don't want to die alone."

"You won't. You're not leaving here. You're a part of this as long as I am. As long as I draw breath, you will be protected."

Tess exhaled her pain and frustration. "You were supposed to be easy… How did we get ourselves into this mess?"

"Well…" he said, drawing the word in with his breath. "It all started with a little red Corvette."

Her memory of that day brought a laugh to her lips. Daire pulled her close and kissed her head.

A mess was an understatement. There was still so much to resolve. So much to understand. Olympus owned Daire, and it was right that it should. The world needed him. The least she could do was respect that he'd dedicated his life to a calling. One that had been picked for him. From the moment he was born, he hadn't been able to avoid it.

Tess was alone. Her mother was gone. Her father was unable to be a father. And Daire? His heart was hers, so it was her responsibility to do everything in her power to protect it… while shielding hers from the pain of its isolation. The past was gone, and she didn't have a clue what lay ahead.

TO BE CONTINUED...

Thank you for reading this tale!
If you can, please take the time to review.

~

Ask your local library for more Scarlett Finn
novels!

~

For all things Scarlett Finn
check out:

www.scarlettfinn.com

BOOK TWO

To Die For
HONOR
SCARLETT FINN

OUT NOW!